BENEATH THE SURFACE

Heaton Wilson

First published 2022
by Rowanvale Books Ltd
The Gate
Keppoch Street
Roath
Cardiff
CF24 3JW
www.rowanvalebooks.com

A CIP catalogue record for this book is available
from the British Library.
ISBN: 978-1-913662-91-2

For Jon.

'The past lies beneath the surface, intransigent truth. Remembered or not, what we say and do remains, always.' – Meredith Hall.

PROLOGUE

Mary's breathless cries of passion were a familiar refrain in the desirable, up-and-coming village of Cardale. But they were about to be cruelly cut short.

The sequence was devastating in its inevitability. The stone wall of her detached thatched cottage buckled under the impact of 3.5 tons of tractor at just after 1 p.m. The roof collapsed, crashing onto the bed, carrying it and its lusty occupants down through the floor into the living room.

Villagers abandoned their Saturday brunches and gathered to gape. Some peered through net curtains in curiosity, while others sat at the bar and offered their humble opinions.

There was unanimous agreement at the Frog and Firkin; Mary MacDonald and Geoff Pegg hadn't stood a chance.

The landlord was said by one of the local wags to have 'brought the house down' with his impromptu speech from behind the bar. 'It's what she would have wanted,' he was alleged to have said. 'The earth moved, and she went out with a bang. I hear Geoff was so worked up, they struggled to nail the lid of his coffin down.'

But when the laughter—and the shock—had died away, one question lingered.

Was it really an accident?

1.

Eric Sykes got the news that morning: he'd successfully completed his Initial Crime Investigation Development Programme, taking him one step nearer the rank of Detective Constable.

He couldn't wait to tell everyone at Lorry and Mark's wedding, but it was not to be. DI George Creasey dispatched him to check on a report that a tractor had *ploughed* (George was pleased with his pun) into a thatched cottage in Cardale.

Eric was not amused. Nothing ever happened in Cardale, apart from the annual country music festival he'd managed to spend his young life avoiding. But he'd got his motivation back by the time he parked up on the green by the shop, wrinkling his nose at the distinctive aroma of burning wood and silage. It wasn't the first time he'd had cause to remind himself of one of his dad's favourite sayings: *'Every day is an opportunity to show what you're made of.'*

He locked the car and followed the sound of voices, taking a right turn at the phone box. And there they were, about 50 yards away; most of them in wellies. Most of them large and loud.

He ducked under the length of tape being slowly unrolled by a burly PC.

'Thanks,' said Eric.

'Thankless job, this,' said the PC.

Eric tutted and walked on, up a street that looked like a set from Miss Marple. The black-and-white houses were crowded together into one long terrace, with front doors that opened onto the cobbled street. Eric smiled to himself as he pictured them struggling to fit through the doors.

A few paces further on, the street opened out slightly.

It was as if a giant fist had punched the house in the face. Only this was no fist; it was a green farm tractor, now half buried. Mounds of matted reeds lay everywhere, weighed down against a fresh breeze by slabs of plaster, roof timbers and pieces of furniture—a mangled bed frame, floral seat cushions, an upside-down rocking chair, a big old television.

Claire Pearce stood out in her white, hooded forensic suit. To Eric, she looked like an angel; even more so when she arced an arm to wave him over.

She'd joined Ashbridge division as a trainee six months ago. All the blokes fancied her. She was pretty with her red hair and sky-blue eyes and a sprinkle of freckles on her cheeks. Eric had always wanted a sister, and he wished it was her. She was the ideal candidate: same age, twenty-three; same personality—serious about the job, determined to do well, always positive.

She'd first got a chance to shine when her boss, universally known as Forensic Phil, needed treatment for a heart condition. He was back at work now but still taking it easy. Claire was clearly loving the extra responsibility.

Eric high-stepped over a mound of stones. 'Got it all sorted?'

Claire frowned. 'I wish.' She pointed towards the back wall of the house. 'We've got two bodies.' She could see his discomfort and moved closer to take his arm. 'They're a hell of a mess, and they've got no clothes on. And they're stuck together, if you know what I mean.'

Eric pretended to be interested in something at his feet. 'What, you mean they were... at it?'

Claire giggled at his embarrassment. 'Hard at it, yeah. You sure you want to look?'

Eric wasn't sure at all, but he took a deep breath, and nodded.

***

The ruins of the original Ashbridge Town Hall, with its stunted columns of yellowing stone, wouldn't have been Jane's first choice for a wedding, but she couldn't fault it as a spectacle.

Dark red canvas sheets were stretched between pillars to protect against the unpredictable September weather. Lorry was equally colourful in a deep purple corset top with a matching full-length feather skirt. Her bouquet of blood-red roses matched her lipstick.

Guests in varying degrees of Goth costume were standing in a circle. The celebrant was in the centre, in a conventional black trouser suit, standing next to a nervy-looking Mark. Jane thought he looked like a magician in his black velvet jacket, white gloves and top hat.

Classical music was playing. Phil whispered in her ear: 'Wagner.' Jane nodded, though she thought it sounded more like Led Zeppelin.

She'd been dreading the wedding for weeks. Deciding what to wear had been irritating enough. It all brought back the memory of Allan proposing to her in Lyme Regis six months ago. That moment had felt like a turning point in their relationship. And so it proved. His head had been turned by a big company buying his paper; hers by a triple hit-and-run murder investigation and the promise of promotion by the Chief Constable.

The end result was that Allan got rich and cleared off, while she caught a killer and was turned down for promotion because she'd upset the Army along the way.

So here she was, still single at thirty-nine, still a DCI, still at Ashbridge and still not sure if she should move on. She'd told herself that if it wasn't for Mum's increasing frailty and confusion, she probably would.

But whenever she thought about moving on, the memories crept up on her: the good times with big, clumsy, childish Allan, the only man who'd understood her, made her laugh, made her feel safe.

They'd met on her first murder investigation—the Fiona Worsley killing—and she'd never forget the first time he'd held her in his arms. She'd been sure he was the one, but—

Lorry caught her eye as she walked past. Jane mouthed one word: *beautiful*. That was a first. She'd never called one of her detectives that before. Lorry smiled and the music faded as she reached Mark's side.

They held hands as the celebrant spread out her arms and raised her face to the sky, turning a full 360 degrees so her voice filled the space.

'Welcome one, welcome all! This is a great day. This is Mark and Lorry's great day. Let's hear it for Mark and Lorry!'

Jane stopped clapping when she felt her phone vibrating in the pocket of her red Reiss jacket—not exactly Goth, but it matched the décor. She turned slightly to check. *Two fatalities at house at Cardale. Eric.*

She showed it to Phil, who nodded. They edged towards the back, whispering apologies. She saw movement to her right. George Creasey had obviously picked up the message, too.

The applause died down, and as they stepped out through an archway wreathed in garlands of black flowers, she could hear Mark repeating the vows: 'I take you with all your faults and with all your strengths. I offer myself to you with all my faults and strengths…'

They waited for George to join them. It was a normal shopping day, and the Goth theme had attracted a crowd. No surprise—a Goth wedding was more interesting than walking down the aisle at Tesco. Then Phil reminded her that anything was better than a supermarket on a Saturday morning.

Jane spoke quietly as George appeared. 'There's no point all of us going, is there? Will you stay, George? We'll try and get back for the reception, okay?'

George didn't argue. He'd grown very protective of Lorry. 'Give me a shout if you need anything, ma'am.'

'Is Ross here? I haven't seen him.'

George smiled. 'You're lucky. He's in disguise. Top hat and tails, can you believe.'

Phil grinned. 'Good for him. You should have dressed up too, George.'

'No need. Wife says I look like an undertaker anyway.'

2.

Jane walked slowly towards the house.

The site had been secured and onlookers pushed back. White canvas marked the spot where the bodies had been found.

Away to the right, where the back wall of the house was mostly intact, Eric was interviewing someone next to an ambulance. Claire was nearer, looking ghostly white as she pecked about amongst the debris. Jane suddenly felt her age, remembering what her mum used to say: '*You know you're getting old when the police look so young.*'

Inspector Alex Gledhill handed them disposable suits and overshoes and talked as they pulled the gear on.

'Tractor driven into a detached house, causing collapse. Two bodies. Naked. No prizes for guessing what they'd been up to. A Miss Mary MacDonald and Mr Geoffrey Pegg. They haven't been touched other than by a doctor to confirm death. No other victims or injuries that we know of. The driver of the tractor was unhurt. He's with Eric now. We're establishing an incident room at the pub down the road, ma'am.'

'Sounds good. Thanks, Alex.'

Jane hopped on the spot as she pulled on the over-shoes. Wearing trousers to the wedding suddenly seemed the right call.

Phil was still struggling to get his arms into the sleeves, so she helped. 'Take it easy, Phil. No rush.' She waited as he zipped up then leaned against a patrol car to pull the overshoes on. 'Do you want to check in with Claire? I'll have a look round and talk to Eric. We'll take it from there.' She turned to Alex. 'How does it feel, Inspector?'

'I was quite happy as a sergeant, ma'am. But I couldn't say no.'

'Well done. You deserve it. If you're celebrating later, I might let you buy me a drink.'

He grinned. 'You're on, ma'am.'

Jane watched Phil walk towards Claire. He'd been back a month; three months since the heart operation. It felt too soon but he'd passed fit, and she couldn't blame him. Work was his life, and it would probably be the death of him. She could relate to that.

She turned to scan the crowd on the other side of the blue and white tape. They looked middle-aged and above: well off, well fed and enjoying the drama. Two faces didn't quite fit, though, in their hoodies and beanie hats. Too far away to tell their age or distinguish male or female. Sightseers, probably.

Jane walked a few steps towards the tape, allowing her mind to wander. It helped to shut out the noise.

Cardale was a small place, so chances were that most villagers knew the victims. And once they learned the bodies had been found naked, the gossip would spread like bushfire. She chuckled to herself. What was she thinking? They probably already knew.

9

There'd be a lot of name-taking and house-to-house enquiries to do. She tapped out a reminder on her phone and turned to study what was left of the house.

It was hard to see how a tractor could accidentally swerve off the road. It was narrow, but the terrace opened out in front of the cottage, and she could see one or two passing places further up the lane towards open countryside. It was just possible, she supposed, that an oncoming car had been speeding, giving the tractor no choice but to get out of the way. There was no CCTV, so they'd be lucky to trace it, if that was the case.

The next best explanation was mechanical failure, or human error. Or maybe driving under the influence? But, she reasoned, you'd have to be beyond plastered to smash a tractor into a house at speed, surely?

If all of those options were ruled out for whatever reason, there'd be only one left. It was deliberate.

She watched as Eric helped his interviewee up into the ambulance then started talking to one of the uniforms.

Eric stopped to look at his notebook. It was as if he was ticking things off. Jane smiled. She remembered when she'd started out twenty years ago. The fear of missing something, skipping a vital process at the start of an investigation, spending hours writing lists of things to remember.

He walked over, looking controlled. It was a far cry from the time she'd had to put him on disciplinary for playing on his phone instead of keeping watch on a private room at the hospital. It had proved to be his turning point, and now he was becoming an important part of the CID team at Ashbridge. She would have been justified in kicking him out at the time, but she'd always trusted her instincts. Eric was allowed one mistake.

'All okay, Eric?'

'Yes, thank you, ma'am. I was just talking to the tractor driver. I could smell alcohol on him, so I've asked one of the guys to get him breathalysed. He was a bit shaken up, so they're having a quick look at him in the ambulance first.'

'Good. What's his story?'

Eric looked down at his notes. Jane noticed he was no longer blushing every time anyone so much as looked at him. A few months with George, Ross and Lorry had obviously cured him of that.

Eric looked up. 'Rob Simmons. He was in the pub like he always is after his Saturday morning shift on the farm. He usually delivers hay today. There are quite a few smallholdings round and about, apparently. Loads the bales into the bucket at the front. He parks up near the pub when he's finished—swears the farmer lets him—then drives back to the farm this way. Says he suddenly lost control. Wasn't going particularly fast but couldn't do anything about it. He seems genuinely shocked, so...'

They watched as the driver stepped down from the ambulance and was escorted to the patrol car.

'How old is he?'

Eric consulted his notes again. 'Twenty years old, ma'am. Employed at Marsh Farm up the lane there for the last year.'

'Okay... Two people are dead, so we'll need a holding charge of dangerous driving. Then start gathering the names and addresses of the gawpers. Including the two in the hoodies, if you can. I want them all to know we're on the case. Might make the guilty blurt out some useful info and the innocent feel safer in their beds, if that's the right expression.' She held Eric's gaze. 'Keep it up, Eric. It's a bit traumatic, so don't be surprised if you feel a reaction later. Hopefully, we can wrap things up here and still make it to Lorry's reception before they eat all the cakes.'

***

The wedding cake was meant to look like a Transylvanian castle, and when Lorry and Mark joined hands to plunge the knife through the black icing, the strawberry cream filling leaked out like blood.

George turned to Jag and his wife, Moraji. 'I thought this was a wedding reception. Looks more like a murder scene.'

Jag shook his head. 'I can't see from here.'

'You're lucky, mate—' George stopped, embarrassed. Jag had lost sight in one eye when he was beaten up while checking out a storage depot. He was only just gaining the confidence and the ability to resume CID support work part-time.

Moraji smiled at George. 'It's okay, George. Jag actually does feel lucky.'

Jag nodded. 'Yes, and I thank you, George, for helping me get back to work.'

George grunted. 'Well, now you're settling back in, it won't be long before you can start making my coffee again, right?'

Jag let out his trademark high-pitched giggle, which seemed to bring the whole reception to a standstill.

Moraji hated attention, which George thought was odd for a teacher. 'Jag!' she hissed. 'They're all looking at us!'

Lorry laughed and waved. 'Jag! You made it! Ladies and gents... give a warm welcome to one of the best— my friend and colleague, Jag, and his lovely wife, Moraji. Jag has got the most hysterical and contagious laugh I have ever heard. It's the only reason we invited him.'

That set Jag off again, and the giggling spread, much to Moraji's annoyance. She whispered in George's ear. 'He's always doing this to the kids. Sets them off laughing. It's like living in a cage of hyenas.'

Waiters in tailcoats wearing black eye makeup walked solemnly round, carrying trays of bleeding cake.

Lorry's mingling eventually brought her to them, and she gave hugs all round as Moraji raved over her dress and make-up.

'I've always been a bit of a Goth,' Lorry said. 'I've had to push it to one side because of work. But Mark wanted it to be my day, so it was his idea for us to do it this way.' She laughed. 'He can't stand it really, bless.'

She didn't wait for a response. She pulled George to one side. 'Where's the boss?'

George took another bite of cake and took his time replying. 'Oh, just a call out. Sounds like an accident.'

'Oh God! Where?'

'Come on, Lorry, love. It's your wedding day.'

'George... I do know that. Come on, tell me. Please.'

'Okay. Well, a tractor ploughed into a cottage at Cardale. Two people pronounced dead at the scene.'

Lorry looked shocked. 'Oh God! I know people there. Have you got names?'

'If I have, you don't want to know. Come on, just enjoy your day. Jane said she was hoping to get back to see you before long.'

'No, George, you don't understand. I mean I've got good friends there. Please. You have to tell me, just in case, otherwise I'll just worry.'

'All right. One was called Geoffrey Pegg, the other a Mary MacDonald.'

'Oh, that's a relief. I don't know them.'

'Oh, charming.'

Now it was Moraji's turn to giggle.

3.

Jane crouched down next to Phil and Claire. Around them, four techs in white protective suits sifted through debris.

They could hear raised voices down the street. More sightseers. The uniforms were shouting to get everyone to go home, but Jane knew reporters would stick around. In the meantime...

'Any conclusions, guys?'

Phil nudged Claire. 'Go on. You've done all the work.' He grimaced. 'But first, help me up, will you?'

She held on to his hand to give him some support, then reached into a pocket and pulled out a small notebook.

'Victim one. Mary MacDonald, aged thirty-six, lives at this address. Victim two. Geoffrey Pegg, around mid- to late forties, with an address at Salford Quays. Both certified dead at the scene and now on their way to us for the PM.

'Looks like they were in bed together when the tractor hit the front of the house and it collapsed. Injuries consistent with being crushed, and if that wasn't enough, they were probably suffocated by the quantity of heavy material that landed on top of them.'

Jane shook her head. 'Ouch. Were they completely buried?'

Claire nodded. 'Only Mary's hand was visible. Mr Pegg was lying underneath her, so she suffered the most visible injuries. The back of her head was smashed in, and she had major trauma to her back and legs. He probably died from suffocation.' She glanced warily at Phil. 'But that's for the post-mortem.'

'Any suggestion of anything other than the tractor causing this?'

Claire shook her head. 'No ma'am. The house is heated by LPG and the engineer has been out to check. Electricity, the same. No faults reported. No evidence of explosion, or fire.' She stopped to check her notes again. 'Eric said he'd contacted the council so they could get a building inspector in to have a look, too.'

Jane whistled softly, impressed.

Phil perched on a stone. 'Excellent work. I need to get back and do the PM. Do you want to stay here and finish off?'

'Happy to, sir.'

He smiled. 'Sorry you missed the wedding, Claire.'

'Oh, that's okay. I would have looked bang out of place in my flowery dress.'

Jane laughed. 'Okay, thanks, you two. It's looking like an accident. But I need to know more before I sign off on that.' She half turned. 'If you see Eric before I do, remind him we need to identify next of kin, if he hasn't already, and to pass that on to me asap so I can break the news.'

She walked over to the tractor. The back end was remarkably untouched. The registration plate dated it at four years old, and what was left of it looked in good condition. Phil had already had it taped off so one of his team could take a closer look.

If she was the coroner at the inquest, she'd have no hesitation in concluding these were accidental deaths. But something about it all niggled at her.

She walked towards the tape cordon. She could see a few people drifting away, the excitement, no doubt, being replaced by the need to get a pint and a takeaway before *Strictly Come Dancing*.

There was a time when she and Allan would have been thinking along similar lines. Saturday night in usually meant a Chinese from up the road, then feet up for a telly-fest.

She wondered how much his life had changed since they split up. He was probably more of a Michelin-star restaurant man now: on a bloody good salary, a director of NW Media, and a quarter of a million in the bank from when they bought out his paper...

A voice interrupted her thoughts. 'DCI Birchfield! Can we have a word, please?'

She looked up to see a TV camera pointing in her direction, three reporters with notebooks, and one holding a smartphone.

***

Chief Supt Roy Cooke leaned back in his chair and sipped Darjeeling.

He put the cup carefully back on its saucer and glanced at Jane's case notes on the screen. 'So, what do we know about this couple? Apart from the fact they were screwing.'

Jane raised her eyebrows. It seemed every male in the station, and all the journos at the scene, were only interested in the sex angle. She'd stayed patient, despite the crass line of questioning from one TV reporter: 'Is this a first for you? Two people dying during sex. Were they married?'

She wanted to tell Roy to grow up. But she took a deep breath and decided to ignore it, just as she'd stonewalled the reporters. 'Sketchy details. Eric is still knocking on doors. We're trying to talk to next of kin to let them know before we give out any information, but Mary's mum lives in Scotland, and Geoffrey's family is in Spain. Both single. No kids. No answer from either family yet. But everything points to it being an accident.'

'No doubt in your mind?'

Jane paused. He was doing it again. Trying to force her into a judgement so she could take the blame if it all went wrong. At least she knew him well enough to think before she answered. 'There's always an element of doubt, as you know.'

He flicked her a glance. 'Yes, Jane, I know. But it's up to us to come up with a definitive answer so we don't get press hysteria. We've got a runaway tractor and two dead bodies in the village where the leader of the council happens to live. And, who knows, maybe a sex scandal as well.'

Jane tapped her teeth with her pen and couldn't resist winding him up. 'Hmmm. Well, we'd better eliminate him as a suspect, then.' She paused. 'Anyway, everyone's so obsessed with the sex angle, I expect you'd be disappointed if there *wasn't* a scandal.'

He wasn't amused. 'Maybe you're right. I do apologise. But it wasn't him on top of that woman.'

Jane kept her voice steady. 'If you want the facts, *that woman* was on top of him. It pays not to stereotype, doesn't it?'

His discomfort was gratifying, although he hid it by drinking the last of his tea then standing up abruptly.

'You need to bear in mind that a lot of influential people live in Cardale. The sooner we can confirm it was an accident, the better. We need to track down next of kin urgently, of course. We don't want them reading it in the paper first.' He cleared his throat and changed to a more conciliatory tone. 'Are you calling in at Lorry's reception later, by the way?'

'According to George, the food's all gone and they're currently thrashing around to weird music at high volume.'

'So that's a no, then.'

Jane just smiled and put her notebook away as she walked to the door.

He stepped in front of her, invading her space. Preventing her escape until he was ready? 'Quiet night in?'

She opened the door and felt the cool air from the corridor on her face. 'Always is, these days. What about you?'

'Same.' He moved away as the door bumped against his shoulder, took his jacket from the back of the chair, then stopped suddenly. 'We never did have that drink, did we?'

'No, we didn't.' Jane knew she couldn't hold out forever. She'd already made too many excuses.

'Well, shall we?'

'I'd love to, but can we make it another night? Sorry. I've still got to speak to their relatives, and after that, I'll be ready to just crash tonight.'

He grinned. 'Could have chosen a better expression, Jane.'

'Sorry. I'll need to be in early tomorrow as well, so...'

He shrugged his jacket on, then flicked through something on his phone. 'No problem. Let's aim for midweek, shall we? How about Thursday? My treat.'

Jane put on a happy face and hoped it was convincing. 'Okay, yes. Thursday it is. Well, have a good weekend.'

'Thanks muchly, Jane. You too.'

***

Allan flicked into cruise control and let the Lexus do the hard work.

He hated motorway driving. He hated car driving, if he was honest, and wished he'd said no to the company car, and yes please to a company motorbike. A Triumph Rocket 3 would have done nicely.

He'd fallen for the status trap: top-of-the-range smartphone, luxury car; he'd even gone shopping for new made-to-measure suits.

It just wasn't him, but it seemed like the right thing to do at the time. He'd never been director of a company before, never had a fit PA before—he'd had more than one dream about the leggy Ruby—never known the feeling of not having to worry about money.

NW Media had made him a six-figure offer to buy out his paper, the *Ashbridge Free Press*, and a tidy salary to join the board as their lead on newspaper development. The only thing that had saved his sanity was that he'd insisted on being given special responsibility for his old paper.

He'd even been signed up to lead a national campaign to raise standards of journalism in Britain.

The company had made him feel special, but he still worried that he'd made a mistake. Not only had he walked away from his life's work, grafting at a news desk; he'd walked out on Jane.

It had been okay at first. The feeling of righteous indignation, that it was all her fault, had kept him going for a couple of months. He'd taken a few women out to flirt with in posh restaurants. But he'd never taken it further. He always ended up comparing them to Jane.

His smartphone buzzed on its dashboard mount. *Meeting with Sue in 30 minutes.*

Allan rested an elbow on the driver's door and massaged his forehead. It had been an innocent text from Sue about a marketing meeting that had triggered the breakup with Jane. She'd misunderstood and he'd gone ballistic.

Work had brought them together. And pushed them apart.

He flicked off the cruise control and pulled into the inside lane, ready to leave the M6 and join another monotonous motorway.

***

Phil felt like he'd aged ten years. He thumped down into his desk chair and closed his eyes while he concentrated on his breathing.

The consultant had warned him he might feel short of breath and be more aware of his heartbeat for a while. He was right.

He still walked up the stairs at the station, as he'd done ever since he arrived more than twenty-five years ago. The difference now was that he needed to stop halfway.

He checked his FitBit. The beats per minute were still a bit high, but there were two people waiting on the slab. His was the kind of job where you are constantly reminded that there are other people worse off than you. Like dead, for example.

He nodded at the assistant who'd just finished the prep, and began washing his hands, the water drumming against the stainless-steel sink.

Claire tapped on the door glass. She'd asked Phil a few times how long it would be before she'd be able to do a PM. But she'd need a Level 3 Diploma just to assist, so she'd have to be patient.

Phil bowed. 'Have you got a ticket, madam?'

She grinned. 'I'm happy to pay on the door, if that's okay?'

'All right, but you'll have to sit in the cheap seats.'

Phil watched as Claire moved a chair into position. He'd been overjoyed when she turned up for the interviews. He knew he'd be in trouble for even thinking it, but it was such a nice change to see a young and pretty face around the lab. He knew what people would think, but it wasn't like that. He'd never looked at another woman since Elaine passed. Young people just made him feel young. Lifted his spirits. Claire was so smiley, so endearing.

Phil had always wanted kids, and it was a crushing blow to be told he couldn't.

He wiped his hands dry on a paper towel, scolding himself for being a silly old fool.

He put a hand on the head of the female body. 'Okay, Mary. Ladies first. Sorry to keep you waiting.' He raised his eyebrows at Claire. 'Ready?'

She nodded.

He started the voice recorder and reached for the scalpel.

4.

Jane decided there was a lot to be said for being a singleton.

She'd rinsed away her day under a shower, without having to wait because Allan had used all the hot water in the immersion heater. Now she was lying on the sofa in her fluffy white bathrobe with a bar of nutty chocolate and the old three-bar gas fire on full, listening to her playlist, uninterrupted.

She was so relaxed it was tempting to open the Malbec she'd bought on the way home. But she sipped sparkling water instead and settled down with her notebook to catch up on the case.

The police in Dumfries had broken the news to Mary's mother, and she was planning to travel down tomorrow. But Alex Gledhill was still waiting for his opposite number in Malaga to report back on Geoffrey's next of kin. Both his parents had died recently, but he had a brother still living in that part of Spain.

Mary's mother confirmed that her daughter had never married. She was born in Worcester, studied geology at Edinburgh, but then got a job with an estate agent. She was good at it and had moved down to

Manchester after being headhunted by one of the big agencies.

According to village gossip, she'd had a long list of men friends, though no one was prepared to name names. One of Eric's notes in particular caught her eye: *One lady said she could twist the council leader round her little finger.* She smiled slightly as she imagined the effect that would have on Roy Cooke's blood pressure.

She wondered briefly what it would be like to have an active sex life, but distracted herself by doing a web search for Cardale.

Eight miles NE of Manchester. Pop. 1,235. A rural village notable for farms, mainly arable, some dairy. Percentage of 65+: 57 per cent. Facilities: stores and PO, village hall, public house, church.

Another website confirmed the trend: a thirty per cent increase in population over the last ten years, people escaping the overcrowded city to overcrowd a village.

Jane scrolled down, her attention beginning to wander as the soft music and the warmth of the fire made her feel sleepy. She blinked back into focus and clicked on the parish council page. And there was Mary, listed as the chair of the Cardale Village Association.

Jane yawned and leaned further back into the seat cushion as she thought it through.

Mary was a very active woman in more ways than one, and attractive with her curly blonde hair. Everything pointed to her and Geoffrey's deaths being a freak accident. But as Allan used to say, Jane always went round with a question mark over her head.

She sat up. There he was, back in her head again. They'd been together less than three years, but she was finding it hard to live without him. She reminded herself it had been equally hard to live with him. She wondered if he was happy, and petulantly hoped he wasn't. That he was missing her, too.

She turned the fire down a notch and went into the kitchen to make cheese on toast. Phil Collins was singing about another day in paradise and the Malbec was standing on the kitchen table, looking lonely.

Jane picked it up. 'Hello. Mind if I join you?'

***

Rob Simmons whispered a thank you as DS Paul Rossiter, aka Ross, put a mug of tea on the interview room table.

Ross was all for letting him go after his night in the cells, but George wanted him grilled one more time. 'Make him sweat, then give him breakfast,' was the instruction.

Ross switched the ancient tape on and leaned back. 'Okay, Rob, let's go through it one more time.'

Rob ran a hand through his tousled brown hair. He was slim, but his hands were big. 'I can't think of anything else to tell you.'

'You've told us you were in the pub at the end of your shift. How much did you have?'

'Two pints.'

'Two? What, just real ale, or did you do the whisky chaser thing?'

He looked indignant now. Ross's easy way with people was beginning to work. 'No way! I was driving.'

'Yeah, but two pints is pushing it, isn't it? Your boss knows you do that, right?'

'Yeah. And you should see the state of him sometimes.'

Ross smiled. 'Yeah? Likes a drink, does he?'

'Likes it? I go into the farmhouse late mornings, just to say hello like, and he's sitting there necking the wine.'

'Okay, but he didn't demolish someone's house with a tractor, did he? So come on, how did that happen? You keep saying you lost control. We'll do a mechanical check, but have you got any idea why?'

Rob leaned back and looked up at the ceiling.

Ross could see the dark rings under his eyes. Probably hadn't slept last night, poor sod.

'I wish I knew.'

Ross leaned forward and spoke softly. 'Look, you should have a solicitor with you, and why won't you let us call your mum?'

His eyes were pleading. 'It would finish her off if she knew. She's got a weak heart. Don't tell her. Please?'

Ross sighed. He was so nice, he had to be innocent. 'I won't for the time being. But you've been charged with dangerous driving... Come on, help us clear this up so you can go home.'

He banged his fists on the table, then put his head in his hands, breathing heavily. 'I know!' He looked up, a hint of brightness in his eyes for the first time. 'I remember... I turned left to get to the farm. Must go steady there because the road's narrow and uneven, so it's easy to go off track a bit. But it was okay until...'

'Yeah? What?'

'Well, it's weird. I thought the brakes must be binding because I was having a struggle to hold a straight line. That's why I said it was like losing control. Only, it wasn't the brakes like I said before. I reckon it was the steering. The wheel was like fighting against me and next thing I know, I'm swerving all over the show. Then bang! That was it.'

Ross gave him a thumbs up. 'Interview suspended at eight twenty a.m.' He switched it off and stood up.

'Now we're getting somewhere. Come on you. Let's get you some nosh.'

***

While Rob was mopping up fried egg with a slice of bread, one of Phil's team was flat on the ground in the rain, checking the tractor's steering while trying to ignore the curious attention of a ginger cat. Once done, he warmed up with the car heater on full and tapped out his findings in an email.

Phil gave Jane the gist of it later as they chewed rubbery toast and gulped builder's tea in the canteen.

'Looks like young Rob was right. The steering was all to pot. If you want the detail, the drop arm, drag link and steering arm connections had worked loose on the offside.'

Jane scraped marmalade on her toast so at least it tasted of something. 'Which means, what?'

Phil scratched his head. 'I'd say that when Rob wanted to make a turn, one of the wheels wouldn't respond to the steering wheel.'

'Yep. I can understand that. So that's why he crashed? Not his fault?'

'Doesn't look like it.'

'A maintenance issue, then? A mistake rather than a deliberate act? I hope the farmer's got good insurance.'

Jane sipped tea and let the information soak in. She'd made good friends with Mister Malbec last night, despite her good intentions, and she needed time to reach top gear.

'Remind me, Phil... there was absolutely nothing out of the ordinary on site, and nothing to suggest foul play?'

Phil nodded after a moment. 'That's right. Nothing to suggest any other forces that may have caused the house to collapse. And nothing on those poor people to indicate assault. No entry wounds, nothing in their systems that shouldn't have been there, stomach contents normal. Just horrendous injuries consistent with being crushed.'

'God, what a way to go.'

Phil grinned. 'What, having it away, you mean?'

Jane snorted. 'Oh, please. Not you as well. I meant being crushed.'

Phil looked suitably remorseful. 'That was once a form of punishment, you know.'

Jane prepared herself for another of his history lessons.

'In the old days, the courts felt they didn't have powers to pronounce judgement until the defendant had pleaded one way or the other. Those that refused to plead did it in the hope that they wouldn't have to give up their property if they were found guilty. So, they'd be tied up for day after day, with more and more heavy stones put on their chests until they either gave up and entered a plea or stopped breathing and died.'

Jane sighed. 'I repeat, what a way to go.'

Phil nodded. 'Institutional torture, that's what it was. And it's still going on.'

'What?!'

'No, no, not crushing—or pressing, as it was called. I mean torture. It's still happening, all over the world. I joined Amnesty a few years ago, and you wouldn't believe what goes on.'

'I would actually. Trouble is, there are so many things to care about that most people just give up and do what's in front of them. Like me, probably... Anyway, we've got to move on. This was an accident. We need to parcel it up and get on with all the other cases.' She stopped. 'God, I am so slow today. Unless, of course, the tractor was tampered with?'

'My guy's pretty sure it wasn't.'

'Not enough. I want it in writing. It must be definite. Was it or wasn't it? I'll tell George to let Rob go, with conditions. And then...'

'Yes ma'am?'

'Then I'm going over Eric's house-to-house report. The devil's in the detail, Phil.'

'You think it's the devil's work, then?'

Jane smiled. 'Let's face it, Phil. Neither of us would be that surprised if it was, would we?'

***

Back in the office, Jane looked through Ross's summary of his interview with the driver.

Ross had surprised no one by coming out as gay six months ago, at the start of the hit-and-run investigation. It had made not the slightest difference to anyone, and Jane was proud of that. He was one of the brightest talents she'd ever seen, but he disguised it under a disconcerting veneer of laziness that fooled most people into underestimating him. He also had an abundance of charm that seemed to work with both men and women.

It seemed that the driver had succumbed, too. Ross had got more out of him in half an hour than Alex had managed in twice the time. His conclusion was that Rob Simmons was not guilty of a deliberate act. He'd lost control of the tractor, in his words, *as if the steering had a mind of its own.*

But it was his comments about his employer that had caught Jane's attention. She read Ross's notes again.

RS says Sid Marsh, of Marsh Farm, bought the place when he moved from London with wife, Julie. Regarded as a rookie by villagers; keen to prove he could farm organically and still make money. RS says the word is the farm is in trouble. RS has been there just over a year and has been on the look-out for other work. Says Marsh is a heavy drinker and sometimes smells of weed. RS has heard some talk of a planning application for development at the farm. I'll check that out.

Jane tilted back, still relishing the comfort of her new desk chair, courtesy of Roy Cooke. She'd thought about a charm offensive to get her office redecorated as well, but realised she'd probably hate working in a room painted magnolia. Yellowing white paint and rusty metal windows were far more appealing.

Ross's note had set her wondering. There were enough hints in there to suggest friction, not least the news of a planning application at the farm. Was Sid Marsh so hard up that he wanted to sell land for housing? That wouldn't go down too well. And Mary ran the village residents' group.

Jane glanced at her in-tray, and the case files waiting for her attention. Some of them were new, but others had been lying there patiently for a couple of weeks.

She needed to catch up. But then, two people had just died in an apparent accident, and there was just a chance there was more to it than that.

She folded her arms and frowned as she computed a decision. She'd spend the rest of today reducing the backlog, and tomorrow morning reviewing Eric's notes. Something told her she'd be heading for Marsh Farm soon after that.

5.

Allan frowned as the editor of the *Ashbridge Free Press* ran through this week's news list in her sing-song voice. 'It's a bit light, isn't it, Jenny?'

She didn't hesitate. 'Aye, but I've saved the best till last.'

'I wish you wouldn't. Would have saved me getting annoyed.'

She grinned. Her Scottish accent was as endearing as her permanently cheerful expression.

Allan looked forward to their twice-weekly sessions.

'Och, away with you. Don't be a worrywart.'

Allan cracked a smile. It would be so easy to get into a banter session with Jenny, but he still felt the need to keep a distance. It wasn't easy. 'Right, come on. What's this amazing story?'

'Two people having sex bring the house down. What d'you reckon to that for a headline?'

'Jenny... just tell me. I can't stand the suspense.'

She had a dirty laugh. 'Aye, well. Here we go. Man and woman were having it off in a little place called Cardale. A tractor ploughs into the cottage—did ye like that? *Ploughs*?'

Allan managed to nod and roll his eyes at the same time.

Jenny kept going. 'Well, they were both killed. Whole place collapsed. They were buried underneath. Still attached, if you know what I'm saying there. Thing is, she was like the top woman in the village—hey, woman on top, right? ... Anyways, he was sales director of a company called Universal Energy. They weren't married. The driver was taken in for questioning, charged with dangerous driving, and released on conditions, whatever you call it.'

Allan drank the last of his coffee. The company name rang a bell, but he couldn't work out why. He tapped a reminder on his phone. 'Okay, not a bad story. We're out a day later than *The Times*, though, so you're going to need to dig a bit deeper.'

She gave him a look. 'Was that an attempt at a play on words, at all?'

Allan grinned. 'I'd do better than that if I really put my mind to it... By the way, how do you know what he did for a living?'

'Mike's been toddling around up there.'

Allan nodded. They'd advertised for a trainee reporter a few weeks ago and been inundated. But Mike Brook had stood out. He was a local lad, full of confidence, and with an eye for a story. Not afraid to put himself about, but serious about the profession.

'Great. That's good, Jenny. Let me know if you need anything this week, okay? I'd better get back to my luxury office.'

Jenny rested her chin on her hands. 'Do you miss being the editor?'

'You know what? Yes, I do. But don't worry, I won't be sacking you just yet.'

'I know you won't. Because I'm too good at my job, isn't that right?'

This time, Allan laughed out loud.

***

Gloria MacDonald looked dressed for a funeral, but there were no tears when Phil pulled back the sheet to reveal Mary's face. She just nodded and whispered *yes*, then turned away sharply.

He'd seen just about every reaction over his twenty-five-year career, so he didn't read too much into it.

It was easy to see where Mary had got her good looks from. Gloria was in her sixties but looked twenty years younger. Her face was unlined, her eyes clear blue, and she'd avoided middle-age spread. She carried herself like a model.

Phil discreetly dismissed Eric Sykes, who'd witnessed the ID, with a nod.

'Would you like to come and sit down for a moment, Mrs MacDonald?'

She nodded and followed as he walked towards a black vinyl sofa in the waiting area.

'Can I get you a cup of tea?'

'No, thank you. Just water, please.'

Phil brought her a glass and sat beside her, elbows resting on his knees. 'When did you last see Mary?'

Gloria sipped water and stared out front. 'I should say it was six weeks ago. She comes up to see me—came up to see me—every now and again.'

Phil nodded. 'How did she seem?'

'Her normal bubbly self.'

Phil heard the tremor in her voice and stayed silent. If she wanted to talk, she would.

She dabbed her eyes with a handkerchief. 'She was the life and soul, everywhere she went. People loved her. She was clever too, ambitious. I wanted her to be a teacher, like me. I thought students would warm to her, respond to her. She got a BSc at Edinburgh, you know?'

Phil nodded. 'Geology, I believe? But she chose to become an estate agent?'

'Don't ask me why. It was probably just a whim, an instinct.' She smiled sadly. 'She was like that: impulsive. But she did well for herself. And now, this...'

'If it's any consolation, Mrs MacDonald, she wouldn't have known much about it. It would all have been over very quickly.'

She nodded.

'Are you staying somewhere local?'

She put her glass on the coffee table. 'I found a hotel nearby. The Royal. I wanted to go and see where it happened, you know... Can you tell me exactly what happened, or...?'

'I'm afraid we're still investigating. It shouldn't take too long. Perhaps we can talk again before you go back.'

She smiled faintly and Phil caught the scent of her as she leaned in slightly. 'I'd like that. Thank you for being so... kind.'

***

'This isn't working, Sid.'

Julie Marsh arched her back, which was seizing up after an hour forking over the compost heaps. Sid had built six bays, using wood pallets and corrugated tin sheets, but only two of them were anywhere near full.

She leaned on her fork as Sid spread old carpet over the other heap. He was ignoring her again. It infuriated her that he wouldn't face facts. He couldn't even rouse himself at the news that Rob had written off their only tractor and demolished a house belonging to one of the most popular people in the village.

Julie had lain awake all night, worrying. They were already a laughingstock. Now, this. It could ruin them. She'd always been able to find a way to fix things. Now she just felt beaten.

She remembered staring at the grey light beginning to seep through the bedroom window, and asking herself: where did it all go wrong?

It had seemed such a great idea two years ago. They were buzzing when they made the decision to escape London. They'd read all the organic farming books. Spent hours online. Convinced themselves they'd make such a profit on their London pad that it would subsidise them for at least three years. But they'd paid way over the odds for this place, blinded because it was a great location and the farmhouse had been modernised. And Sid was already compromising, buying chemical fertiliser and weedkiller behind her back.

Julie reckoned their extravagance with the house had cost them a year's savings, and then they'd had to survive one of the worst periods of weather for years.

A combination of dry conditions and lower temperatures had cut wheat and barley yields by at least half. Vegetable production wasn't doing too badly, but there was a lot of competition from farm shops for organic produce, and despite her best efforts to out-shout the other traders at the local markets, Marsh Farm was nowhere near making enough of a name for itself yet.

Sid had stayed positive. He'd worked his way up through the layers at the investment bank, and his mantra was that if he could survive in that environment, running a farm would be a cinch. But his optimism resembled blind faith now, and Julie knew she was in danger of becoming the archetypal nagging wife.

She still had friends in London, mainly at the ad agency in Marylebone, and their weekly video catch-ups had kept her sane.

As she watched Sid trudge back to the farmhouse, she couldn't help smiling as she remembered last week's Facebook video chat with Shelley, one of her best mates. *'If you dare use that phrase "nagging wife" again, I will come up there and punch your face. You're not his little housewife, you're Julie, and you went into this together. So, if he's being a pillock, tell him for Christ's sake. Life's too short, arsehole!'*

Julie shook her head. Shelley was right, but Sid had obviously drunk too much, and there was every chance he'd overreact if she laid it on the line. Even so, she had to find a way of making him see that they couldn't go on like this.

It was one thing having a tractor written off—they could at least claim that on the insurance—but demolishing Mary's house? That would be covered by public liability, but what effect would that have on their insurance premiums next year?

According to her calculations, they could only survive one more growing season without going into debt, and even that assumed favourable weather.

Julie angrily skewered her baling fork into the soggy ground and walked across the yard to check the cauliflower field.

Sid Marsh stood at the kitchen door and watched her. She was losing faith, but she'd soon cheer up when he told her his news. Their money worries would soon be over.

6.

The Policía Nacional in Malaga called Alex Gledhill to say that Geoffrey Pegg's brother did indeed live in the area but wouldn't be able to identify the body, mainly because he was in residence at the Alhaurín de la Torre Prison for drug offences.

George despatched Eric to Cardale to show Mr Pegg's picture around. 'Don't come back till you've got at least one positive ID.'

Ross looked up from his computer as Eric headed for the door. 'Might be worth asking at the farm, mate.'

Eric nodded, quietly pleased with himself for planning ahead.

He'd put a pair of wellies in the boot.

***

Jane cleared her paperwork by eleven and was looking forward to a drive out to Marsh Farm when Phil called with the news that Mary's mother was planning to visit the village later.

'Can you find out what time, so I can meet her?'

Phil sounded vaguely put out. 'She said she'd get there around one and call in at the pub for a bit of Dutch courage before going to the house.'

'Okay. Give her my number and tell her I'll meet her at the pub.'

She put a note on the log reminding Family Liaison to contact Gloria later that afternoon to offer support.

Eric's notes from the day of the accident revealed his diligence, but not much else. There was the gossipy stuff about Mary and her men friends. A few of her neighbours said they could set their clocks by her Saturday sessions. Others admired the way she threw herself with equal enthusiasm into her voluntary work as association chairperson.

Geoff Pegg was hardly mentioned, but one person wondered if he'd been genuinely passionate about Mary or more interested in getting customers for Universal Energy.

Jane shook her head. There was a lot to be said for living in a city. No doubt people gossiped and bitched and complained. But you were less likely to hear it above all the other noise.

***

'You what?'

Julie stared as Sid Marsh poured himself another double and drank it in one. 'Half a million in the kitty. For one field. How's that for a deal?'

'So, it's going to happen, is it?' She put her meek reply down to the shock.

'Planning application being finalised tomorrow. Council says no grounds to oppose. Got the call yesterday. Bit of a way to go, though. Statutory process and all that bollocks.'

'Did you not think it would be a good idea to talk to me about it?' She was talking, but her voice sounded like it was coming from somewhere else. She felt the anger building inside and there was nothing she could do to stop it.

He smiled. 'Remember what we said at the start of this? You're the boss on the agricultural side of things. I'm the boss when it comes to the commercial stuff. You've been beating me up for months about the state of our finances. You wanted me to do something, and I did. This puts us in a great position. We lose our crappiest field—two per cent of our land. We gain financial security. No need to worry anymore, Julie.'

Julie felt something snap inside. 'No need to worry? How do you think the village will react to this? Thirty detached houses with bloody enormous garages, no doubt. Two gas guzzlers each. Tons of tarmac and concrete and building supplies. Heavy lorries clogging up the lanes. On an organic farm? Oh, yes, and we're the neighbours who managed to kill two people when their tractor smashed into a bloody villager's house! No need to worry. You're off your fucking head! And if you think—'

A loud knock on the door. They turned and stared. A pause.

Sid not looking at her, his voice low. Angry. Petulant. 'I'll get it, shall I?'

Julie went upstairs and sat on the bed.

***

Jane heard shouting and hesitated before knocking. Three taps on the horseshoe knocker had the desired effect. There was silence, then the door opened.

She held up her ID. 'Mr Marsh? DCI Jane Birchfield, Ashbridge Police. May I have a word?'

The man looked too frail to be a farmer. He was a couple of inches taller than her, slim and pale. His eyes were strangely out of alignment, as if one was looking at you and the other was more interested in something just over your shoulder. He smiled pleasantly enough, but there was a smell of alcohol mixed in with the sweet and sour scent of manure coming from the yard.

He nodded and stepped back to let her into a large room with a stone floor and an enormous open fireplace. There was a modern table tucked up against the wall by the window, with a computer and a neat pile of box files. The black desk chair looked equally out of place.

He held out his hand. 'Sid Marsh. What can I do for you?'

Jane looked round. 'I hope I'm not interrupting anything. I heard voices...'

He moved towards an armchair by the fireplace and pointed to the other. 'Oh, it's okay. Just Julie and I having one of our regular disagreements.' He stopped. 'Ah, sorry. Was it Julie you wanted to see?'

Jane filed that one away as quite an odd thing to say. Defensive. She let it pass, for now. 'No, not particularly, Mr Marsh. I wanted to talk about the incident involving one of your tractors.'

He shook his head, tutting. 'God! Nightmare. I've no idea what Rob was playing at. He's usually so reliable. We feel awful about what happened. Those poor people.'

Jane nodded. 'Obviously, we need to find out exactly what happened. Especially when deaths are involved.'

He nodded to himself, his eyes looking down. Jane noticed the half bottle of whisky on a side table, partially hidden behind him.

'So, the issue is whether it was driver negligence—a mistake, perhaps; or dangerous driving—we know he was in the pub before; or perhaps a mechanical fault.'

Sid's eyes flicked up to meet hers, but she couldn't read his expression. 'Fault? What do you mean?'

Jane heard a faint creaking noise from upstairs. 'Mr Marsh. It appears that there was a significant problem with the steering mechanism. We think it's more than likely that this caused the tractor to veer off into the house. We're pretty sure Rob Simmons wasn't to blame.'

His face twisted into a scowl, his eyes narrowing, his jaw jutting forwards. It looked to Jane like a bad impression of a petulant child. 'So, what are you saying? It's my fault?'

Jane sat back. 'We're not blaming anyone, Mr Marsh. We simply want to establish the facts. Two people have died. We owe it to them and their families to be clear about how it happened.'

He nodded. She leaned forward again. 'So, in view of that, I'd like to see the documentation for the tractor, please, including the service history. Just for the record.'

He got up, walked over to the computer table without a word and started flicking through papers in a white wire mesh tray.

Jane took another look round the room. First impressions were of a farmhouse kitchen, but that was deceptive. On closer inspection, it looked more like a Sunday supplement image of designer country living. The sofa was clearly high quality, in red and gold fabric that matched the Roman blinds on the windows. The coffee table looked like mahogany, and the fireplace housed a stainless-steel wood-burning stove with a smoked glass front.

Upstairs, the sound of a toilet flushing, then foot-steps on the stairs. Sid Marsh continued his silent search as a strikingly tall woman with a boyish haircut strode up to Jane.

'Hello. I'm Julie.'

'Hi. DCI Birchfield. I'm here about—'

'The accident? Yep. Thought so.' She turned to her husband. 'What are you looking for?'

'Service history for the tractor. Seems to have van-ished.'

Julie winked at Jane, then said, airily, 'It's vanished into a file marked "transport". Let me get it. Hold on.'

Sid looked at Jane as Julie walked quickly into another room. Jane got the feeling he was on a very short fuse. What had their argument been about? Julie must have been doing the shouting earlier. Either it had meant nothing, or she was a very good actor.

'Here it is.' Julie handed the file to Jane, even though Sid had his hand stretched out to receive it. Jane saw his anger, though he quickly camouflaged it by coughing. What the hell had she walked into?

'Mind if I look now?'

'Course not.' Julie sat next to her. Then, without looking at her husband: 'We've got nothing to hide, have we, Sid?'

Jane tried to concentrate as she studied the papers on the coffee table. The tractor had been bought four years ago at a dealer in Macclesfield for just over £55,000. It came with a three-year warranty. For the first two years, it had been serviced on-site by a tech-nician from a garage six miles away, but there were no records after that.

Jane wrote the details in her notebook and glanced at Julie, who was looking through a gardening magazine. She appeared strong, outgoing and artificially relaxed. And she hadn't looked at her husband once since she came down.

Jane cleared her throat. 'Can you help, Julie? I can't find any service record in the last two years.'

'You're kidding me.' Julie reached over impatiently, turning pages over, then left the room, calling over her shoulder. 'Give me a minute. They could be in the wrong folder.'

Jane heard drawers being opened and closed. She was back a few moments later, and though she was looking tense, she kept her voice light. Jane thought she sounded just like a nursery school teacher. 'What happened, Sid? Did you forget?'

Sid looked at her without a trace of emotion. 'Course I didn't.' He turned to Jane. 'They must be somewhere. Can you leave it with me, and I'll give you a call?'

Jane stood. 'Of course. I can give you until tomorrow. Here's my card. Call me by then, whether you find the service record or not, okay? Thanks to you both.'

Julie waved from the door as she walked across the yard to her car. Once out of sight, Jane leaned against a low stone wall and breathed in deeply. The fresh air tasted wonderful, which was more than she could say for the atmosphere at Marsh Farm.

7.

The Frog and Firkin made its intentions clear. The A board in the entrance porch was chalked with the message: *No tea or coffee unless you're having a meal.*

It was just after midday, according to the big old clock behind the bar, and the regulars were already dosing up on beer. Big old jumpers, cord trousers and grey hair. The landlord looked like he'd been rehearsing the part. Big moustache, bigger nose, beer belly and a deep voice that filled the room as he cheerfully repeated and personalised the orders. 'One pint of Bombardier for Charlie. There you go, my little ray of sunshine. The damage is three twenty-five to you, sir. No, thank *you*, my man.'

He acknowledged Jane with a nod as he dished out the change. The old boys turned as one to eye her up, then decided the beer and the horse racing on the wall-mounted television were more interesting. 'Yes, madam. Welcome. What can I get you?'

She said she was here to meet someone, and he walked her through to the dining room at the back. A dozen dark wood tables; red paper napkins and cutlery stuffed into terracotta pots; table mats featuring hunting scenes. And in the corner, her hair glowing like a halo in the sunshine through a little bay window, the only diner.

They ordered vegetable soup and sandwiches: chicken and tomato for Jane, prawn salad for Gloria. Gloria offered Jane a glass of white from the carafe she'd already paid for, but Jane said she was on duty and went to the bar to order a pot of tea.

They made small talk over the soup, about Scotland, the weather, Gloria's hotel—'basic but comfortable'. Jane admired her self-control, her poise, the way she obviously looked after herself, took care over her appearance. She said she'd been a widow for around twelve years. She told Jane her husband, a science professor, had been 'destroyed by a brain tumour'.

'He was such a clever man; it felt even more cruel. He wanted Mary to use her brain. She was clever, too. A first class in geology, you know.' She smiled sadly. 'The only consolation was that he died before she decided to go into estate agency.'

Gloria carefully poured the last mouthful of wine into her glass and looked out of the window. 'Was anyone to blame for this?'

The question came suddenly, and so directly, it caught Jane out. She sipped water and folded her napkin slowly. 'We're still looking into it. It seems to be a tragic accident. I'm afraid it may take some time to prove anything. But we'll find out, I promise.'

Gloria reached into her handbag and stood. 'I want to see where it happened now. I'll pay at the bar. See you outside.'

***

Jane signalled Claire Pearce to take five as she stood with Gloria, looking at the wreckage of the house.

She was relieved Gloria hadn't asked what Mary had been doing in her final moments, but that would probably come out in the inquest. It suggested she hadn't read the papers. Either that, or it had come as no surprise.

Jane pointed to where Mary's body had been found. Claire and her team had bagged and photographed what they needed and cleared debris to form a neat rectangle of bare earth. The sun slid behind a dark cloud as Gloria knelt to place a posy of flowers, bought at a garden centre on her way there.

Jane blinked away a tear as she looked on. She was more liable to cry lately, she'd noticed. Her mum said it was no surprise after what she'd been through. Maybe so, but crying on duty was not in the job description.

She could see Gloria's lips moving, but there was no sound. Saying a prayer or saying goodbye? Jane had always felt there was something mystical in the way that places people die became shrines. She could imagine villagers seeing Gloria's small posy of flowers and adding their own. Jane had annoyed her mum as a teenager by telling her she never wanted to visit her dad's grave because it reminded her he was dead. Seeing Gloria connecting with her daughter made her wonder whether she should make the effort next time.

Gloria let her hand rest on the flowers for a moment, then stood. 'Thank you for coming with me.'

'Thank you for letting me. I'm so sorry. Are you okay?'

She nodded and began to walk back the way they'd come.

Jane called after her. 'I need to talk to the team while I'm here. Is that all right?'

Gloria turned back. 'Yes, I'll be fine. I'll go for a walk. Get to know the village. Thank you again.'

'Ah. Just one thing.' Jane hesitated before deciding Gloria was tough enough for her to try. 'Can I ask... did Mary ever talk about boyfriends, affairs? Whether she was in a relationship?'

Gloria glanced at what had been her daughter's house. 'Oh yes. All the time. She was never short of admirers, Mary.'

Jane couldn't swear to it, but was there a hint of bitterness in Gloria's tone? Gloria was very attractive, but had her widowhood isolated her? Or was it disapproval? 'Did she mention anyone in particular? Any problems?'

'Not sure why this is relevant, but she talked about a farmer last time. Didn't give me a name.' She smiled briefly. 'I'm not sure she trusted me. Said he was married.'

***

Jane had felt the beginnings of a headache but felt better after driving back to the station with the window down and drinking half a litre of water.

She sat at her desk, scrolling through case notes, waiting for Roy Cooke to finish a phone call.

Forensics had found a small plastic zip-lock bag in the rubble of the house, containing traces of white powder. Claire said they'd photographed it where they found it, close to where the open fireplace would have been. Jane took it in to be recorded before Phil got his hands on it.

She made a note to tell Phil to talk to Ross, who was looking into a new outbreak of drug activity in Ashbridge.

The Marshes had been very tense individually and with each other. And Gloria had said her daughter had been seeing a married farmer. Was that too obvious a connection? There must be dozens of farmers in Cardale.

It was obvious that Sid Marsh hadn't had the tractor serviced under the conditions of warranty. It meant he was culpable for the accident, and likely to be the subject of a civil action for compensation. It was questionable whether his insurance would cover him, so the Marshes could be facing financial ruin.

Eric had come back from another morning of house-to-house calls with news that Geoff Pegg had been winning support in the village for gas exploration. Tests had been carried out, and Geoff had told a few people there was enough evidence to justify an application. The villagers Eric had spoken to had all been keen, he said. 'They thought it was great because it would mean jobs and loads of money.'

Jane steepled her fingers. So many connections. And what about the contrast between Gloria's calm control and the undercurrent of violence between Sid and Julie Marsh? Everything pointed to it being just a bad accident, but—

A loud tap on her door and Roy was there, looking anxious. 'Come through, will you, Jane?'

He was silent for a moment. Weighing up his words. He normally just blurted it out.

Jane waited.

Roy sighed and leaned forward, attempting a smile. He wanted to be in control, but he was the first to admit he was a learner. The great unknown was how long his mentor, Chief Constable Hopkirk, would be willing to wait before ripping the L plate off his back.

'Okay, Jane,' he began. 'Here's the thing... I've had a shit morning.'

'Sorry, boss.'

This was coming out all wrong. 'No, no, it's okay. I'm fine. But we have a problem.'

Jane noted his emphasis on the word *we*.

'I've had the press on, closely followed by Councillor Barrett.'

Jane narrowed her eyes, trying to anticipate where this was going, wishing he'd get on with it. 'Right.'

'In a nutshell, Jane, the press is running a story about a planning application for housing at Marsh Farm, and Barrett is bloody furious. The application hasn't even gone in. So how did the press get hold of it?'

'Right. So, okay, sorry—what has this got to do with us?'

Roy sighed. Jane knew where this was heading. *He just wants a problem off his desk.*

'You know Mary was chair of the village residents' group?'

Jane nodded.

'Well, the press has got her on record as saying there'd be new housing at Cardale "over my dead body", or something like that.'

Jane snorted with disbelief, but he wasn't deterred.

'They're not saying it's a motive for murder, but according to Barrett, the *Ashbridge Free Press* is running both stories on the front page. So it's inevitable people will link it in their minds. They're sending a reporter to Marsh Farm to interview the farmer, who, I am reliably informed, stands to make a bloody packet out of the scheme.'

Jane frowned. She could do without this. The *Free Press* was Allan's baby. He'd refused to sell it to NW Media without an assurance he'd stay in day-to-day control. She'd wondered how long it would be before their paths crossed.

'So, what happens next?'

Roy was having trouble sitting still, she noted.

'Good question. The council leader doesn't want an important housing scheme jeopardised by association with this... erm, tragedy. He lives in the village, don't forget. We need to nip it in the bud. If this gets picked up, it'll be a national story.'

'Sorry, sir. When you say *we*... It's not for me to take this up with the paper, is it?'

Roy leaned forward, smiling. 'Well, normally, no, of course not. I'd take responsibility. But in this case, there's no one better placed than you. You know Allan Askew better than anyone. Don't you?'

8.

The note was propped up against his half-empty whisky bottle. *Gone to London for a few days. Need time to think. Julie.*

Sid lay on the sofa and stared at the ceiling. Their relationship had fallen off a cliff since the money worries started. Maybe he'd raised her expectations too high. He'd been famous for that at the bank: persuading investors to put money into his schemes, watching the commission and the bonuses pile up in his accounts.

She should trust him more; that was the problem. He'd never had to worry about money. Always found a way. Downward graphs were for other people. And he'd done it again with the housing development. Massive capital boost, and the developers were keen to get him on the board so they could tap into his investment expertise. With that income, the farm could just be a no-stress hobby. He'd worked out a plan to diversify into flower production. Julie would enjoy that.

Speeding up the housing scheme had also been an attempt to outsmart that pushy bastard, Pegg. Sid and Julie had always opposed Pegg's plans for gas exploration. It would wreck the environment, destroy habitats, poison the atmosphere, clog the roads. But they were in the minority. Pegg had bought the whole village off. He'd even been shagging the chair of the village association.

Sid sat up, feeling angry again. His plan was to get in first with a housing scheme in the hope it would pressure the politicians, and the public who loved visiting Cardale, into resisting further development. Yes, it would be messy. But it was the lesser of two evils.

He thought Julie would see his thinking and be pleased.

But had things gone too far? Would she even come back? She'd be at Shelley's place, peppermint tea and bloody wind-chimes, calling him names in her walled garden in Islington.

He walked to the window, his thoughts switching back to the accident at Mary's place. It was his tractor, his driver, and he'd skipped the last service to save cash. His feelings about Pegg were no secret, either.

He chewed his thumbnail. No wonder the DCI had come calling.

A car was parking up outside. Door slamming shut.

Sid put the whisky in the sideboard, folded Julie's note into his gilet pocket, and crunched a mint.

***

His card said he was Mike Brook, *Ashbridge Free Press*.

No way was he coming in the house, getting his feet under the table.

'It's a nice day. Shall we take a walk?'

They stood with their elbows resting on a gate, looking across the valley. The square grey tower of St Jude's was visible above a line of trees. A light aircraft buzzed overhead.

The reporter got his notebook out, and Sid reminded himself to be careful.

'So, how can I help?'

'Right, yeah. Thanks for the tour. Great place. Thing is, we're running a story about the accident in the village, and we understand it was your tractor.'

'It was. A terrible accident.'

'How could that happen?'

'Ah well, I think you know that I can't talk about something that's under investigation by the police.'

Mike Brook looked surprised. 'So, you're under investigation, are you?'

Sid stopped himself just in time. It was a classic ploy to get him off guard, reacting to the wrong question, giving answers that hadn't been asked for. The throwaway remark had spelt the end for many politicians. 'The incident is being investigated.'

They started walking back towards the farmhouse. Brook tried to establish when the tractor driver would be coming back to work, but Sid gave nothing away. 'He'll be back when he's ready.'

Brook changed tack instantly and pointed off to the right, towards a road junction. 'That's where they're going to build the houses, isn't it? That field?'

Sid stopped. 'I'm not sure I understand. Are you interviewing me about a tragic accident in which two people died, or about a planning application?' He realised his mistake too late.

Brook held his hands palm up. 'Hold on, Mr Marsh. It was just a passing remark, mate.' He paused, smiling, notebook in hand. 'So, there definitely is a planning application, then? It's all happening in little old Cardale, isn't it?'

Sid held it together until the reporter drove away, then sat on the doorstep, head in hands. Cameron, their ageing Springer, came waddling up, ears scraping on the cobbles, and rested his head on Sid's thigh.

Sid stroked his head. 'I've messed everything up, Cammy.'

***

'Allan. It's Jane. Hope you're okay. Can you call me when you get this, please? Usual work number. Thanks.'

She was glad he wasn't there to pick up. Hearing his voice message had been weird enough. They hadn't spoken since the split, except that time he came back to collect some stuff, when they'd behaved like people meeting for the first time. Unsure, hesitant, careful. Socially distanced.

She thought she'd feel stronger with the passage of time. And at least they could both hide behind work this time. Two busy people. Or should that be *too* busy? That's what had finished them off, in the end.

Jane sipped coffee, her thoughts drifting. She was puzzled by what was going on at Cardale. It felt as if the accident had set off a chain of events. Connections she wasn't seeing.

The ring of the desk phone startled her. She took a breath. It was Allan, sounding like he always did. As if nothing had happened.

'Hi Jane. What's up?'

She tried hard to be businesslike, explaining the concern about linking the housing story with the death of two people in Cardale. He claimed he knew nothing about it and that he wasn't surprised she was worried.

'Leave it with me, will you? A story like this isn't going to help anyone.'

'Thanks. I appreciate it.'

'No problem. Erm... are you okay, otherwise?'

Jane hesitated. *After six months, seriously?* She played the game. 'Yeah. Busy.'

She could hear the smile in his voice. 'So, no change there then. I was wondering—'

'Allan. I don't want to be rude, but I really need to go. I'm due in a meeting right now.'

'Oh yes, sorry. Well, I'll let you know the outcome.'

'Yes, great, thanks again.'

She disconnected before he could reply, and paced the room. Just the sound of his voice brought it all back. His comforting presence, his soothing voice... And what was that about? What had he been about to say? She should have let him finish the sentence. First contact for six months and her emotions were all over the place.

She punched the desk drawer. The pain made her wince.

***

Peter Attrill straightened his golf club tie, smoothed down the sparse thatch of grey hair that clung to the top of his head and stepped out into the rose garden.

He'd married Maggie six years ago. Second time for him, third for her. They were happy enough. He had his committees and his golf. She had her garden. He knew better than to offer to do anything other than trundle around on the ride-on mower now and again.

She was wielding secateurs like a surgeon, making the most of the spring sunshine.

'I'm off then, Maggie.'

She turned to kiss him lightly on the cheek. 'Oh God. I forgot. It's the big vote, isn't it? Good luck, dear.'

He winked. 'No luck involved. It was all sorted a couple of days after Mary died.'

Maggie carefully snipped away another length of stem and placed it neatly in the trug. 'Poor girl.'

'I know. At least we're safe from runaway tractors here, eh?'

'Oh Peter! Don't.' She laughed. 'Except you on your mower?'

'Ha! Show more respect.' He put a hand on her shoulder, suddenly serious. 'Anyway. Wish me luck. Here I go.'

Maggie watched him go out onto the lane through the white wrought-iron gate. She smiled to herself. Usually, he'd turn right for the pub. But not today.

***

Allan told Ruby, his PA, he wanted to see Jenny, the *Free Press* editor, in his office, in half an hour.

For the first time since he'd become a director at NW Media, he felt angry. Let down. Jenny usually did a great job. She was spikey but hard working, and full of original ideas. Best of all, she consulted him.

So why the skulduggery over this story? Why not talk it through? She must have known that linking a housing development to a tragic accident wasn't just poor judgement; it was an embarrassment to him. He'd set the *Ashbridge Free Press* up to be a community paper: one that didn't look for sensation, cared about its readers, was sensitive to local opinion, not afraid to tackle controversy, and above all, balanced.

He sensed Mike Brook's influence. He was bright and very pushy: not bad attributes for a reporter. Ambitious, too. Maybe he sensed a national story that would put him on the map and Jenny was finding him hard to control.

He realised he was clenching his fists and tried to release the tension by stepping out onto his eighth-floor balcony, admiring the view, trying to think positively.

One good thing had come out of it: he'd spoken to Jane. It was great to hear her voice, and now he'd got an excuse to call her back.

Six months apart had done nothing to make him feel any better about himself. He'd walked out on her after a pathetic row about a text from the marketing director, Sue. Jane read it and got completely the wrong end of the stick. But he'd overreacted, big time.

Righteous indignation and the distractions of his new job had kept him going at first. But now his new wealth and status meant little. It was good not to have to worry about money. But he'd never loved anyone as much as Jane. And he'd thrown it away.

Allan turned his back on the view and walked back to his desk. The light on his phone was flashing.

9.

Peter had been prepping his maiden speech ever since Aaron Barrett suggested he should stand for election as village association chair.

He'd been flattered, but he knew why Aaron had tapped him up. He'd done a bit of canvassing for him at the last council elections and, more importantly, had always been a strong supporter of gas exploration in the area. There was no in between with Aaron. You were an ally or an enemy.

Aaron had convinced him the village was about to be presented with a once-in-a-lifetime opportunity to put itself on the map.

He remembered his words as they'd gone into a conspiratorial huddle over a pint: 'We need to show unity of purpose, Peter. You and I can see the clear economic benefits. There'll be the usual hippy hysteria about birds and bees. But we both know the environmental impact will be marginal and temporary, and the rewards will be massive, and permanent. Not just for the village, but the whole district. We can't be NIMBYs.'

The hall was full tonight. Peter looked up from his notes at the rows of familiar faces. The village hall stage was mainly used for am-dram productions better known for their comedy value than their quality. This was the first time Peter had been on the stage, and he could understand why nerves got the better of the village thespians. But at least he had the words in front of him, and overacting wasn't his style.

He acknowledged the applause with a nod as his election was confirmed, and he scraped his chair back so he could stand. Maggie told him his voice would project better that way. And he'd look more dominant, Churchillian. He liked the sound of that.

'Thank you for putting your trust in me. But of course, this isn't about me. Let's remind ourselves what the village association is. An association like ours is a group of people living in an area who have come together to take up issues of common concern, like housing, community, the environment.

'For it to be successful and effective, it should represent and include all residents. A collective voice is a powerful voice. Being united with other people who share your living environment means you can influence the quality of services and improve quality of life.'

He paused and was gratified to hear a brief burst of applause. He could see Aaron nodding his approval in the front row. Then he caught sight of Sid Marsh. He was on the end of a row, slouching in his chair, getting disapproving looks. Probably drunk. Again.

Peter cleared his throat. 'So, with that in mind, it is my pleasant duty to confirm tonight that Universal Energy have submitted a formal application for permission to drill for gas at various locations around the village. You don't need me to tell you what good news this is for—'

'Good news? Are you mad?' Sid Marsh staggered to his feet, shouting. 'They'll destroy the village, kill wildlife, destroy habitats, pollute the atmosphere. Want me to go on?'

Peter kept his tone reasonable. 'No, thank you. You've made the same point many times.'

But Sid was not to be silenced. He walked jerkily down to the front and turned to face the audience, his right hand gripping the edge of the stage for support. Peter could see the venomous looks he was getting, but Marsh was oblivious.

He spoke in a slurred shout. 'You can't agree to this! Don't let them kid you. They want it because they're the bloody landowners and they'll make a fortune. You won't. Your nice little village will be wrecked, and they'll be laughing all the way to the wine bar.'

A voice called out from the back. 'You'd know all about that. Sit down, for God's sake. You're drunk.'

Peter caught Aaron's eye as the audience laughed and clapped. It was as expected. Sid was tanked up and going way over the top. No one in their right mind would dare to take his side.

He was inadvertently guaranteeing the opposite of what he wanted.

***

Sid sat on his own in the corner of the pub, while Peter held court at the bar. It had gone well.

Aaron patted Peter on the back and steered him away to the end of the bar. 'I think we can call that done and dusted. Between you and me, it'll be a similar story at council tomorrow. Our one and only Green councillor will have a fit, of course, but she's a bit like Marsh. No one pays her a blind bit of notice, and who in their right mind would vote Green?'

Peter laughed and checked his watch as Aaron moved off to collar someone else. The real ale was going down nicely, and there was time for one more. He looked over at Sid and shook his head. He'd been steadily accumulating pint glasses on his table and was now drinking shots and staring at the fire.

He was just about tolerable if he carried on behaving like a bar-room bore. But Peter knew he could make life very difficult if he sobered up long enough.

Sid stared at the fire through hooded eyes. He vaguely remembered ordering a toasted sandwich at the bar. God knows when that was. He'd skipped lunch and dinner, so it had been a token effort to soak up the alcohol. It felt like the room was moving now, so it clearly hadn't worked.

He slowly shifted position so he could see the bar. There they were, keeping their distance, looking down their noses at him. That was nothing new. They'd sneered since he moved into the farm and told everyone it was going organic.

He heard the shout for last orders and walked to the gents at the back, then stood outside, taking deep breaths.

He'd made a fool of himself tonight. He was starting to wonder if he was losing his mind. No wonder he was on his own.

A man he vaguely recognised came towards him from the beer garden. 'Fancy a smoke? Your favourite.'

Sid nodded and accepted a light. His brain was foggy from the booze. But as he dragged the smoke deep inside, he felt the sharpness come back.

The man moved in close and handed him an envelope. 'Here you go, mate. Plenty in there for you. Bit extra this week. Good stuff an' all. Usual price for you.'

Sid pulled his wallet from his jeans pocket, roughly grabbed a few notes and handed them over without counting.

The man's face was hazy, shadowed by the lighting behind him, as he slowly counted up. He nodded. 'Yeah. Nice one. Anyway, people to see. Enjoy yourself. See you next week.'

Sid flapped a hand and walked back inside, stuffing the envelope into his jacket. His head was clear already. Walking straight, thinking sharp. Just like he always did. He ordered a double Scotch and remembered Rob Simmons.

He tapped out a text when he got back to the table: *No more farm work, sorry. Sure you'll find something else. Thank you!*

He heard his name amongst the chatter at the bar. They were getting louder. Sid shook his head. Amateur drinkers.

One voice got louder, rising above the others. Soon, it was all Sid could hear. 'That's him. The pisshead in the corner. His bloody tractor killed two people! How's he got the nerve to come in here, eh? Tell me that!'

Then the landlord. 'All right, that's enough. Come on. Let's not have any unpleasantness.' He came over to Sid's table and spoke quietly as he started clearing the glasses. 'Sorry about that, young man.'

'It's okay. Thanks. Used to it. I made a pillock of myself at the meeting.'

'We're all pillocks from time to time.' He leaned in closer. 'There's one or two getting aggressive over there. Time to get off home, eh?'

Sid could feel the effects of the coke wearing off. He fixed his eyes on the door and started walking. He heard the laughter as he bounced slightly off the doorframe.

After the light and the warmth of the pub, the night felt cold and damp, dark and silent. He sobbed. He felt sick and his head throbbed. All he could think of was that he was on his own now. What was there at home, apart from Cammy? Tears dripped off the end of his nose. What had happened to him?

He stumbled on a loose paving stone, then heard laughter as people came out of the pub. He turned left into a lane so they wouldn't see him.

It was even darker here, like being in a tunnel, and everything seemed louder. The trees rustling in a fresh breeze, running water, his breathing shallow, irregular.

Then footsteps behind him, getting nearer.

10.

Ross put the phone down and frowned at George.

'That guy, the tractor driver, says he's been sacked.'

'And good morning to you, too. So what? I'm not surprised.'

'It wasn't his fault though, was it?'

George reminded him that nothing had been proven; the farmer had lost £50,000-worth of tractor and could be facing a pay-out for compensation. Saving a few quid on wages was a no-brainer.

'Yeah, okay. But why do it by text at eleven at night?'

'Let it go, son. The way he runs his farm has got nothing to do with us. Least of our worries. Now, come on, we need progress on that drug case.'

'I'm on it, boss.' Ross swiped through screens on his tablet. 'I gave the guys at National Crime Agency a bell, and they told me about a couple of hard lads they caught smuggling cocaine from Costa Rica. They're pretty sure they've been active for years, just got a bit too ambitious. And they reckon they've got contacts round our way.'

'Hellfire.'

'Exactly. It gets worse. They added a chemical to their stashes to bulk out the powder—more money for less product. It's used for de-worming cattle.'

'Christ!'

Ross grinned. 'You're very religious today, boss.' George grunted and hid a smile. 'So anyway, they got sent down for twenty years, and the NCA are hoping they'll start talking. Might even identify the lowlifes who are spreading this stuff all over Ashbridge.'

'Good. The sooner we can get some names, the better. Any other leads?'

'Not really. The boys in the city have passed on a few. I'm just working through those now.'

'All right, nipper. Keep me posted. This is more important than bloody tractor drivers—hey, hang on a minute!' George stopped and looked through the online case notes. 'Yep, here it is. Knew it rang a bell. Have a look at Claire's forensic report from the tractor incident.'

Ross nodded and tapped in his password. He opened the file, then stared as George came over and jabbed a podgy finger on the screen. 'Holy Moses!'

***

Jane rested her chin on her hand as she read through yet another case report, her fourth that afternoon.

Her task was to review and prioritise in line with the new mantra of cost-effective policing. She was cynical, like most of her colleagues in Greater Manchester. The politicians spouting this line would be the first to complain if their own house burglary was pushed to the bottom of the pile.

It was just a soundbite ahead of the local elections in a few weeks' time. No one had yet produced any guidance on whether domestic abuse was more of a priority than peddling drugs, or whether fake roof repairers conning vulnerable older people out of their meagre savings merited more police action than burglary.

She ticked a few boxes on the spreadsheet and was about to pick up the next folder when her phone rang. She checked the screen. Allan.

'Hello again.'

His trademark chuckle was a reminder of how much they'd laughed together. But he quickly turned serious. 'Yes—hi Jane. I just wanted you to know that I've spoken to the editor, and we won't be running that Cardale housing story.'

'Oh, that's good. Thanks for sorting it.' *God, this sounds so formal. Were we really going to get married six months ago?*

'Yeah, no problem. The thing is, we've picked up on another story... and I think you should know.'

Jane felt herself tensing up and tried to relax her shoulders. 'Okay.'

'Did you know the council and the village association have given the okay to gas exploration in the area?'

'What? In Cardale?'

'Yeah. And the guy who died in that tractor accident was the main man promoting it.'

'Geoff Pegg?'

'Hmmm, yes. He was the sales director for Universal Energy.'

'And more than cosy with the woman who ran the village association.'

'And the leader of the council is a member, so you can see why we're interested. We're not doing anything silly with the information, beyond stating it as a fact, but I thought... you know...'

Jane flashed back to meeting Allan on her first murder investigation.

A councillor had been killed by a blow to the head with a hammer. Allan had had a relationship with her, but it had ended a few years before. He'd felt obliged to help Jane, and he'd been very useful. They'd ended up living together soon after.

And here he was again, being helpful, supportive.

She tried to keep her voice polite. 'It certainly puts an interesting twist on it. Thanks, Allan. I'll make a note on the log, and we'll keep an eye on that angle.'

'Okay, glad to help. And Jane?'

'Yes?'

'It's been a long time. I wondered how you'd feel about meeting up for a drink. Just to reconnect, you know. I feel bad about walking away. It was stupid of me. If nothing else, we could surely be friends, couldn't we?'

She felt completely off balance, unable to find words, unsure how she felt. Her gut reaction was to be angry, bitter. *That's what jilted women do when they're in victim mode, isn't it?*

When she spoke, her voice sounded as if it was coming from somewhere else. 'Well, yes. Why don't you let me have a few dates that you could make, and we'll take it from there?'

'Okay, yes, I will, thanks.' She could hear his disbelief, or was it relief? 'Thanks, Jane. I'll text you soon. Great! Okay, well... see you.'

'Yes. Bye, Allan.' The familiar pattern of four rhythmic taps on the door told her Phil was outside. 'Got to go, someone's here to see me.'

She put the phone on the desk slowly, composed herself, then pressed the button that told Phil he could *enter*.

He hurried in, then stopped and looked at her curiously. 'Jane? Are you okay?'

'No, I'm not. Something tells me I've just made a big mistake.'

***

Maggie Attrill checked herself in the hall mirror as she tied her hair in a ponytail and flicked it through the back of her baseball cap.

She'd been working on her weight since walking out on her second husband seven years ago. She'd been happy with him, until she found out he'd been bonking someone else for two years.

She'd been determined not to be a victim, not to let the feeling of rejection ruin her life. So she turned it into an opportunity. She vowed to get fit, feel proud of her body. Now, she drank only water, avoided red meat and made sure she had her five a day.

She'd just turned fifty and was feeling better than ever. The pleasure of being able to wear skin-tight leggings hadn't worn off. And she quite liked the second glances she got from much younger men.

It was Wednesday, and time for her morning run. She usually did a 3k. Friday was a 5k, and her current target for Sunday mornings was 9k.

She called up the stairs. 'Right, Peter. I'm off!'

No answer. Probably staring at his computer already.

She walked to the gate, started her watch, tugged her top down so it covered her bum, and set off at jogging pace.

She'd planned to run to the church, then up the lane past Mary's house before looping round back home via the dairy farm. But she instantly felt good and turned left just after the pub. It was a narrow lane and a bit of a climb. She'd read that putting in one or two hills was a good way of building strength.

She made it halfway up before stopping to catch her breath. She was glad she did. It was idyllic here. Hard to believe this was just a few yards from the village. The only sounds were the gentle rustle of leaves and the creak of heavy branches, the chatter of a blackbird, the trickle of water.

A streak of colour caught her eye in the ditch, and she moved a few steps closer.

'Oh my God!'

The man was lying on his back. His face was horribly grey and streaked with a mix of what looked like blood and dirt. But she knew who it was.

Maggie reached for her phone and dialled 999.

11.

Gloria MacDonald heard the sirens as she walked back to her hotel room after a late breakfast.

She was still waiting to hear when Mary's body would be released for burial, and it was making her anxious. Why the delay?

The sound of the siren alarmed her, reminded her about Mary. She could see the blue lights from her window. It looked like an ambulance, and it was heading up the steep road towards Cardale. Moments later, a police car, heading in the same direction.

Everyone she'd spoken to had said the same thing: 'Oh, nothing ever happens in Cardale.'

Well, that was clearly not true.

She remembered Mary chatting, the last time she came. *'Cardale is full on, mum. It looks so twee, but don't be fooled. They're all crazy. I like coming to Edinburgh. It's quieter.'*

Gloria sat by the window and picked up her phone, flicking through pictures of Mary. She toyed with the idea of calling that man Phil at the police station. He'd been so kind and understanding. Maybe he'd know what had happened. But she knew he wouldn't appreciate being bothered.

She looked at her watch. 9:35. *No point just sitting here all day, worrying.* She put on her gilet and asked reception to order a taxi.

***

The policewoman was asking her lots of questions, but Maggie was more interested in why Sid Marsh had come down this lane last night.

It wasn't on his way home. In fact, if he'd carried on, he would have ended up out on the A road between Ashbridge and Oldham.

Peter had come to mollycoddle her within minutes of her call. He told her Sid had made a complete fool of himself at the meeting.

Maggie knew the feeling. The policewoman was treating her like an idiot, nodding absently when Maggie told her she should find out why Sid had been here in the first place. There was a red-haired girl in a white suit looking closely at where the injured man had been lying, and Maggie could tell she was listening. But the constable wasn't interested.

'It looks like an accident,' she said. 'Slipped and banged his head. He got very cold and wet so he's suffering exposure, and that's a nasty head wound, but he'll be okay. Now, what about you? You've had a shock. We should get you checked.'

Maggie just scoffed. 'Oh, there's nothing wrong with me. I've seen worse. But I'm telling you now, this was no accident.'

The PCW gave her a patient smile. 'All right, Mrs Attrill. I've made a note of that. Now you should get off home and let us do our bit, okay? If there's anything to find here, our Claire will find it.' The red-haired girl looked up and smiled and called out to Peter. 'I think a sit down and a cup of tea will help, sir.'

Peter lost his mind, as he usually did when faced with a pretty woman. 'Of course. I'll go and make you one.'

Maggie and the constable snorted in harmony. 'I think Claire meant a cup of tea for your wife, sir.'

Peter cleared his throat and took Maggie's arm. 'Ah yes. Come along, dear. Let's get you home.'

Maggie walked to the end of the lane with him, then stopped and pulled her arm away indignantly. 'Oh, sod this, Peter! I'm not a little old lady!'

'Darling, no need to shout.'

'I don't care who hears me. I'm fed up with being patronised. I came out to have a run and that's what I'm damn well going to do. I'll see you later.'

Peter watched her go, then turned towards home, shaking his head. He heard a voice from over the wall. Aaron. Laughing.

'Bit of marital strife, matey?'

'Hmmm.'

'Don't worry, old chap. I'm sure all the lads in the village will understand.' His face appeared over the garden wall. 'They all fancy Maggie, you know. Anyway, who was that being taken off to hospital?'

Peter updated him. Aaron nodded. 'Well, well, what goes around, comes around, eh?'

'What do you mean?'

'His tractor kills two people. He goes against the village on the gas licensing. He even has the nerve to set himself up as some god of organic farming, trying to make the rest of us look like village idiots. Now he's in hospital. I'd call that justice, wouldn't you?'

***

Jane asked Doreen on the switchboard to put a call through to Marsh Farm.

'Sorry, me love. No answer. Want me to keep trying?'

Jane realised that the more she asked Doreen for help, the more likely she was to talk to her. At her, more accurately. 'No, you're all right, thanks. I'll try again later.'

An hour later, Jane was rolling her shoulders to prevent them cramping up after another session hunched over a pile of case files. Then Phil told her the news, and she was able to prioritise finding out what happened to Sid Marsh.

Soon, she was standing by the ditch in Cardale, where Claire was up to her ankles in muddy water.

'Victim is Sid Marsh. Wound on the back of his head consistent with hitting this stone.' She knelt to point to a boulder half concealed by vegetation, then leaned towards the side of the ditch. 'Marks here show where he may have slipped, so it suggests an accident.'

She hesitated.

Jane raised her eyebrows. 'But...?'

'Well, ma'am. He smelled of drink even after a few hours down here. And he had an envelope in his jacket. Cocaine, I think. But it's just something one of the women said...'

Jane nodded as Claire explained, then messaged Phil to go to the hospital to check on Sid Marsh, and phoned George. 'I need to talk to a Maggie Attrill. According to Claire, her husband or partner is called Peter. Can you check for any previous on either of them, and Sid Marsh? Particularly drug use.'

George made a slight choking sound. 'Drugs, ma'am. Again?'

'Yes, George. Sid Marsh was found in a ditch this morning with cocaine in his pocket. It's either his or he's a dealer, or someone planted it on him.'

'Bloody hell! Ross is on the case right now. It looks like a gang moving in on Ashbridge.'

'Yeah, I remember. This is getting interesting. Tell Ross to book in to see me later. Mid-afternoon, ideally.'

Jane disconnected and walked up the lane in the direction they guessed Sid had been walking. Why had he come this way? Had he been so off his head he didn't know where he was? Or was he meeting someone?

It was a steep climb, but the views from the top were worth it. She took in a few breaths of the cool air and leaned on a gate. The big blue-and-white sky, clouds like sliding cathedrals, a couple of birds spiralling high above, trees and hedgerows, lush fields, distant farm buildings. Allan would love it here—*stop it, Jane!*

She'd spent a restless night trying not to think about him, trying not to wonder how it would be to see him again, arguing with herself about whether to call it off. By three in the morning, she'd decided it would be better to go ahead and get it over with so she could move on. One way or another.

She turned, leaning back against the gate, looking down across Cardale, trying to focus. It wasn't a murder investigation, but it was every bit as complicated. She processed what was known so far...

Two people dead in an apparent accident: one of them a sales director for a gas exploration company about to start drilling, the other led the village association. White powder found in the rubble confirmed as cocaine, but no trace of drug use from the post-mortems. A few days later, the man whose tractor demolished the house is seriously hurt in what seems to be another accident. Cocaine found in his jacket pocket. Was he a user or a supplier? And then the other stuff: a housing development no one knew about yet, and Mary allegedly saying 'New housing over my dead body,' and planning applications going in for gas exploration? Oh yes, and the leader of the council lives in Cardale...

Walking back down the lane, she could hear the snap of logs being chopped, and the clatter of hedge trimmers and lawn mowers. A woman in a wax jacket and a purple headscarf carrying a wicker basket called out 'good morning', then crossed the road near the pub and unlocked the door of her black-and-white timbered cottage.

It was so normal it felt unreal.

***

Ross slid his phone into his inside pocket and relaxed against the headrest.

The call from George had set him on a new train of thought. He knew he'd become obsessed with the drug smuggling angle. Ross could picture himself taking them on in Ashbridge—what a way to make a name for himself. But common sense told him the wealthy thugs at the top were nothing without the users, the punters who were prepared to beg and steal to feed their habit.

It was a pyramid. Money for some, misery for most. The people at the top raked in the profits, but their dealers were well rewarded too, otherwise the system broke down. The more customers they got, the more they made. Then they could afford to recruit others to do the legwork. They built up an income of their own. And so it went on.

Ross drummed his fingers on the steering wheel of his beloved XR2. So, the best place to start is at the bottom. Find the users.

His tenant, Amy, was barmaid at the Feathers, about five minutes' drive away. He'd only talked to her generally about investigations, even though they'd met during the hit-and-run murders, just over six months ago. The three victims, all ex-Army, used to meet up for a few pints at the Feathers every Friday.

She'd never given even a hint that there was drug use there, but pubs and clubs, and the streets around them, were the obvious place to start looking, and if he talked to the landlord first, she wouldn't get in any bother.

He started the engine and let it tick over for a minute. It all made sense. Then, with a bit of luck, he could convince Jane to let him check out the scene in Cardale—the one place where they knew cocaine was being supplied.

12.

Aaron Barrett loved the buzz of press conferences. Other politicians found them intimidating. But he thrived on the flash of cameras, the array of microphones, the clamour of questions.

And today's—his double act with Alistair Grant, CEO of Universal Energy—was going well. The plan was to come across as semidetached. Neighbourly without being overfriendly.

As Alistair put it over coffees in the Mayor's Parlour at the Town Hall: 'We're in it together but keeping our distance. Right?'

The cabinet had nodded the deal through without discussion. Aaron's Conservative Group had a majority, so the council meeting last night had confirmed the decision, despite predictable opposition from the only Green councillor, the loud and permanently annoyed Labour Group Leader and a noisy handful of supporters in the public gallery.

And now, what they were calling 'a landmark deal' was going public. The *Daily Express* had even turned up for this one.

Aaron did most of the talking because most of the questions were about the impact on the local environment and economy.

He looked directly into the camera as a BBC bright spark asked him what he'd say to a roomful of protestors.

'Environmental impact: minimal. Economic impact: massive. This project delivers a vital, clean, safe and *local* energy supply for the Greater Manchester conurbation. The price we pay for that will be the development of a few fields in the area around Cardale. Weigh that against the investment Universal Energy will be making in the local economy. Jobs, infrastructure, maintenance, transport, road improvements. And when the supply runs out, the company reinstates the land, plants more trees than were there in the first place. Take it from me, this is good news for Ashbridge, for Manchester—indeed, the whole country.'

***

Felicity Crowther sipped peppermint tea and held the old transistor radio up to her ear.

The red and cream campervan she'd lived in for the last three years was parked up in a wooded valley in Cheshire, and the reception was scratchy. She flicked her hair out of the way, her indignation building as she listened.

She turned it off and yelled through the window. 'Jack! Come on, we're packing up.'

The old van lurched as Jack stepped inside, using an old tea towel to wipe engine oil off his hands. 'What? Why? It's nice 'ere.' His accent was rural Devon. 'I ain't finished servicing 'er yet.'

'We're reactivating Strawberry Fields Forever, that's why.'

'Get in! What's goin' on, lovely?'

'Drilling for gas in the most beautiful countryside you've ever seen. They'll destroy habitats, ruin the landscape...'

Jack scratched his head. 'You're kiddin' me.'

She stared. He was hard work sometimes, but loyal to the cause. He used to play rugby for Exeter, and he'd spill blood to protect her. In fact, he had done exactly that when they'd joined the HS2 protests and the police got heavy-handed. She'd watched amazed as he took three of them out at once.

'Why would I be kidding you, Jack? Do I look like I'm joking?' She sighed. 'Come on, just pack the stuff and let's get going. I'll make a few calls while you finish off. We're going to Cardale.'

'Never 'eard of it.'

***

Jane stopped at the gate to Maggie Attrill's house, phone to her ear.

'Thanks for the update, Ross. Yes, let's focus on the users. But hold off Cardale for a while.' She paused. 'Meet me at the hospital in an hour. We should be able to talk to Sid Marsh by then. Yep. Okay. See you then.'

She was about to tap on the elaborately carved front door when she saw a familiar figure on the other side of the road.

Jane jogged up behind her, calling her name. She stopped and turned. Didn't look pleased.

'Gloria,' Jane said. 'What are you doing here?'

Her hostility was a shock. 'What does that mean? Why shouldn't I be here?'

Jane kept her tone pleasant. 'Sorry, just an expression. I was surprised to see you, that's all.'

'Well, my daughter lived here. Died here. And as you very well know, I am still waiting for her to be released so I can take her back home. I think I have a perfect right to be here.' She paused. 'If you must know, I heard sirens from the hotel this morning. Saw the ambulance coming this way. I wanted to see what was going on.'

Her anger and aggression were such a contrast to the last time they'd met. Was it just coincidence that she was here and Sid Marsh was in hospital?

'Okay, I understand. The farmer whose tractor ran into Mary's house has been taken to hospital with a serious head injury. He was found in a ditch this morning,' Jane explained as gently as she could.

Gloria stared back. Not a flicker of surprise. 'Oh, I see.'

'It looks like it may have been an accident, but—'

She laughed, disbelieving. 'Oh, I get it now! I'm a suspect. My God! I don't believe this!' She started to walk away and recoiled as Jane put a hand on her arm. 'Get your hands off me! Don't you think I've been through enough?'

'Gloria... You're not a suspect.'

'Wonderful! So, I can go on with my life then, can I?' Gloria was losing it; her voice broke as it got louder.

Jane could almost feel the eyes of the village turning on her.

'Oh no! I can't, can I? Because you won't let me take my beautiful daughter home!'

She walked off quickly before Jane could reply, her heels clicking on the uneven pavement.

***

He opened his eyes slowly, and it was like looking through a letterbox into bright mist.

A face, moving close. A deep voice. 'It's Okay, Sidney. Just relax. You're in hospital. You've had a bump on the head, but you're going to be all right.'

His own voice. Soft, far away. 'Julie...'

'Your wife? Yes, we called her. She's on her way to see you. Don't worry. You just need to rest, all right?'

A sound. Like a lorry reversing. Beeping. 'What...'

'We've got you connected up to some machines until we're sure everything's working. Try to rest now.'

Head feeling heavy. Dark again. Silence.

***

Ross grimaced as he sipped the coffee. He pushed the cup and saucer to the edge of the table.

There was something unsettling about hospital catering. This looked like any other café, and it had the usual buzz of conversation, but Ross couldn't get away from the thought that he could be sitting a table away from a brain surgeon, or someone waiting to go in for chemo, or worse. And there was always a background aroma somewhere between disinfectant and school dinners.

He smiled, remembering bringing his grandad in before an appointment. He'd sniffed the air like a dog. *'Don't make any difference what's on the bloody menu,'* he'd said. *'It all smells the same.'*

'What's amusing you then?' Jane sat down opposite and ripped open a sandwich as if she'd not eaten for a month.

'My grandad. He hated coming in here. Always had a moan about something.'

'Hospital food's all right these days.' Jane took a bite and dabbed her mouth with a serviette.

Ross briefed her on his visit to the Feathers. Amy had told him everyone knew there were always one or two dealers hanging around outside the pub.

'I was wondering if I could go and check out Cardale next, ma'am?'

Jane sipped her ginger beer. 'No reason why not. But...'

Ross dabbed biscuit crumbs off his plate. 'What is it, ma'am?'

Jane smiled ruefully. 'You know me. I don't like to get side-tracked. There's already plenty going on in Cardale. Too many connections, too many questions. I've just interviewed the woman who found Sid Marsh, and she's the wife of the man who's replaced Mary as chair of the village association. Coincidence? Connection?' She checked her watch. 'We'd better get moving. Keep an eye on Sid Marsh as we talk and give me your thoughts after, okay?'

It was a five-minute walk to the ward, and Ross hadn't realised how unfit he was until he tried to keep pace with Jane. She asked him how it was working out, inviting Amy to move in with him and pay rent.

'It's pretty good,' he said. 'She's a good mate.' He smiled. 'And she pays on time.'

Sid's bed was in a corner, by the window. A tall, blonde woman was already there. She stood and shook their hands as Jane did the introductions. Ross noticed she didn't look either of them in the eye.

Jane tried to lighten the atmosphere. 'So, how's Sid getting on?'

Julie sat in an armchair and put a hand to her forehead. Her voice was flat. 'He's doing okay, apparently.'

Jane flicked a glance at Ross, and he raised an eyebrow in return. She turned to Sid, who still looked out of it. 'Hello again, Sid. Remember me? Can you tell us what happened?'

His voice was surprisingly strong. 'Not much I can tell you. I heard footsteps. Next thing, I'm in the ditch. Felt cold and my head hurt. That's it, really. Must have blacked out. Feel okay now, though.' He pushed himself further up in bed. 'When can I go home, do you know?'

Jane smiled. 'No idea, sorry. Just a few more questions. Did you hear any voices you recognised?'

He shook his head slowly. 'I remember hearing people coming out of the pub. They were loud. Been celebrating. Gas licence. Pillocks.'

'You're against the idea, then, Sid?'

He nodded, then stopped, looking uncomfortable. 'Yes, you could say that.'

'What about everyone else?'

Julie broke in angrily. 'Oh, let's get to the point, shall we? The whole village thinks it's a great idea. Everyone, except us. Sid spoke up at the village meeting last night. One of them got their own back. That's why he's in here now. He's just too scared to say it.'

Sid stared straight ahead. Jane wondered how this couple had stayed together with so little warmth between them. Was his opposition motive enough for the attack, though? She nodded at Ross.

He cleared his throat and leaned forward, speaking gently. 'Sid. We found cocaine in your pocket. You know it's illegal. I have to ask you where you got it.'

Julie stood suddenly and turned away, facing the window.

Sid looked at Ross and licked his lips. 'I paid for it.'

'Okay. Who did you buy it from, and where?'

'Round the back of the pub. No idea who he is. He just meets up with me every week or so.'

Jane tapped Ross on the shoulder and indicated five minutes. She took Julie's arm and they walked out of the ward.

***

She was still thinking about Julie that night when the text from Allan came through.

Drinks at 7 on Friday? A x

Jane sipped orange juice as she tried to make her mind up. Yes, no, or maybe another time?

Her uncle and mentor, Bill, a blunt Yorkshire detective, always used to tell her that we know the decision we ought to make. *'Don't think too hard. You know what's right, so just do it.'*

She tapped her answer and pressed send.

***

Allan snatched up his phone as the vibration alert shunted it across the desk.

She'd replied straight away. *Friday OK. Where?* So formal, but maybe that was to be expected.

The Warehouse? Send.

They'd been there before. It had been called something else then—was that their first date? He could feel the tension in his shoulders and tried to shrug it away. But was it any wonder? Six months apart after three years living together. Not a great track record.

Part of him couldn't believe he'd taken the lead. He'd always been the passive one, happy to go along with things. Or so he thought.

Her reply...

Yep. See you there.

Allan hesitated for a second. Keep it formal or lighten up a bit? *Great. Looking forward to it. A x*

He'd had time to come to terms with his own stupidity. He'd walked away from Jane in a temper and lived off his righteous indignation for a few weeks. Until he started to realise what he'd sacrificed for the sake of making a point. He'd told himself he was just being strong, assertive. But he knew he was the complete opposite when it came to his relationship with Jane. She was stronger, and his tantrum was a pathetic attempt to redeem himself, restore a bit of pride.

He knew he needed her. He hoped she needed him, too. He had to try one more time.

He added *Jane - drinks* to his Google calendar and took a last look at his emails before heading back to his flat in Angel Gardens. One from Aaron Barrett. *Statement from the Leader's Office: Cardale protests.*

Allan pressed speed dial as he forwarded the message. 'Jenny? Check your emails then get Mike and a photographer over to Cardale, will you? Sounds like World War Three is about to start.'

***

Jane wrapped the last slice of veggie pizza in cling film and put it in the fridge. It looked lonely on the shelf with only milk, yoghurt and orange juice for company.

She tried to unravel her feelings about seeing Allan again. She knew she wanted to. As she'd told her mum over a coffee at Aunt Betty's last week: 'He drove me mad, but I miss him.' Her mum had just nodded and said in her matter-of-fact way that she still missed Jane's dad.

Leaning back and closing her eyes, she could hear the silence. Meeting Allan was a chance to get out and talk to someone about anything other than work. Still, it amazed her that she could feel isolated when she was in a full-time, demanding job, living in a terraced house in a busy suburb of Manchester.

It was obvious Julie Marsh felt the same. She'd confessed in their chat at the hospital that she had suspected Sid was taking drugs but had turned a blind eye.

'I've discovered there's a limit to the number of times a day you want a confrontation,' she'd said. 'So I spend my time holding everything together.'

Jane had noted the name of Julie's friend in Islington. It was her alibi for the night Sid was attacked. One for George to check tomorrow.

She moved to the kitchen table without knowing why and tried to find something else to think about. It didn't work. The events at Cardale were troubling her, and she was sure a common thread was lying just beneath the surface.

She was struck by how many strong women were involved: Mary herself, her mother Gloria, Maggie Attrill, Julie.

Mary had died in bed with Geoff Pegg. She'd never been short of men and had told her mum about an affair with a farmer. Who was that? Sid? Gloria was good-looking, too, unlikely to be without male company for long, and she'd been in the village the morning Sid was found.

Maggie Attrill looked after herself, running round the village in Lycra and a skinny top: a complete contrast to the photo of her portly, ruddy-faced husband on the sideboard—the man who had replaced Mary as chair of the village association. What's more, she was the one who had found Sid Marsh, a few hours after he'd made a nuisance of himself at her husband's first public meeting.

And then there was Julie, who'd had a shouting match with her husband not too long before he was found in a ditch. She'd told Jane over a tea at the hospital that she was close to divorcing him. She'd known about the cocaine but had let it go because he'd promised her it was only occasional. She admitted the farm was a financial disaster and she'd not been consulted on plans for the housing development.

Jane found it hard to believe Julie wouldn't have seen any correspondence or overheard phone calls. But the anger and frustration in her eyes had seemed genuine.

'He never talks to me about things,' she'd said. 'I think I'd be better off on my own.'

Jane massaged her forehead with her fingertips. Was there a link to Mary and Geoff Pegg's deaths? Or was she seeing connections that had no significance?

The sound of her phone was magnified in the tiled kitchen. She snatched it off the table on the third ring. Alex Gledhill, very brisk. 'Sorry to disturb you, ma'am. We have a public order incident at Cardale. Protests about gas drilling. We've got reinforcements coming in from Bury and Oldham, so we're handling it, but in view of what else has been happening there lately...'

'Okay, Alex. On my way.'

***

The drilling site was close to Marsh Farm.

Jane counted more than twenty vehicles parked on the lane, most of them white vans or campervans. The yellow wall in the distance turned out to be a line of police. She showed her ID, and one of them dragged a six-foot-high metal barrier to one side to let her through.

Her car bounced over the grass, bringing back vivid memories of being thrown around in the back of dad's car as they parked up at his favourite farm festival.

Alex waved and walked over as she stepped out onto the flattened grass. 'All quiet so far, ma'am.' He pointed away to their right. 'They're setting up camp over there. We've already had words with their leader.'

'Who's that?'

'Felicity Hawthorn, ma'am. A few of the Manchester lads recognise the name. Apparently, she spends her life making a nuisance of herself on environment protests all over the country. Made a career of it. Got herself on *Question Time* a few times, I'm told.'

Jane nodded. 'A celebrity then. Well, let's hope she behaves. But when you see what they're doing to the countryside, you must have some sympathy.'

She waved Alex away as his radio crackled, and walked further into the site to have a look round.

Earthmovers on caterpillar tracks were inching down the slope into the valley floor. Men in blue overalls and yellow safety hats were bolting metal panels together under the glare of LED lamps mounted on poles.

Further down the valley, a meeting was going on outside a large caravan with a hatch in the side. Jane smiled to herself. The catering van, of course. Behind it, a structure resembling a cut-off Blackpool Tower was being wheeled into place on the back of a truck.

A smaller digger to one side looked like a silhouetted beast pawing the ground. The air out here was cold and fresh, and voices seemed to carry.

Jane shook her head. In different circumstances, she'd be joining the protestors. They had reason to be angry. As she got nearer, the noise and smell of engines and the shouts of workers got louder. She looked back up the slope. At least this blot on the landscape was hidden from view.

She was startled by a workman built like a prop forward who'd jogged up behind her. His blue padded jacket was labelled 'Security' in white reflective material.

He was slightly out of breath and his eyes were bright with excitement. 'DCI Birchfield?'

Jane briefly wondered how he knew. 'Yes?'

'Can you come with me, please? There's something you need to see, ma'am.'

'Ah. You need Inspector Gledhill. He's in charge of the police operation tonight. I'm just observing.'

He nodded but gestured to her to follow him anyway. 'He asked me to find you. They've found a body.'

13.

Journalists adored Felicity Crowther. She seemed to know instinctively how to look and where to look. She delivered her lines in soundbites, with pauses that made them easier to edit, and never tired of requests for 'just one more, Fliss.'

She lived in a campervan with a washroom the size of a kid's wardrobe, but still managed to look groomed. Her supporters called her 'model girl', and she'd lost count of the offers she'd turned down to pose for glamour magazines. Her standard response was to remind them that the only thing she cared about was protecting the environment from what she called 'the cancer of capitalism and the grubbiness of greed'. She was quietly proud of that one—it had made it into *The Guardian*'s 'quotes of the year' list.

She told friends she'd be taken a lot more seriously if she was a man, but that only added to her determination to make Strawberry Fields Forever a national movement. And though it rankled, if her good looks meant the organisation got more airtime, it was a price worth paying.

Right now, she was smiling into a TV camera with the drill site below and behind her, visible through the security fence.

She kept her head still and spoke slowly and clearly. 'Ashbridge Council are deluding themselves if they think the people of this country are prepared to sit back and let them destroy the countryside and decimate precious habitats for the sake of poisonous fuel that the world no longer wants or needs. There is a better, cleaner way, and we are not moving until the threat to this beautiful corner of the world is removed. We're not going anywhere until the rape of our planet is ended. Strawberry Fields Forever! Thank you.'

She gazed meaningfully into the camera, then turned away. Jack stepped in to shield her from the reporters and steer her towards the protestors, who were obeying her instructions to keep their distance from the police. She could hear some of them singing.

Jack put an arm round her shoulder. 'What's the plan, lovely?'

She smiled up at him. 'We go back to our camp. Sing a few songs. Let them think we're a bunch of pussycats. Then we'll hit them.'

Jack punched the air. 'Yes! Come on!'

***

Ross sat back and rubbed his eyes. He'd been staring at his computer screen for over an hour.

He was on his own in the Ashbridge CID room for the first time since he'd joined five years ago. George was normally last man standing, but he'd shuffled off an hour before, grumbling about his wife inviting her friends for drinks. Lorry was still sunning herself on honeymoon in Crete; Eric Sykes had got the day off and Jag was still on part-time hours.

Ross was reading up on drug trafficking. Around 3,000 people died in the UK every year from drug misuse; cocaine production in Columbia was at an all-time high and crack cocaine use was one of the biggest factors behind violent crime.

As if policing the problem wasn't tough enough, the National Crime Agency had to contend with a few corrupt port and airport officials who were taking cash to turn a blind eye. And at local level, criminal gangs were grooming young, and not so young, vulnerable people. They depended on them for the County Lines supply network that cut across police boundaries, using untraceable mobile phones and a constantly shifting storage and distribution network.

The more he found out, the more he wanted to do something about it. For the first time since he came to Ashbridge, Ross was seriously considering moving on. This was the sort of challenge he felt he needed: operating undercover, having access to the latest technology, working in the big cities, where the action is.

He shook his head as he remembered that in Ashbridge, he couldn't even get permission to go to Cardale.

Jane was a great boss, but Ross couldn't understand why she seemed more interested in a tractor accident than the probability of a major drug cartel moving in.

He checked his watch. 9 p.m.

He thought back to his chat with Jane at the hospital after the interview with Sid Marsh. She hadn't said he could go to Cardale. But she hadn't said no, either. So, there was no harm in having a look, was there? If he put his foot down, he'd have at least an hour at the

Frog and Firkin before last orders. Time enough to clock any dodgy activity.

He called Amy and she answered straight away. 'Hey you, what's up?'

'Fancy coming for a drink?'

'Yeah, if it's not the Feathers. It's my only night off this week.'

'I know. You did mention it. Several times. I thought we could go out to Cardale for a change. Try the village pub.'

'It's a bit posh, innit? You sure they'd let you in?'

'Cheeky sod. I'm your landlord, you know. Show a bit of respect. Yes or no?'

'Yes, sir, Mr Landlord. But give me ten minutes to change.'

'What into? A handsome prince?'

'You wish.'

***

Jane stayed close behind as the security guard shouldered his way through.

A thin, thoughtful-looking man in a yellow jacket and white safety helmet was standing on the edge of a trench, leaning back against a small digger, studying his fingernails as he talked quietly into his radio.

As Jane approached, he ended the conversation and nudged his glasses up onto the bridge of his nose. He looked like someone who enjoyed being in charge.

'It's not a pretty sight, I'm afraid.'

Jane kept her voice level. Another patronising male to add to the list. 'It never is, I can assure you.'

She scanned the faces that were pressing ever closer, hoping to get a peek, and called out, 'Can you please stay back? Give us some room.' She turned to Glasses Man, and said, more brusquely than she intended, 'What's your name?'

'Alan Taylor. I'm the site supervisor.'

'Right, Alan. Make sure this whole area is cordoned off, will you? I want everyone back at least ten yards. Have you seen Inspector Gledhill?'

'Yes. He's around somewhere. Said he had to make some calls.'

'Good. Okay. Let's have a look.'

He stepped sheepishly to one side as Jane moved closer to the shallow trench, holding up her right hand to shield her eyes from the glare of the lamps.

The body was flat on its back. Traces of fabric were visible. Decomposition was obviously at an early stage.

Glasses Man moved to stand beside her. 'We've only just begun preparing the site for test drilling. We'd only been going for about ten minutes when one of the lads noticed something in the bottom of the trench. They stopped the digger and climbed in to dig by hand.'

Jane nodded. 'So the body hasn't been moved?'

He shook his head. 'The gaffer is going to go ape. Don't suppose we'll be doing any drilling for a while yet.'

'That's a fairly safe assumption.' She turned to face him. 'All right, Alan. Thanks for your help. Could you step away now? We need to be sure there's no further contamination of the site. And if you're in contact with the inspector, can you get him over here asap, please.'

He began to walk away, but Jane called him back. 'Whatever you do, don't let the press anywhere near this area, and no one is to say anything about what we've found until we're ready. Understood?'

He raised a hand in acknowledgement as he walked away.

Jane felt the adrenaline surge as she switched into investigation mode. She knew it would be a matter of minutes before someone blabbed to one of the reporters.

She put a stray square of cardboard down and knelt on it to get a closer look. The eyes were caked in dirt. Blue trousers—denim jeans?—and what looked like trainers were visible, but the rest of the body was still half covered in earth, so it was difficult to tell if it was male or female. The legs looked as though they were raised higher than the torso.

Alex crouched down next to her, told her Forensic Phil was on his way. Jane looked over her shoulder to see that a few uniforms were herding everyone back and tying incident tape to street irons to form a barrier.

Alex pursed his lips, thinking. 'You know what? It looks like a freshly dug grave, ma'am.'

'That's what I was thinking, Alex. The body looks intact, too. If I had to bet on it, I'd say he or she was buried less than a couple of weeks ago.'

14.

A scrum of reporters trapped Jane on her way back to the car two hours later.

She gave in to the clamour of shouted questions. Behind them, the yellow glow from floodlights in the valley gave the impression of a volcano about to erupt.

She raised her voice above the growl of generators the size of vans. 'I'm sorry I can't tell you very much. As you know, a body has been found on the site. We have a forensic team in position, and until their work is done, there is very little more we can say.'

A woman's voice pierced through all the others. 'Does this mean that drilling has stopped?'

Jane narrowed her eyes against the light. 'Sorry, you are?'

'Felicity Crowther, Strawberry Fields Forever.'

'Ah, okay, Felicity. Yes, drilling has stopped for the time being. Thanks everyone. We will issue a further statement tomorrow. Now, please excuse me, I must get back to work.'

Jane was impressed. The hype about Felicity was justified. It was rare for a non-journalist to be allowed to gate-crash a news conference. She walked to her car and made a mental note to find out more about her.

As she drove to the station, she was preoccupied with the thought that the world was losing its mind. A life had just been lost. Someone had been murdered, dumped in a hole and buried. Yet all the questions being yelled at her were about what impact this would have on the drilling operation.

She blinked a few times to refocus her tired eyes and vowed that the day she stopped valuing human life was the day she quit her job.

***

His name was Keith Castle.

He was married, without children, and lived on a street of terraced houses with back yards, just off the main road through Ashbridge towards the Pennines. His wife had been hysterical when George broke the news. She told him he was a handyman at the Spinnaker Leisure Centre and had become, in her words, 'increasingly fond of a drink'.

Briefing Jane, George said she was feeling isolated because he spent so much time out in the evenings. George said he'd be following that up with Keith's employers, but in the meantime, he'd found a few minor offences on his record, including shoplifting, petty theft and drunk driving, most of them a long time ago.

Forensic Phil joined them after a few minutes and reported that Keith had suffered a stab wound through the back of the neck, severing the carotids that supply blood to the brain, and into the spinal cord.

Phil sat down wearily. He seemed to be ageing, though he ran through his notes with his usual thoroughness.

'Whoever did this knew what they were doing. An ordinary knife, like a pocketknife, might have been survivable, just, but this was done with a long blade. They were taking no chances.'

Jane sighed. 'A professional job, then.'

Phil nodded. 'Possibly, yes. But in Cardale?'

'That's what's on my mind. Why there? Why him? He must have upset someone, big time.'

'Or he had information...'

'Yep.' Jane tapped her pencil against her teeth. 'Would there have been a lot of blood?'

'Yes, but there was no sign of it. Suggesting that it was done somewhere else and the body was taken there later.' He rubbed the grey stubble on the top of his head. 'They'd wrapped him in a bedsheet, too. No clues on that so far either, not even a label. You could see where it had been trimmed off.'

'They've thought of everything, then. But I keep thinking about that location. Why there, in that field? Anything from the PM?'

Phil shook his head. 'All I can say with a fair degree of certainty is that the poor lad died about a week to ten days ago, that he was killed somewhere else and transported there not long after. He was in pretty good condition, physically.'

'Meaning what? He worked out?'

'I don't know about that. I'd guess from the state of his heart and valves that he was a runner. He was a healthy chap, anyway.'

Jane took a sip of coffee. 'Well, he did work at the leisure centre. Okay, Phil. Knowing you, you haven't finished yet, am I right?'

'Not by a long chalk, ma'am. I'm going back to the site once I've got my notes sorted. The whole area has been trampled, but let's be positive; there's always something to find. I just need to look harder.'

'I need to do the same. There's a link between this and the tractor accident—must be. Something's going on. But what the hell is it?'

George reached for a ginger nut from the plate on Jane's desk. 'If it's anything like the villages you see on the telly, we'll never find out, ma'am.'

Jane smiled. 'Don't be so negative.' She began typing, then looked up. 'I'm just sending out an instruction for house-to-house enquiries in Cardale. Let's flash his picture around, see if anyone recognises him.'

***

It was a relief she didn't have to spend time clearing her lines with Roy Cooke. He was away at another conference on community policing.

It was some consolation for the fact that she was no longer acting as Chief Super. She hated conference rooms with a passion, and PowerPoint presentations were the stuff of nightmares. She'd missed out on promotion, but at least she was doing what she did best: cracking cases, working closely with her team, sifting evidence.

But events in Cardale were troubling her. So much so that she knew she'd have trouble finding the right words when she eventually briefed Roy. She needed to make sense of it, but it still felt out of reach.

Were there any links between the three events: a tractor smashing into a house and killing two people, Sid Marsh being found in a ditch with a head wound, and the murder of Keith Castle?

She eased the car up to 25 mph as the road opened out into a dual carriageway, then eased back again as she saw the queue at the next set of lights. She braked gently before rolling to a stop. One thing she'd learned was to take her time. It was too easy to get a theory in your head and then make the facts fit.

Her phone flashed a reminder from its cradle mount on the dashboard. *Allan. The Warehouse. 7pm.*

Jane didn't feel at all anxious about seeing him again. In fact, she was desperate for a night out. It was a chance to wear her skinny jeans, slap on some makeup, talk to someone not connected with police work.

She was just meeting her ex. It happened all the time. What could possibly go wrong?

***

Julie plumped up the cushions and helped Sid settle in the armchair. He smiled and reached out to take the mug of tea she was offering.

'Thank you. Are we friends again?'

Julie blew on her tea to cool it, but it was still too hot to drink. She put it on the side table. 'It depends.'

'On what?'

'You being straight with me. I want to know everything, and I want us to talk everything through. No more secrets.'

He nodded, watching her over the rim of his mug. 'Agreed. Go on.'

Julie took a breath. 'We're in a mess. We're going to get hammered for compensation because you didn't keep up with the servicing of that bloody tractor. Who's going to underwrite us after this? Our premiums will go through the roof. And that's the best-case scenario. There's a strong chance we could face criminal negligence charges. So, we can't carry on here, can we?'

Sid's hands were shaking so much, she almost felt sorry for him. But she couldn't let him off the hook. She was tired of being passive. She knew it was partly her fault that they'd got into this mess. She could hardly sleep from fretting.

Sid put his mug down. 'Okay, you're right. I'm sorry. I've messed everything up. But I promise I'll put things right...'

He blinked, trying to clear his head. The tablets they'd given him in hospital were starting to wear off and the dull ache at the back of his neck was spreading into his right shoulder.

Julie would never know the burden he'd been carrying lately, a burden he couldn't share. He wasn't as strong as her and he wanted to plead infirmity, delay the discussion, but he knew how badly she would react. Instinct told him he could find a way through this, but common sense was kicking in. Maybe he'd had too high an opinion of himself. This was the harsh reality of life; he was no longer cloistered in the cosy closed circuit of corporate banking.

He leaned forward, trying to ease the pain. Julie looked so strained, and yet so beautiful. It hurt him to think of the damage he'd done; of what they'd been through.

He reached out a hand, and she took it. 'I agree. Let's do it. Let's start again.'

15.

She suddenly felt nervous, despite her best intentions.

This was where their story had begun. But the place had changed, and so had they.

Gone were the leather sofas and dark wood coffee tables. In came bistro tables, barstools with red leather seats, abstract art, and waiters strutting like catwalk models.

As Jane pushed in through the heavy glass door, she saw Allan straight away, looking too big for his barstool. He was by a pillar near the window onto Market Street, his head down, studying his phone.

Jane had tried to reason with herself since she got home after work. There was nothing to be nervous about. They'd been separated for six months, yes, but before that, they'd had three years together. It wasn't as if they were strangers. Checking her eye makeup in the bathroom mirror, she'd decided to treat tonight as a chat and a drink with an old friend.

She wasn't sure she wanted them to get back together anyway. She missed him. But did she just miss a physical presence?

She put on a smile and startled him by dragging her stool out noisily.

'Oh God, sorry, Jane! I didn't see you come in!'

'Too busy on your phone, I see?'

He looked vaguely guilty, and she wished she'd made it sound more obviously jokey, but there was no time to dwell on it. Their nervousness seemed to speed everything up. He stood and offered to get the drinks in.

Jane sat down and checked the menu. 'I think it's table service, actually. Shall we have wine?' She flinched internally—taking control already.

He pushed back onto the stool, squirming to get comfortable.

Jane smiled. 'I'm not impressed by the seating, are you? Do you think we'd be better off down at the pub? It's not far to the Wheatsheaf.'

They found a table in an alcove, and Allan seemed to relax as he clinked his pint against her wine glass. 'Cheers, Jane. Erm, I suppose I should say thanks for coming, but that sounds a bit formal.'

'Well, it does feel strange, doesn't it? Hard to know what to talk about. But how about we catch up on each other's news? I don't really want to look back, do you?'

He shook his head. Jane thought he looked older. A little bit of grey at the temples, a few more lines round the eyes. It suited him. He'd spent some of his new wealth on himself, too. A smart jacket and open-neck shirt instead of his traditional night-out gear of rugby shirt and jeans. And his phone looked so big it had to be expensive.

He frowned slightly, then looked into her eyes. 'I only want to look back long enough to say sorry for the way it ended. I was in the wrong, and if I don't get that out of the way, I'll never have a chance of enjoying tonight.' He smiled at last. 'Hope you don't mind.'

Jane resisted the sudden urge to put her hand on his. 'No, I don't mind a bit. I overreacted, so it's as much my fault.' She pushed back into the seat, putting a bit of distance between them. 'So, come on, how's life?'

They stayed till the bell rang out for last orders, talking easily, naturally. Allan walked her to the taxi rank at the end of the street, and Jane was tense as a teenager about the best way to say goodnight.

A cab was waiting, and they hesitated. Eventually, Allan held out his hand. Jane took it, then leaned in to kiss him on the cheek. He turned his face to return the kiss, his hand on her back.

At that moment, she could easily have invited him back, and she spent the ride home wondering what stopped her. There was an ache inside as she lay in bed that night. Allan was making the right noises about work, but it sounded hollow, as if there was something missing. Something he wasn't saying. She wondered what signals he'd picked up from her. Was he lying awake too?

***

George slurped his tea and listened as Eric chatted with Ross.

Eric was going on about how he'd gone top of the league in an online football game and was trying to convince Ross to sign up so they'd both get game codes. It was all gibberish to George, but Ross got his attention when he told Eric he'd gone out for a pint in Cardale last night.

'I took Amy to the village pub,' he was saying in his lazy drawl, which seemed even lazier first thing in the morning. 'It's all right. Nice place but too many geezers in check shirts and cord trousers for my liking. Snooker table in the back room, though. Wasn't all bad.'

George called over to them. 'So why did you go there, young man? What were you up to? I thought Jane told you to keep away.'

Ross looked offended but managed a wink for Eric's benefit. 'Amy just wanted a change, boss. She's fed up of the Feathers, so we thought we'd have a jaunt in the countryside.'

George wasn't convinced. 'Oh aye?'

'Yeah. While I was there, I just kept an eye open. I did wonder if there was any drug business going down, but there was no sign of it. No dodgy characters.'

Eric chipped in, beaming. 'Except blokes in tweed waistcoats and flat caps!'

Ross smiled. 'Ah, nice one, young Eric.'

George gave Ross one of his death stares. 'I don't think our DCI would be very impressed if she knew where you were last night.'

'I promise, it was purely social. I didn't flash my ID or question anyone, and I only went to the pub. Genuinely, George, I only went because Amy wanted a break.'

George scratched his ear slowly, and Ross knew he was building up to something. 'Right. So, while you were there, keeping an eye open, as you said, how come you didn't find out that a body had been discovered about half a mile away?'

***

George's deadpan delivery always amused Jane, and she laughed as he explained how he'd embarrassed Ross.

'You're a hard man, George.'

'My wife thinks I'm soft.'

'She's wrong; tell her from me.' Jane stirred her coffee and broke a digestive biscuit in half. 'So, do you want to let Ross loose on the drugs angle now? He's done some digging, but I get the feeling there's more to be found.'

'Yes, ma'am. I wondered whether Castle's name crops up with any of his contacts.'

'Okay.' She pushed the plate of biscuits across the desk, and George took one. 'What else do we know about Keith Castle?'

'Nothing much yet, ma'am. There's no evidence of big spending or saving. Nothing out of the ordinary at work. Seems he was an ordinary bloke. Just did his job, enjoyed a workout at the gym three times a week—God knows why—and liked watching football on the TV. The only thing we have is his wife's comment that he'd started coming home a lot later.'

'So, another woman?'

'That or doing drugs, maybe.'

'Okay, George. Have another chat with his wife, see what else comes up. Tell Ross to check, discreetly. I'm calling a team brief for this afternoon. I need to talk to the boss first.' She rolled her eyes. 'He's not going to be happy.'

'When is he ever?'

'Fair point. But I'm getting it in the neck already for putting a stop to the drilling. The protestors love me, but Roy's anticipating trouble from his friends in high places, as he likes to call them.'

George shook his head and reached for another biscuit. 'I'd rather have friends in low places, myself.'

***

Jane rapped her pen on the table.

Jag's arrival had given them a lift. He was looking as smart as ever, and uber cool in his sunglasses, though they were only to hide the fact he'd lost sight in one eye and had reduced vision in the other. He'd hardly sat down before Ross and Eric were demanding a demonstration of the software he was using to magnify text and convert text to speech.

Jane had never forgiven herself for what had happened to him on the last murder case. But Jag hadn't lost his spirit, or his commitment to the job, and she'd vowed she would do whatever it took to get him back on the team.

She took a quick sip of water and looked round the room.

'Okay everyone. Here we go again... A murder inquiry. I'm pleased to have Jag back with us. He's going to be keeping the record of events up to date, so make sure to keep him posted. Our record keeping—or should I say mine—was a bit slapdash last time. That is not going to happen again. All right?'

They nodded, then turned as Phil and Claire walked in.

Jane pointed at the whiteboard. 'The victim is Keith Castle, late thirties, married, no children. Previous history of minor offences. We think he was killed elsewhere before being buried in a field in Cardale. Death was caused by a knife with a long, wide blade, and it was done by someone who we think knew where to strike to cause the maximum damage.

'First line of enquiry: why Cardale, why that field? Was it just coincidence that the same field was being used for test drilling by Universal Energy? Which, by very strange coincidence, was Geoff Pegg's employer. He, you remember, died with Mary MacDonald when a tractor hit her house. It could be that Geoff was a regular at the leisure centre where Keith worked. Who knows? George is going to investigate all that and check knife sales locally.

'Even stranger coincidence—if any of us believe in such a thing—Geoff and Keith's deaths weren't that far apart. So, was there a connection between the two of them and/or between Keith and Mary? Okay to follow up on that, Eric?'

He nodded. Jane paused and looked across the room. 'Are you keeping up okay, Jag?'

He looked up and smiled happily. 'Yes, ma'am. I'm recording and transcribing into a Word document as you speak.'

'Better make sure I make sense then.' She carried on. 'Third strand: the local farmer Sid Marsh was under the influence of cocaine as well as drink when he was found in a ditch. So, is there a connection there? Ross is checking to see if anything is known about Keith in the local drugs scene.'

Ross sat back in his chair and gave the thumbs up. 'Yes, ma'am. I'm working the streets tonight.'

George snorted. 'Would you mind rephrasing that?'

Jane smiled and leaned back against the table. 'Okay, thanks everyone. You know how manic it's going to get, so catch up on sleep tonight. It could be your last chance. And remember, it's dangerous out there, so no one works alone. All right, let's go!'

***

She'd talked to Allan about the case last night without giving away too much detail. He'd knocked back his second pint, then thought for a minute. 'You know what it reminds me of? The Russian doll thing. You know, you open one and there's another inside, and another, and another.'

The image had stayed with her ever since. Jane sat at her desk and logged into the case folder on the screen. A prompt came up: *Security reminder: change your password.*

She keyed in *russianDoll5.*

***

Universal Energy was a darling of the stock market, and much of it was down to its boss: the self-proclaimed 'local boy made good', Alistair Grant.

Tall, slim and fond of tailor-made suits and gold cufflinks, he was also fond of relating his humble beginnings. His father ran a chip shop in Miles Platting six days a week; his mother worked as a cleaner. Their mission was to save enough to pay for the best education for their only child.

Alistair was a popular after-dinner speaker, and the story was well worn now. 'I was a weedy youth,' he'd say. 'But I managed to avoid being beaten up by carefully selecting the boys I'd invite round after school. It was an invitation to die for, ladies and gentlemen.' He'd pause and smile. 'Fish and chips, on the house! Well, after that, you can imagine how popular I became. And untouchable! That is how, with all due modesty, I have managed to retain my youthful good looks.' Pause for laughter and applause.

His enemies took it as proof of his ability to manipulate from an early age. But he reached a whole new level after he passed the entrance exams for Harrow—his passport to privilege.

Now, at the age of forty-eight, his Italian-leather contacts book was neatly inscribed with the rich and the famous, and he was the billionaire head of the UK's largest independent energy supply company.

He'd negotiated deals for gas exports with some of the biggest nations in the world. He'd won respect by being open about his homosexuality—and sympathy, too, when he revealed in a magazine interview that he had not yet found true love.

But none of it mattered now as he sat back in his office chair, with tea in the pot and a china cup and saucer on the mahogany side table. A map of the world took up most of the wall facing him. Each black dot was a Universal Energy distribution centre.

Already today, he had signed a supply contract with Ukraine and chaired a video conference with his national unit heads. But for all the good news, the only project that was causing him a headache was about ten miles away in Cardale.

Aaron Barrett, the council leader, had promised him it would be straightforward. But there were two hundred protestors surrounding the security fence, and they hadn't even started drilling yet because they'd unearthed a dead body.

He leaned forward, dropped one sugar cube into the one-cup teapot and stirred it once. He checked his watch. It needed another minute.

This was his one break in a working day that began at 7 a.m. and ended when his driver came back to collect him at 6 p.m. He called it his think-tank time, and staff knew better than to interrupt.

He gazed at the map. So, what to do about Cardale? It was a small scheme but showed potential for a few million cubic metres of gas, which was not to be sniffed at.

However, every day without progress was money lost. Alistair had drummed into his team the mantra that every site must operate as a standalone business. It either makes a profit or it gets shut down.

Time was up. Alistair poured the tea and sipped slowly. He put the cup gently back onto its saucer and walked to the window. Manchester was growing upwards. There was so much housing, office, retail and leisure development it reminded him of Singapore a few years back. He'd seen the signs there long ago, and Universal's Asian arm was its most profitable by far.

The demand for accessible, reliable energy wasn't going away, and Manchester could be the next big success story.

How perfect it would be if he could supply all his hometown's needs from a local source. He turned back to his desk. There was so much at stake, and it was personal. The Cardale site would be the fulfilment of a dream: giving something back to the city he loved. A fitting legacy.

He pressed the red button on his control pad. 'Could you get Aaron Barrett on the telephone for me, please?'

***

Jane watched as George wrestled with the lid of a plastic container. Every fibre of her being wanted to tell him, *'Just prise one corner up using that little flap...'*

Luckily, he worked it out and looked up. 'Would you like to try one, ma'am? Wife made them last night.'

One bite of the shortbread was enough. 'Can I take another?'

George looked suitably pleased and reached in his jacket pocket for his notebook. He cleared his throat. Jane bit into her second square of shortbread and waited.

'You asked me to go back through the records, ma'am. Previous similar stabbing incidents.'

Jane felt the gentle buzz as the sugar did its work. Now for the caffeine. She sipped her third coffee of the day and nodded.

'We have what looks like an exact match. Stockport area. Three years ago. Knife in the back of the neck. Body buried. No one found, ma'am.'

Jane thought George looked awkward for some reason. 'What aren't you telling me, George?'

'The investigation was led by Simon Hopkirk, ma'am.'

16.

Jane had driven home without remembering the journey.

One minute she was in the station car park fending off Roy Cooke, who was annoyed she'd forgotten their drink date. The next, she was zapping the car remote and standing outside her front door.

She imagined her brain must have resembled the burned-out inners of a knackered computer before its final journey to the recycling centre.

She'd even forgotten to call in at the supermarket: a mistake that was only made apparent when she opened the fridge, convinced she'd find half a bottle of Sauvignon with her name on it. Half a bottle of two-day-old milk didn't quite cut it.

She threw her keys on the table and sat down, closed her eyes and tried to zone out, but the silence didn't soothe. If anything, it magnified the noise in her head. Meeting Allan had been a mistake. She missed his bear hugs more than ever now.

All her experience seemed to have jumped out of the window. She felt overwhelmed by what was proving to be the most complicated case yet. *Cardale connections*. It sounded like a board game, which was bad news because she'd hated them with a passion ever since her dad had swindled his way to victory at Monopoly every Christmas.

Maybe this game was all about money, too. Was that at the centre of what was happening in Cardale?

There were so many possibilities it was impossible to unravel them, or even to know where to start.

Jane went upstairs and turned the immersion heater on. She'd promised to go round to her mum's tonight, but it wasn't going to happen. A hot bath with music and candles was, though.

She splashed cold water on her face, drank a glassful and started to feel vaguely human. Ten minutes later, she'd thrown her clothes into the linen basket and changed into what she called her slob gear—baggy joggers and her cosiest fleece sweatshirt.

She knew it would take the ancient heater at least an hour to manufacture a bath-sized portion of hot water, so she decided to drink tea and brainstorm the case again.

By the time she'd finished, her sheet of A4 resembled a circuit board.

She hadn't had any contact with Hopkirk since the hit-and-run murders, when he'd told her he couldn't offer her promotion because she'd ignored orders and accused an Army brigadier of a cover-up.

She stabbed the yellow highlighter over his name and drew another line to connect it to the name in capitals in the centre: *KEITH CASTLE*.

Jane poured another glass of water from the tap and looked at her handiwork from a distance. The answer was in there somewhere, and she was going to find it.

After she'd nipped out to the supermarket.

And after she'd soaked in the bath.

***

Aaron Barrett ordered a double Irish and joined Peter Attrill at the table in the corner.

Aaron had a temper on him tonight, and Peter had already sensed their 'cosy chat' would be anything but. Neither of them noticed Mike Brook sitting on his own a few tables away, his head down, nursing half a pint of bitter.

'I had Alistair Grant on the phone this morning,' Aaron told Peter indignantly. 'Long story short, he wants me to get the police off that site so they can get on with the job.'

Peter nodded slowly, buying time to come up with a non-contentious remark. 'Easier said than done,' he said hesitantly.

'Exactly! Much easier said than done, you are correct.'

Peter took courage and volunteered a few more words of wisdom. 'Needs careful handling, doesn't it?'

He winced inside as he realised his mistake. Aaron never had time for careful. His philosophy was to wade in and make noise, and he made that clear again, loudly. 'Bollocks to that! I'm going to kick someone's arse. They've pratted about long enough. They're costing the project a few thou a day and it can't go on.' He looked closely at Peter, who was studying a beer mat. 'Can it?'

Peter felt obliged to agree. 'Erm... no, certainly not. Do you... I mean, do you want me to do anything?'

Aaron's response caught him off guard: 'How much have you had to drink?'

'Just a glass after dinner, and this pint. Why?'

'Can you drive me up to the site? Let's get this sorted.'

***

Ross kicked his shoes off, lay back on the sofa and smiled as Bess climbed up to rest her head on his lap.

He'd surprised everyone by offering to adopt her, mainly because her previous owner, Thomas Armitage, had been convicted of the Ashbridge hit-and-run murders a few months ago. One of the last things he'd said to Ross before he'd been sent down was a request to make sure Bess was given a good home.

He stroked her head. 'What do you think, Bess? Is this a good home?'

She replied by grunting softly and stretching her legs.

Ross laughed. 'That's a yes then.'

Ross had never seen himself as a dog owner, but there was something about Bess. She had been a racing greyhound, kicked out because she developed arthritis. She was put in the station kennels when Armitage was arrested, and everyone suddenly became a dog lover.

They knew she'd be put down once her owner was locked up. Ross couldn't bear the idea, and the clincher came when Amy agreed to move in with him as a house share. She worked nights at the Feathers, which meant Bess wouldn't be alone all day.

Amy and Bess had made it feel like home, and Ross had started to look forward to getting back there after work. He'd even given up the poker sessions. Neighbours he'd never spoken to before would come up and talk to him on Bess's walk to the park.

She grumbled sleepily as he gently moved her head so he could escape. Once safely in the kitchen, he chose a beer from the extensive selection in the fridge.

He sat at the table to review his notes from a day spent chatting up local drug pushers. Jane and George would be pleased, and the work gave him a buzz. The more he got into it, the more he wanted to specialise. It was an evil trade that ruined lives, but it was also a massive challenge because it attracted such devious characters.

He'd checked out the criteria for joining the National Crime Agency, and it looked like he stood a chance. But that was for another day.

He sipped French lager from the bottle and began noting down all he knew about the secret life of Keith Castle.

Bess stretched out to fill the sofa and started snoring.

***

The combination of soothing music, calming candles, a hot bath and lightly chilled prosecco seemed to be working.

The microwave pinged to summon her to the kitchen. She scooped a ready meal for one onto a plate and sat at the table in her bathrobe with a towel round her head, feeling decadent.

She'd spent so much at the shop she couldn't fit it into her bag for life. Luckily there'd been a parking space outside her door when she got back. Even better, the good-looking neighbour with grey hair and a suntan helped her carry some bits as far as the hall. And he didn't make jokey remarks about the number of wine bottles.

The fridge was now respectably full—prosecco, white wine, milk, cheddar cheese, a shelf full of ready meals, yoghurt and tomatoes—and on the worktop next to the hob, a white bowl piled up with apples and satsumas. And a couple of bottles of Malbec.

She made short work of the prawn curry and rice, washed out the container and stacked one plate and one fork into the dishwasher.

She stopped. One plate! What had happened to her? She was independent, but she certainly wasn't designed to be alone. It hit her that everything about tonight had just been a distraction. She missed Allan. Needed his love, his support, his bad jokes.

Never mind solving the Cardale case. What about her life, her future? How about a plan for cracking that problem?

She felt hollow. The silence was claustrophobic and her Pilates breathing technique didn't work. The tension in her head was a sure sign of a migraine.

Her phone lay dark and silent on the table in front of her. All she had to do was pick it up and press a few numbers.

She filled her glass with prosecco, grabbed the phone and opened her contacts. Allan was the first entry.

***

Much to Peter's alarm, they were waved through security, and he was inside, feeling like a zoo animal, being watched by a crowd from the other side of the metal barriers.

Some of them had heckled as they walked from the car park, but Aaron had sneered. 'Don't worry about them, matey. They're scum.'

Aaron was setting a fast pace. Peter's heart thudded as he tried to keep up, his eyes fixed on a circle of bright light where two white figures were crouched down.

Peter looked on, dragging in deep breaths of country air with a hint of red diesel, as Aaron knelt next to the chap in the white suit and patted him on the back.

'Good Lord! Phil? Haven't seen you for bloody ages, man! Last I heard, your ticker was about to give up the ghost. Good to see you! Want a hand up, chum?'

Phil nodded and grunted as he stepped up the ladder, with Aaron on one arm, and Claire on the other.

'So, what can we do for you, Aaron?' He winked. 'As if I didn't know.'

Aaron smiled, and belatedly remembered to introduce Peter, who nodded, looking twice at the red-haired lady, who he remembered from when they found Sid Marsh in the ditch.

Aaron was suddenly oozing charm. 'Well, Phil, we all just want to know when you'll be finished here so we can get on with the drilling. Alan here has got a lot of chaps being paid a fortune to sit on their arses, and it would be marvellous if we could just get on with it—save everyone time and money, right, Alan?'

The site supervisor nodded, quietly proud to be included in the conversation by someone he'd been told was a VIP.

Phil smiled. 'Hello Alan. And there was us, thinking you were bringing tea.'

Aaron laughed, his voice seeming to boom across the valley. Peter secretly hoped the protestors couldn't hear it. It would just wind them up even more. But there was no stopping Aaron now. 'So, Phil, what's the verdict?'

Phil looked at Claire, looked at the trench, looked at Alan, and finally looked across to the drilling tower that loomed to their right. Claire smiled at his playacting. They'd already started packing up. He was really milking this.

'Oh, we'll be gone first thing tomorrow. After that, it's all yours.'

Aaron gossiped happily all the way off the site, but the smile was wiped off his face when they were confronted by Felicity Crowther and Mike Brook.

Aaron nudged Peter's arm. 'Leave the talking to me.'

Peter had no intention of doing otherwise, and just nodded.

Mike Brook smiled brightly. 'Evening, Councillor Barrett. Can I ask how long you have been on the payroll of Universal Energy?'

Aaron didn't hesitate, though Peter could see he'd been thrown off balance. 'Good evening, Mr Brook. If you have any serious questions, I'll give you an answer, but if you're going to talk rubbish, I think I'll get an early night.'

'Do you deny telling your friend here that the CEO of Universal Energy had told you to come here tonight and get the police off the site so they could start drilling?'

Peter heard muttering from the group standing behind Felicity and started to look for an escape route. But Aaron laughed, though his eyes were steely.

'Tell me, Michael. How long have you been working for Felicity Crowther? She's got you asking the questions for her now, has she? So much for the independence of the *Free Press*. Still, if you must know, I instigated a discussion with Universal Energy—our partners in this project—about the impact of the delays to a project that is openly supported by the council—check the minutes if you don't believe me—balanced by the need to allow the police time for a thorough investigation. We agreed that since I was coming up here tonight anyway, I would find out what could be done, and Peter, the chair of the Village Association, agreed to join me.

'And the result of that, we are pleased to say, is that drilling is now cleared to start straight away.' He turned away. 'Now, if you'll excuse us. Some of us have got work to do in the morning.'

'You're getting in early to make Barrett's tea, are you?' Felicity got a few laughs and jeers for her parting remark.

Aaron had had enough. He stopped, turned and walked up to them. 'If you dare print or repeat any accusation that questions my integrity as leader of the council, I promise you will regret it.'

The jeers and the name-calling followed them all the way back to the car. Peter was ready for a whisky when he got back to the sanctuary of his thatched cottage. Maggie was stretched out on the sofa listening to Verdi, so he poured a glass and sat in the recliner by the bay window.

Maggie looked at him with a curious expression and turned the music off. 'Keith Castle was a friend of yours, wasn't he?'

Peter hesitated. 'Well, not a friend as such... But yes. Not seen him for a while, though. Why?'

'It was his body they found at the drilling site.'

17.

Jane hadn't been driving more than ten minutes before Roy Cooke was on the phone.

The sound made her jump. She'd been lost in thought, wondering what had stopped her calling Allan last night.

She put the call on speaker as she edged through the morning traffic. When she saw the queue at the first set of lights, she decided it would surely have been quicker by bike.

'Morning, sir,' she called out.

The Chief Super was in no mood for pleasantries, and his voice sounded even more harsh through the car speakers. 'Jane, I'm getting earache like you wouldn't believe about the delay to drilling up at Cardale. How much longer is Phil going to spend on his hands and knees with a bloody magnifying glass? It's costing the company thousands a day, and for what?'

Jane took her time over the reply. She wanted to enjoy the moment, sad though she knew that was. 'Well, it is a crime scene—a murder investigation, sir...'

'Yes, I do know that! But how long does it take to sieve soil and check for traces? He's been up there for nearly two days!'

Jane waited till the lights turned red again, then delivered the punchline. 'He's finished now, sir.'

Silence. Then... 'Jane? What? Are you taking the p—'

'No sir, Phil told me late last night. The site's cleared and drilling can start. If they're still determined to ruin the environment, of course.'

Roy cleared his throat. 'I agree with you on that. But we are where we are. It's not for us to judge. Anyway, thanks for letting me know. So, what's next?'

Jane hit the brakes sharply as the next set of lights snapped to red. 'I'm getting a bicycle, sir.'

'What??'

Jane smiled and pushed the button to disconnect the call.

***

There was no sign of Roy at the station, but there was a message from Ross among the alerts on her computer screen.

Good result last night, ma'am. Please check the log. Ross.

Ross reported that a few drug pushers recognised Keith Castle's photo, though they were carefully vague about when and how they'd seen him. Ross said their reticence may be because he was working for the same supplier, and they didn't want to be known as squealers.

Another contact had told him Keith had been absent from work for around two weeks before he was killed.

Jane massaged her forehead as she re-read the note. Everything seemed to date back to when that tractor demolished Mary's cottage. Was that apparently random and unpredictable event the trigger that detonated a deadly chain reaction? If so, the deaths were linked, and so was the attack on Sid Marsh.

Jane remembered a conversation with her mum during the hit-and-run murders. They'd been talking about how solving murders was like doing a jigsaw. You had to be methodical: find the corners, then the straight edges, and work your way in. Then her mum had innocently pointed out that, while that was true, everything is ruined if there's just one piece missing.

Jane shook her head. In this case, it felt like the corner pieces were missing, and she couldn't find the right place to start.

She sighed and opened the rest of the case log. There was a new note from Phil. *Lab analysis shows Mr Castle had been taking anti-depressants.*

Jane scrolled back a couple of days. Yes, there it was... Keith's wife had told George he seemed fine and showed no sign of having personal problems. There was no medication in the house and his GP hadn't seen him for months.

She sat thinking for a moment, then pushed her chair back roughly and grabbed her car keys.

There was only one location that connected all the events in Cardale. It was time for another visit to Marsh Farm.

***

Gloria MacDonald sipped her white wine spritzer and nodded her thanks as Peter Attrill pushed the saucer of olives closer to her.

She noticed his hand was shaking slightly and wondered if it was nerves, or illness.

She'd heard he'd taken over from Mary as chair of the village association. Maybe the responsibility was too much for him. She remembered Mary laughing about the time it took up: '*If they paid me by the hour, I'd be a zillionaire, Mum!*'

It was no surprise that the memories of her seemed to be flooding in, rather than receding. They'd told her they'd be releasing the body so she could plan for the funeral. She wanted to take Mary home to Scotland, but so much of her life was here.

Gloria stabbed a black olive with a cocktail stick and dunked it in her glass.

Peter raised his eyebrows and smiled for the first time since they'd sat down. 'I thought they only did that with cocktails.'

Gloria smiled. 'Well, yes, but I have a vivid imagination. Makes me think of holidays in sunny places. Happy thoughts seem to be at a premium these days.'

He nodded sympathetically and seemed to relax. He took a swig of his pint. 'So, thanks for the invitation. You said you needed some help?'

Gloria leaned forward, and Peter felt himself drawn in. It was hard to believe she'd recently lost her daughter; she seemed so composed.

'Well, Peter. I'm keen to learn more about the village that Mary loved so much. Find out about the people. Pick up the gossip. It all helps to connect me to her, if that makes sense.'

'Of course. I can tell you she was very popular...' He stopped, realising he was in danger of saying completely the wrong thing. 'She was popular with all of us. Kind-hearted, cheerful, helpful—and strong, too. She had to be to run the association.'

'Why? Is there a lot of controversy? Disagreement?'

Peter needed time. He wasn't as quick-witted as Aaron, who could answer any question without blinking or pausing. He suddenly felt on his guard but wasn't sure why. Gloria was sharp, just like Mary had been. The same good looks. The same razor edge?

She sensed his discomfort and tried to nudge him. 'I suppose that's a silly question. There always will be disagreements. I imagine not everyone was happy about the drilling, or the housing development. And...' She leaned forward, whispering, so close her cheek was almost touching his. '... she said quite a few locals were, shall we say, a little too fond of illegal substances. Is that true?'

The look on his face was enough.

He cleared his throat noisily and drained his glass. 'I have heard the rumours but I've no idea if any of it is true.'

Gloria wouldn't let it go; he was starting to sweat. She smiled. 'I don't think there's any secret about it, Peter. I heard that cocaine was found in the rubble at Mary's house. Obviously, as her mother, that concerns me. I'd really like to know where it came from and wondered if you could help.'

He felt cornered. His mouth was dry, and his brain had shut down. All he could think was that he needed to end this conversation.

'I'm sorry. I need to be somewhere else. I don't know if you know, but I used to run a dairy farm. Used to supply all the milk round here. Sold it not long ago, but they keep me on as a kind of advisor, you see. Anyway, they apparently need an urgent chat. Completely forgot.' He stopped, realising he was babbling, then gave her a weak smile. 'Do excuse me.'

Gloria just smiled and raised her glass. 'I quite understand, Peter.'

He left the pub in a hurry and headed for home.

***

Jag sat back in his chair and closed his eyes.

The doctor told him he should take at least a five-minute break from close work every hour to avoid overworking his good eye. But taking time out had never come easy, especially now, after months of enforced idleness and daytime television.

He lifted the eyepatch and soothed his damaged eye with a wet wipe, then repositioned it and leaned forward to resume his search of photos on the NCA drugs database. Ross warned him it would be a hard slog, but Jag was glad to help. Even so, he was surprised by how many people seemed to be involved.

Quite a mix, too. Young, middle-aged and older; black, white; smart, scruffy; male, female—there were no barriers to employment here.

His mission was to see if there had been any sightings of the murder victim, Keith Castle. So, it was a case of combing CCTV stills of dubious quality, as well as the official mugshots.

Face recognition software was doing most of the hard work for him, and it had come up with more than a hundred possible matches.

He scrolled down slowly, leaning closer even though screen magnification was on full. Keeping his good eye fixed on the screen, he reached out to grab his water bottle. He was just about to take a drink when the software pinged, as he had programmed it to do if there was a particularly close match.

And there it was!

Jag dragged the picture Ross had sent him alongside the CCTV image that had come up as a ninety-nine per cent probability of a match with Keith Castle.

It showed him in a series of photos putting small packets into his jacket. They were being handed to him from a parked van.

Jag wanted to jump up and punch the air, but his doctor wouldn't have approved, so he sent a message to Ross instead.

***

The *Ashbridge Free Press* headline took up most of the front page, with a picture of Felicity Crowther and a group of banner-waving protestors.

ENOUGH IS ENOUGH!
Cardale protestors vow to stop the drilling.
Jane turned to an inside page to read the story.
Environmental activist Felicity Crowther says the decision to drill for gas in green fields at Cardale is 'the devil's work'.

She warned energy giants Universal Energy that hundreds more protestors were on their way to the site from all over Britain. She added: 'We're prepared to do anything to protect the environment, even if Ashbridge Council can't be bothered to honour its climate change obligations. Aaron Barrett is so determined to do Universal's bidding he's been trying to cut short a police investigation into the discovery of a body on the site. That's how much they value profit above human life.'

Jane folded the page and took in the view through the windscreen from her vantage point above the village. An undulating mosaic of trees and fields and hedges set against a backing track of birdsong. The drill site was hidden from here, but that made it even more sinister. It made her think of a stealth bomber; invisible until it thundered into view and wreaked destruction.

She would be interviewing Felicity later and hoped she could remain objective. It was hard not to agree with her, but her inflammatory language begged the question: how far would she go to win?

Allan's paper had gone in hard, and she was proud of him for that. But was that because his company cared, or were they motivated by profit too? A local controversy is good news for sales, he used to say.

As always, more questions than answers.

She obediently responded to the ping of her phone. A message from Ross with a picture of Keith Castle, caught in the act of supplying drugs.

Another ping. A message from George: Lorry was back at work.

Jane leaned back against the headrest and closed her eyes, concentrating on deep breathing, willing herself to relax the tension in her neck and shoulders.

It didn't work. She needed to make sense of it all. Then there was just a chance that she could relax.

Next stop, Marsh Farm.

18.

Maggie quickly dented Peter's hopes of a quiet afternoon.

'I hear you were in the pub with Mary's rather glamorous mother.'

Peter kept the *Free Press* in front of his face for a moment to hide his surprise. Lowering it slowly, he put on a disinterested tone. 'Yes, she wanted to talk to me about her, knowing I'd taken over as association chair.'

Maggie sipped her herb tea and raised an eyebrow. 'I wonder why.'

'Why what?'

'Why she felt the need to talk to you. And why you didn't tell me.'

Peter folded his paper roughly in half and dropped it on the carpet. He kept his voice even. 'She just wanted to know more about Mary's life here. I didn't mention it simply because I've got so many other things to think about, as you know.' He paused, trying to think of a way to lighten the atmosphere. 'Anyway, which of your spies gave you this insider information?'

Maggie was wearing running shorts. She tucked her legs under her and swept her hair back. Not for the first time, Peter wondered how on earth he'd managed to marry such an attractive woman.

She smiled in that way of hers that made him uneasy. 'Wouldn't you like to know? Anyway, stop ogling my legs and tell me the truth about Keith Castle.'

'What do you mean?'

'He's been found dead, not far from here. You knew him. You surely realise it's only a matter of time before the police start knocking on doors? And if you knew him, they're going to want to question you... closely.' She looked out of the window then turned quickly to catch the expression on Peter's face. 'See? You're anxious. Don't you get it? Not only are you starting to look like a suspect, but you're also making me wonder.'

'Wonder what?'

'Come on, Peter. I'm not a fool. You've been spending an awful lot of time in that den of yours, and you and Barrett are thick as thieves. Something's going on, and I'd quite like to know what it is.'

Peter sighed elaborately and leaned forward for emphasis. 'Nothing is going on. I've just got a lot on my plate, that's all.'

She stood, pulled her sweatshirt off over her head to reveal a tight-fitting running vest, and tied her hair back into a ponytail.

She walked towards the back door, then turned, pointing a finger. 'I guarantee the police won't be satisfied with an answer like that. I'm certainly not. I'm going for a run. I hope you're ready to talk to me when I get back. Otherwise...'

'Otherwise, what?'

She walked out and slammed the door.

***

Sid Marsh looked frail, but he said he was following doctor's orders and walking every day.

'I feel guilty. Julie's doing all the work.'

Jane heard her laughing in the kitchen. 'So, what's new?' she called out.

They both seemed more comfortable together. Jane knew from her own experience, though, that people put on a show for the outside world. Maybe these two were just good at it.

She thanked Julie for the tea and took a bite of fruit cake.

Jane held her phone out so Sid could see the image of Keith Castle. She watched him closely but kept the tone casual. 'We're trying to identify this man. Do you recognise him?'

He shook his head. 'It's not very good quality. No idea who that is.'

She showed Julie, who studied it carefully; something Sid had not done. 'No, sorry. I don't recognise him. Who is he?'

The contrast in their responses was pronounced. Jane swiped to the next picture.

Sid shook his head again. 'Am I supposed to know him?'

'No. It's not compulsory. But it's important you co-operate. I remind you, we're investigating a murder. His body was found on the drilling site just down the road from here. His name is Keith Castle. No one is accusing anyone. We just want everyone to realise the importance of our investigation, and to think hard and tell us what they know. Starting with you. I have one more picture, but can I ask first—does that name mean anything to you?'

Sid looked shocked but said nothing. Jane showed him the third picture. He looked closely this time, holding the phone nearer, taking his time.

'I know who it is now. He's the guy who used to supply my cocaine.'

Julie turned to Jane. 'Do you have any more questions? Only, I think Sid needs a break now. He gets tired so easily.'

'Of course. Drug use is not my priority just now, but we now have a connection between your husband and the victim. I need to find out who killed Mr Castle. So, any help you provide—both of you—will go a long way towards making the use of illegal substances even less of a priority. Understood?' She paused to finish her tea. 'Just one more thing, for now, Sid. Did you see this man on the day you were attacked, and do you know who else he was supplying in the village?'

Sid sat up straighter. 'Someone came to sell me some stuff out at the back of the pub, but it wasn't him. It was a guy I hadn't seen before, but he acted like he knew me.'

Jane flicked a glance at Julie, who nodded her permission. 'Can you describe him for me?'

'He looked a bit like him, but I was pretty much off my head on booze that night. What else did you ask me?'

'Who else was he supplying in the village?'

'There must have been quite a few. Don't know who. But he used to say it was one of his best rounds. A nice little earner, he called it.' He stopped, massaging his forehead. 'There was something he said: *People call me their milkman.*'

***

Jane parked near the village hall and was so deep in thought she didn't register Maggie Attrill's cheerful greeting as she ran past.

By the time she realised, Maggie was about twenty yards away. Jane called out, 'I was on my way to see you!'

'Peter's in. Won't be long!' Maggie yelled back, but carried on running.

Jane made her mind up there and then that she was going to get fit. But running just wasn't her thing. The last time she'd run anywhere was from the car park to the supermarket to dodge a heavy shower. Maybe it really was time to get a bike. It would get her moving and be one less car on the road. And she could pull rank and have first call on the pool car if she needed it. The decision was made by the time she reached Attrill's cottage.

Peter's middle-aged demeanour came as a bit of a shock after Maggie's athletic youthfulness.

Jane showed her ID and introduced herself. 'Mind if we have a chat?'

He obviously did mind. 'What about? I am rather busy.'

Jane glanced at the newspaper he was holding. 'Ah, don't worry. It won't take long. We're just trying to identify someone, so we're asking as many people as possible.'

He stepped to one side and waved her in without a word. Not for the first time in Cardale, Jane caught the aroma of whisky.

He pointed to a cream panelled door, and Jane pushed through into a bright kitchen fitted with white units, an oval oak table and chairs. A cream-enamelled Aga took up the whole of one wall, and a vase of red and pink roses stood out against the terracotta tiles on the windowsill.

Peter did a fair impression of a waiter, pulling out a chair for her and pushing it in behind her as she sat. She refused his offer of a drink and ran through the routine stuff before opening the gallery folder on her phone.

'I simply want you to look carefully at these photos and tell me if you recognise the man. It doesn't matter if you don't know his name. We're just interested to know if he's been seen around Cardale lately. I need to tell you that this is a murder investigation, so your co-operation is very important.'

As he reached for the phone, she noticed a tremble in his hand. He took his time, swiping through the pictures, then handed it back without making eye contact. 'No, sorry.'

'That's a shame. Are you sure? Would you mind looking again?'

He sighed and rested his elbows on the table. There were dark patches under his arms, and he was breathing heavily. He shook his head and handed the phone back.

'Are you all right, Mr Attrill?'

'Yes, of course. Why do you ask?'

'You seem a little anxious.'

'Like I said, I'm very busy. Got a lot on. So, if you don't mind...?'

He held the door open for her, and Jane stepped outside. She turned as she walked towards the gate.

'Right, thank you, Mr Attrill. Can you tell Maggie I'm sorry I missed her, but I'll be back to check with her too?'

If he took that as a warning, he didn't show it. 'Yes, yes, I will. I'm sure she'll tell you the same thing. Sorry I can't be of more help.'

Heavy rain had been forecast by an annoyingly cheerful radio presenter, and Jane ran back to her car as the first drops began to fall. By the time she'd slammed the door shut, the rain was bouncing off the windscreen and she was out of breath.

She sent a note to George asking for a background check on Peter Attrill, and another to Ross telling him to put all his energy into exploring the drugs network.

She started the engine and put the heater on full to clear the glass, just as a message came through from Phil. *Mary's mother invited us to the funeral on Friday.*

***

Chief Supt Roy Cooke checked his tie in the mirror and brushed a speck off the sleeve of his suit jacket.

He could hear Jane talking in her office next door and checked his watch irritably. The chief constable of Greater Manchester would be in the building within a couple of minutes, and she was still chatting.

Simon Hopkirk had said it was just an informal visit, and they'd known each other a few years, but Roy didn't believe that for a minute. There had to be another reason.

His desk phone buzzed, and he picked up straight away.

Doreen was on the front desk today, and he really wished she wasn't. She was hyper, as usual.

'Oh hello!' she said, as if him answering his own phone was a surprise. 'The chief constabulary is here, sir!'

'Chief constable, Doreen.'

'Yes, that's what I said. Shall I send him up?'

'No, Doreen. Do not do that. Please just tell him I will be down in a moment to meet him, and please see if he wants anything.'

'Right! Yes! Erm... a brew, you mean?'

'A cup of tea, or coffee. Ask him which he prefers, all right?'

He put the phone down to cut her off, just as Jane tapped on the door and walked in. 'Good,' he said. 'Right. Quick word?'

Jane nodded and accepted his invitation to sit.

'I have no idea why he's visiting today,' he said. 'What about you? Any thoughts?'

'Not really, sir. Unless he knows we're looking into a case that has similarities with one he was leading a few years back.'

'Ah, of course. The stabbing. Same M.O. as the Keith Castle job, right?' He paused. 'Hmmm. Maybe. But why come here? He could easily do a video call.'

'No idea. I may be completely wrong, of course. It might just be a courtesy call. How are we getting on together, that sort of thing.'

'And what's your answer?'

'Honestly, I think it's working well, sir.'

Roy smiled and checked his watch again. 'We'd better go and say hello.'

Jane laughed. 'Definitely. Doreen's on today, isn't she?'

***

Felicity Crowther wiped condensation from the glass and looked out across the field as more tents and campervans arrived.

Her rallying call through blog and Instagram had brought at least another hundred protestors to the site. They were making headlines locally and nationally, too. But she still felt dissatisfied.

She sipped peppermint tea, nibbled an oat biscuit. Jack had been impatient last night. All she'd wanted to do was close her eyes and disappear into the sleeping bag, but he was bright-eyed with rough cider and eager for direct action. She'd distracted him by suggesting a bit of action in bed instead. He was still there, gently snoring, and she was beginning to think he was right.

Her Strawberry Fields Forever movement had won support because it grabbed headlines, and occasionally got results. As she always said: 'Think of it as the Hundred Years War. We're not going to win every time, but we are making people think, and we're winning over politicians, too. It's going to take a long time. But that's the only real way to achieve change.'

She watched the field slowly come to life as people emerged, stretched and greeted one another, and wondered how much longer they'd be happy to stand at the barriers chanting slogans and waving banners. How long before they got bored and moved on?

She rinsed her cup under the tap, then sat on the bed and punched Jack's shoulder.

'Come on, you big lump. You wanted action, so let's have some.'

Jack slowly opened his eyes as the words sank in. 'Seriously?'

She nodded. 'Very.'

He sat up and kissed her, instantly awake. The campervan lurched under his weight as he walked to the sink and drank a mugful of water. 'What's the plan, captain?'

Felicity smiled. 'Don't breathe a word yet. We're going to break through that bloody security fence tonight.'

'Yes!' Jack punched the air, then groaned and nursed his hand. He'd also punched the van roof.

19.

Simon Hopkirk was clearly relieved to escape Doreen's clutches.

Roy suggested they go to his office first, and he readily agreed, but had the good grace to thank Doreen for the cup of tea. Jane smiled quietly as Doreen blushed, then patted her on the arm before following them up the stairs.

The chief constable waved Roy away when he offered more tea or coffee and smiled at Jane.

'This is just a courtesy call. I wanted to see how you're both getting on. And, with all due respect, Roy, particularly Jane.'

Jane couldn't hide her surprise. 'Me, sir?'

'Yes, of course. I gave you a bit of a dressing down not too long ago over the Army business. So, I want to hear how you're coping now. It was a setback for you, I know, but I see you're already deep into a complex investigation?'

'Sir. I'm okay. Completely understand. You did what you had to do, and I'm happy enough now. Roy and I are getting on fine, and this case is certainly a challenge. But I like to think it's what I do best, so...'

Roy butted in. 'I'd echo that, sir. Jane has been a great support to me, and if she was disappointed by the outcome re the Army, it certainly hasn't affected her work, or our relationship.'

Simon crossed his legs and leaned back a little. 'Excellent. So, down to business.' He stopped and smiled. 'Yes, I know I said it was a courtesy call, but neither of you really believed it, did you? I've thought about that Army cover-up allegation, and I asked my team to do some more digging around. The upshot is that the Crown Prosecution Service agrees there is a case to answer.' He turned to look at Jane. 'It's my roundabout way of saying you've been vindicated, Jane. We will be formally interviewing the brigadier. I'm here because I wanted to apologise for questioning your judgement, and to say—with Roy's blessing, I might add—that the offer of promotion is back on the table.'

Jane tried to respond but could only smile and flick a glance at Roy, who nodded his encouragement.

'No need to say anything yet, Jane. As before, I have a position in mind for you, but first, I need to know you would be open to taking the opportunity to move to HQ and work directly with me.'

Jane was buzzing with conflicting emotions, but she knew her answer. 'Yes, sir, I would. Thank you!'

***

Allan used to relish his moments alone with Ruby.

On the surface, it was all very business-like, but she would occasionally hitch up her skirt and perch on the edge of his desk. Her legs were long and tanned, and she was so close he could breathe in her perfume. It felt dangerous, tempting. He'd wonder if she was making a play for him. But he told himself he was being a fool.

Now it was making him feel uncomfortable, and he invariably found an excuse to stand and pace around as he dictated a memo.

Today, at least, she sat across the desk, legs crossed demurely, notebook on her knee, pen poised, as Allan ran through the top ten projects in his in-tray.

He'd reached number three when the phone rang. Ruby stretched across to pick it up.

'Good morning. Mr Askew's office; how can I help?'

She listened for a moment, then covered the receiver. 'It's Jenny on the line. Says she must speak to you.'

Allan was happy to be interrupted by his editor, though he disguised it behind a sigh as he reached out for the receiver, now fragrant with Ruby's perfume.

'Jenny, hi.'

'Morning, boss. We've got a tip-off the Cardale protests are going to get a bit spicy tonight. Okay if I go out there with Mike?'

He loved the way she got straight to the point. 'Of course, it is. You don't need my permission to chase a good story.'

'Och, I know. I only rang just to see if you'd heard anything yerself, from the council maybe?'

Allan covered the receiver and asked Ruby if there had been any messages for him relating to the Cardale protests. She shook her head.

'No, nothing's come my way, Jenny. Tell me what time you're going out there.'

They were driving out around 10 p.m., and Allan asked her to be careful and keep him posted.

Ruby looked at him expectantly. 'Sounds exciting.'

Allan would have liked nothing more than to go up to the site with them. But he smiled at Ruby, asked if she'd mind sorting out a coffee for them both, and reluctantly grabbed the remaining papers from his in-tray.

As soon as she'd closed the door behind her, he stood and walked slowly to the window. He needed air, not paperwork. He slid the balcony doors open and stepped onto the teak boards.

Hazy sunlight was reflecting off the steel and glass tower blocks that seemed to be springing up so quickly. The traffic below sounded more like breaking surf. He breathed in deeply through his nose and remembered how uncertain he'd been about selling his paper to NW Media. He still felt caught between the novelty of not having to worry about money and the regret at missing out on the thrill of the journalistic chase. And losing Jane.

He closed his eyes, allowing the cloud of thoughts to dissipate.

When he opened them again, the clouds had parted and only one thought remained. He knew exactly what he had to do.

***

Lorry was full of stories about her honeymoon: the villa in Crete with its own path to the beach, the white-walled houses and bright red flowers, seafood platters, warm sea and sunshine. Ross wanted to know when she was going to give him the souvenir she'd promised. But Eric stole the show by telling her how nice she looked with her suntan.

'Thank you, Eric, that's sweet of you. I'm not used to compliments.'

Ross shook his head wearily and turned to Eric. 'I'm disappointed in you.'

Lorry laughed and produced three gift bags, just as the door opened and the chief constable walked in.

'Morning everyone. Please, relax. I just wanted to say hello and get a feel for how things are going. According to Roy and Jane, you are the best detective team in Greater Manchester.' He smiled. 'Would you go along with that?'

Ross was first with an answer. 'Sir, if we are, it's because we work for the best DCI.'

Lorry stared at her desk. Ross was known for his glib answers, but she knew he meant it.

'Yes, I agree, Jane is one of the best,' Simon said. 'George, you've been here a few years. Is everything okay? Do you have the resources you need?'

George had remained standing out of respect. 'Yes, sir. We're pleased to have recruited Eric, who has settled in very well and is doing good work. Our only real issue is that Jag is unable to do more than a few hours a week.'

Simon leaned against the conference table. Eric couldn't take his eyes off the uniform: the badges and buttons catching the light, his gleaming white shirt. He just hoped he wouldn't have to say anything. But then the chief constable turned slightly to look at him, and his heart began to pound.

Simon smiled. 'Welcome to the team, Eric. I've heard good things about you. Keep up the good work, okay?'

'Yes, sir!'

'About Jag. Jane and Roy are committed to finding a way to reintegrate him, and I will back that all the way. Please be patient, and don't hesitate to speak out if you believe lack of resources is getting in the way.'

He turned to Lorry, and soon they were chatting like old friends about Crete, until he checked his watch and apologised for having to get back to work.

As the door swung shut behind him, George brought them back to earth. 'Right. Stop gawking and get on with your casework. Lorry?'

'Yes, boss?'

'You've been away for two weeks. Time you did some catching up. Mine's a strong coffee with milk.'

***

Gloria MacDonald's invitation had emphasised that the service was to be a celebration of Mary's life. She had written a message by hand at the bottom of the card: *Please wear bright and colourful clothes.*

She'd told Phil she wanted to reunite her daughter with her father at a family grave just outside Edinburgh but felt it was important to allow her friends in the village to give her a send-off.

It was only when Jane stepped out of the car and opened the passenger door for Phil that she realised she was wearing the clothes she'd worn for Lorry's wedding: red jacket and black trousers.

Phil was looking cool in a white linen jacket and blue chinos, but he seemed so much frailer than usual, and she instinctively linked arms as they walked slowly along the gravel path to St Jude's.

'I don't like funerals,' he whispered. 'Especially when they're called celebrations. I want people wearing black and crying bitterly when I go.'

'I'm sure I could manage that for you, Phil. Now come on, put on a happy face, but let's keep an eye out.'

'Not sure I've got the co-ordination to do both. Anyway, what for?'

Jane rolled her eyes. 'You know what for... We want to see how people react. Any signs of awkwardness, guilty looks, body language.'

'And who's missing.'

'Exactly. We'll make a detective of you yet.'

'No, you bloody won't!'

Jane was about to hide her smile but realised, at a 'celebration', smiling was just what Gloria wanted. She was waiting at the grey stone entrance porch in a sky-blue jacket and skirt with a white carnation pinned to her chest.

The vicar next to her was a surprise: tall and slim and blond, and under thirty.

Gloria welcomed them with a polite smile and an invitation to sit anywhere. The vicar took Jane's hand in both of his, then did the same for Phil. The front six rows were full, and Jane steered Phil towards a pew further back.

Eric Sykes was already in position. He'd met most of the villagers from his house-to-house calls, and she wanted him there to compare notes afterwards.

She spotted Aaron Barrett, and Maggie and Peter Attrill, but there was—perhaps understandably—no sign of the Marshes.

Phil leaned in conspiratorially. 'How did you get on with Hopkirk?'

Jane played it cool. 'It went well. He's still talking up my chances of a promotion, anyway.'

'No one deserves it more.'

Jane nudged him with her elbow. 'Behave!'

His reaction was drowned out by the sound of the church doors closing, followed by a sudden blast of organ music as Gloria and the vicar walked slowly up the centre aisle. They sat side by side beneath the dark wood pulpit, weak sunlight insinuating itself through the stained glass behind them.

As the music faded, the vicar launched into the service.

'Welcome. We're here to remember Mary MacDonald. But not just to remember, but to celebrate her life. A life that shone brightly, spreading joy and happiness...'

At the end of the service, the organist played 'Ode to Joy'. Jane stayed at the back to observe as the congregation filed out. The only ones to catch her eye were the Attrills. Peter looked quickly away, but Maggie smiled and nodded.

Shaking hands with Gloria outside, Jane asked how long she was staying in the area.

'I'm taking Mary back home tomorrow.'

'I'm so sorry for your loss.'

'I know. I'm sorry I've been a bit of a cow.'

Jane put a hand on her arm. 'You haven't. I promise you I will keep looking into what happened, so please keep in touch.'

Gloria dipped her head, reached into her bag for a tissue and dabbed her eyes. 'I will. Thank you both.'

As they said their goodbyes and turned away, Eric stepped in and looked to Jane. 'Excuse me, ma'am.'

'Yes, Eric?'

'You asked me for any observations. Well, the only thing I noticed was the Attrills.'

Jane took his elbow and steered him away. 'Go on.'

'I don't know if it means anything, but they always seemed like, you know, very close. But in there, I could see them talking, but it was like they were arguing. She looked really angry with him. Erm, well, that's it, really.'

Jane looked at Phil, who raised his eyebrows. 'Good work, Eric. That's interesting. I never did get a chance to talk to his wife. I'll make a point of doing that.'

Eric smiled, relieved. 'Will that be all, ma'am?'

Jane looked round to see the Attrills pushing through the church gate into the lane.

'Actually, Eric, why don't you and I take a stroll into the village and call on the Attrills? Phil wouldn't mind waiting for us, would you?'

Phil smiled happily. 'Not at all, I've always wanted to look round this churchyard. There's supposed to be some fascinating gravestones going back to the seventeenth century.'

Jane winked at Eric. 'We'll leave you to it then.'

***

They sat round a wooden table on the lawn, and Maggie Attrill brought tea and cakes.

'I'm sorry. Peter's got so much work on now. He's up in his room. I can get him down if you—'

'No, no, don't worry.' Jane smiled. 'It's you we wanted to see. I missed you last time I was here.'

'Ah yes, Peter said you called round. I was out running, I expect. Tea for both of you?'

They nodded and waited as Maggie poured carefully into china cups, then passed round a plate of small cakes. Eric got stuck in as Jane sipped tea.

'I'll be blunt with you, Mrs Attrill.'

'Maggie, please. And being blunt will be a refreshing change. Nobody says what they really think these days.'

'Indeed. Well, I must admit my conversation with your husband left me feeling vaguely suspicious. It was as if he was hiding something.'

Maggie put her cup and saucer on the tray and looked across the lawn towards a rose border. She sighed. 'If I'm honest, I feel the same way. He's changed.'

Jane caught Eric's look and nodded as he pointed to the notebook on his knee. 'Do you know why?'

'Well, it's coincided with him taking the reins at the association. I didn't take much notice at first. After all, it's a new thing for him, and he's had a quiet life for a few years—he used to be a farmer, you know—so I thought he was just feeling the pressure, but...'

'Yes?'

'I think there's more to it than that. Maybe I'm being oversensitive, but he reacted very strangely when I told him about the body that was found at the drill site.'

'In what way, strangely?'

'As soon as I told him the poor man's name, he went very quiet, cut me off and disappeared into his room.'

'And your conclusion was...?'

'That he knew the man. In fact, the more I thought about it afterwards, the surer I was.'

'What made you so sure?'

'I said to him point blank that he knew him. It was like a shot in the dark, but the look on his face told me I was right.'

'But how would he have known him? You've presumably heard: Keith Castle was a low-level drug dealer.'

Maggie put a hand to her mouth. 'Oh God.'

'What is it, Mrs Attrill?'

'Please don't tell me Peter's been taking drugs.'

'We're not saying that. Do you think it's possible?'

Maggie looked back at the house, then leaned forward, lowering her voice. It struck Jane how quickly her shock seemed to vanish. 'I pray to God it's not true. But the way he's been behaving, the way he's changed... well, it makes you wonder.'

Jane nodded, waiting as Eric caught up with the note-taking. She put her cup and saucer on the table. 'I know this is difficult for you, but there may be nothing in it. Let us continue our investigation, but please keep an eye open, and call me if you have any more thoughts, all right?'

Maggie nodded and reached across to take Jane's business card.

She sighed. 'I will.' She stirred the teapot. 'It's true what they say about country villages, isn't it?'

'What's that, Mrs Attrill?'

'Oh, just that everything looks so lovely, until you dig underneath.' She paused. 'More tea?'

20.

Eric made his way back to the station with instructions to put the interview notes on the log and incorporate any results from George's background check on Peter Attrill.

Jane found Phil on a lichen-coated bench under a yew tree in the graveyard. 'Anything interesting?'

Phil nodded contentedly. 'You find the same names cropping up in little villages like this. There's a few Attrills, and a couple of Barretts.'

'Not surprising, though. A small place like this.'

'True. It suggests strong family connections.'

'Yeah, well, I find it scary. Unhealthy.'

'Maybe... They must have been people with influence. They didn't just have mossy gravestones. We're talking proper tombs. Well cared for. You don't often get that these days. People move around too much. No one settles, puts down roots. That's why everywhere looks the same, wherever you go.'

Jane smiled and checked her watch, pointedly. 'So, what's this telling us, Phil?'

Phil pushed himself upright with a grunt. 'Sorry. Another of my lectures. But the point is, the further back a name goes, the higher the chance of tensions and rivalries.'

'Family feuds.'

'Exactly!'

Jane sighed. 'As if Cardale wasn't complicated enough.' She could feel the peace of the graveyard seeping into her, but she fought it off. If what Peter was saying was true, it was just an illusion anyway.

She rattled the car keys. 'Come on. Let's get back. We've got a murder, two apparently accidental deaths and a possible assault to sort out.'

Phil nodded. 'Yes, and this is making me wonder if the answer lies in the past.'

***

'So, what have we got, George?'

'Not a lot, ma'am.'

'No previous on Peter Attrill?'

'Squeaky clean, by the look of it. He's lived in the area all his life. Farming family. They owned a lot of land, several farms, and he inherited the lot when his father died.'

'Must be worth a packet, then. Makes you wonder why he wanted to take over running the association.'

'Probably a power trip. He sold up all the farms but still acts as a kind of advisor to one of them.' George shuffled through the notes on his lap. 'Yep, Bailey's Farm.'

Jane tapped a pencil against her chin. 'Did he own Marsh Farm by any chance?'

George ran a finger down a list. 'He did, yes. It was called Meadowtree Farm at the time.'

Jane pulled a face. 'That's really naff...' She stood and walked to the window. 'There's another connection. He sold it to the Marshes not that long ago. And according to his wife, he's been acting strangely since we found Keith Castle's body up there.'

George nodded at her back, waiting.

Jane walked back to her chair, and leaned back, gazing at the ceiling, then sat up straight. 'Let's run a similar check on Maggie. When did they get married? Was she involved in any of the farms? Not sure I trust either of them. Plus, we now have a direct link between Peter Attrill and our murder victim.'

George coughed. 'A tenuous link, though, ma'am.'

'Tenuous is better than sod all.'

***

Felicity watched as the protestors gathered in the middle of the field. Some sat cross-legged on the grass, while the older and less flexible stood with arms folded.

Felicity took a deep breath. She needed to hook them in, and the only way to do that after days of passive protest was positive action.

'Okay, everyone. Today's the day!'

A few of the regulars were already doing clenched-fist salutes. One of them called out. 'All right, Fliss! Let's go!'

She joined in the laughter. 'Hold on! Here's the plan... We're going to break through onto the site tonight. We're going to raise our game, let them know they're not going to get away with killing our countryside.'

She paused, looking round, gauging reactions. She lowered her voice, slowed it down.   'I'll understand if some of you would rather stay back. So, there's no pressure. Your support is appreciated, whatever. But just so we have an idea and can make plans, could I have a show of hands? Who wants to be on the front line with me?'

She turned to Jack and grinned. 'Wow! That looks like ninety per cent of you. Thank you! Right. We've got around four hours till dusk, so let's gather here then. Can our group leaders join me in an hour so we can run through the details? Then it will be up to you to share the info, as usual. And now, like the man said, let's go!'

***

Jane sipped coffee and studied George's notes.

There was something odd about the way Maggie had openly cast suspicion on her husband. Wouldn't her instinct be to protect him?

Turned out she'd been a successful entrepreneur when she married Peter, with a chain of health and beauty salons across Lancashire and Cumbria. She'd sold up and moved into his place at Cardale.

Jane whistled softly as she tried to do the maths. Peter was already filthy rich from selling off the farms he inherited. She was wealthy in her own right. And now, she spent her time jogging round Cardale and tending to her roses. The more Jane thought about it, the more questions it threw up.

Meanwhile, Peter had jumped at the chance to take over the village association, and—according to the minutes of his first meeting—had spoken out in favour of the drilling operation, despite the protests of the man who'd bought one of his farms, Sid Marsh. Was he in it just for the money, or did he have another reason, linked in some way to the historic Attrill and Barrett family connection Phil had found?

There was nothing in George's report that suggested the Attrills were spending lavishly. But statements showed they were building up substantial savings through a range of investments. That suggested they were still earning money from somewhere.

Money could be the glue that bound them together. Was their chocolate-box cottage lifestyle just a front?

Jane stopped. Thoughts of Allan were intruding. Again. Money and career had put paid to their relationship.

She found herself thinking about him more and more these days: reminders, triggers, bringing it all back. He wouldn't go away, even in the middle of a murder inquiry.

She forced herself to focus. There wasn't enough evidence against the Attrills to divert resources from the drugs line of enquiry. But then again… the drugs racket was all about money. The stereotypical image was of callous villains getting rich while poor, vulnerable people sought temporary escape from their sad lives. But not all drug users were poor or vulnerable. Stats suggested that drug taking was rife among the professional classes, too.

Jane tapped quickly at the keyboard to send a message to George.

When it was done, she drank the last of her coffee, picked up her phone and scrolled to Allan's number.

***

Lorry stood behind Jag as he demonstrated the screen magnification on his monitor. They had the office to themselves.

'Wow! You could read that from down the road.'

Jag laughed. 'I hope not. There's some sensitive stuff on here.'

Lorry patted his shoulder. 'It's great to see you back at work, mate. So, what are you up to?'

Jag swivelled round to face her, and Lorry couldn't hide her surprise. 'Jag! You're not wearing the eyepatch! Does that mean...?'

He shook his head. 'No, I still can't see through this one, but the doctor gave me some new eye drops and he wanted me to keep it uncovered more often. Let the fresh air in, he said, and the light.'

'Ah. Okay. Well, that's good news.'

'It is, thanks.' He stopped, and Lorry noticed he seemed awkward suddenly. He quickly moved on. 'Anyway, Jane asked me to stay up to speed with the Marshes. You know they're facing a court case over the tractor accident? So, I'm in touch with them about that and watching out for any bank transactions, that sort of thing.'

'Great. Found anything yet?'

'Their solicitors are trying to negotiate a settlement. They're admitting they skipped a service and check-up on the tractor but said it had been regularly serviced to that point, and they're claiming driver error had to be considered.'

Lorry raised her eyebrows in disbelief. 'So, it wasn't all their fault? Unbelievable! And they've got the nerve to blame that young lad?'

Jag stroked his chin. 'I think they have a chance, to be honest. He did own up to being in the pub just before it happened. He told Ross he'd only had one drink, but the landlord said he'd had at least a couple.'

Lorry tutted. 'Idiot! So now he could be setting himself up for charges, could he?'

'It does look that way. But he was breathalysed and came in just under the limit, so...'

'It's a grey area.'

'Like every case, isn't it? Always another angle.'

'True, young man.' Lorry smiled. 'So, how long before it's settled, do you think?'

'The way the lawyers are exchanging messages, it could be over within the week.' Jag stood slowly and arched his back.

Lorry instinctively put her hand in the small of her back and pushed.

Jag cleared his throat. 'I hope you don't mind me asking, but am I right? You are having a baby?'

Lorry laughed in disbelief. 'Hey, don't beat about the bush, will you? But yes, you're right. How did you know?'

'Sorry. I can see the signs.' He paused. 'I remember when Moraji got pregnant. There was something about her, like she had inner happiness. I think you have it too.'

She put a hand on his arm. 'Aww, Jag, that's lovely! I haven't told anyone yet. So...'

Jag smiled. 'Please. Your secret is safe. But don't leave it too long.'

'Why not? George and Ross wouldn't notice if I was due next week.'

***

Ross stamped his feet and shivered in the shelter of the cypress trees that bordered the Frog and Firkin's car park. The lights glowed warm inside, and he could hear laughter. It wasn't helping his mood.

He tried to distract himself by going back over the sequence that had led him here. It looked as if Castle had been recruited by the gang that controlled the eastern half of Greater Manchester. Ross was hoping to nail whoever had taken his place tonight, and the NCA people were counting on it, too.

Helping them was all the motivation he needed. It would be a nice addition to his CV when he sent his application in. He just wished the wind would drop.

George had needed persuading that he'd stand a better chance working alone, but he'd finally got the okay, as long as he carried a radio.

Sid Marsh used to get his stash delivered here, and Ross had reluctantly accepted that hanging round here night after night in the cold country air was his best hope.

As George said: 'No one's going to admit they're taking the stuff, so we must nail the lowlifes that are selling it. Someone killed Castle and buried him in that field, and the odds are it was a local. Right?'

Ross wasn't totally convinced Castle's murder was a local job. There was a good chance someone further up the ranks had either ordered it or carried it out.

The back door of the pub opened, sending an elongated rectangle of light onto the grey shingle. Ross stepped back and waited. Whoever it was had gone into the toilets. He heard the door close then open again, then the rapid click of a lighter. Ross sighed. Just another fag break.

Then he heard the crunch of footsteps. Someone was walking into the car park from the lane, wearing a hoodie with the peak of a baseball cap just visible. He walked on the balls of his feet, making as little noise as possible.

Smoking Man stepped out and they exchanged a few words. Ross quickly zoomed in with his phone camera and grabbed a few shots. The car-park lighting was feeble and it was difficult to see anything clearly, but it was worth a try. A momentary flash of white confirmed that the hooded man was handing over a package.

Ross was about to run over to nab them both but stopped to think. They were far enough away to make a run for it, and he'd lose them.

But if the dealer left the way he came, he could grab him. The guy doing the buying would be back in the pub, feeling smug. But Ross could easily pick him out later by the smell of cigarette smoke, not to mention the packet in his pocket.

Ross picked his way behind the trees to position himself near the car park entrance, holding his breath and hoping he hadn't made the wrong call.

The trade was done. Hoodie called out 'Thank you', which sounded far too polite for a drug dealer, then turned back the way he came.

Ross waited till he reached the lane, then stepped out, holding his ID card in one hand and a torch in the other. Hoodie froze, temporarily blinded by the torch.

'Evening, mate. Ashbridge Police. What are you up to then?'

Ross was ready for the next, inevitable move. Hoodie turned to run the other way, but Ross stuck a foot out and he fell to the ground. Pocketing the torch, Ross pulled him roughly to his feet and dragged him round to a table under the illuminated sign at the front of the pub.

'Right. Pull your hood down, mate. Let's have a look at you.'

'What for? I haven't done anything.'

'Really? Let's start with supplying drugs. And let's say, for the sake of argument, that you, mate, are under arrest. You do not have to say anything, but anything you do say may be taken down and used in evidence. Do you understand?'

He nodded.

Ross sighed. 'So, let's start our little conversation by you telling me your name and what you were doing back there. After you've taken your hood off. Come on. Show me your face!'

He slowly pulled it back.

Ross couldn't hide his shock. 'Rob Simmons? What the hell?!'

21.

'The tractor driver? You're kidding me.'

Ross shook his head. 'Nope.'

'So, what did he say?' Lorry asked.

'Not much. Whoever he works for has got him well trained.' Ross thumped his desk. 'Stupid bugger!'

'Well trained or scared out of his wits.'

Ross nodded. 'Bit of both, probably.' He ran a hand through his hair and grimaced. 'I can't believe I fell for his innocent victim act. By the time I got him in the car, I'd forgotten about the guy in the pub, too!'

Lorry chewed the end of her pen. 'Hmmm. Makes you wonder if the house demolition really was an accident.'

'Why?'

'He's a drug dealer. They found drugs in the ruins of Mary's house, didn't they? He'd been in the pub just before. Was he getting a bit of liquid courage, or dropping some stuff off for a customer? Had he got orders to get rid of Mary or—what was he called…?'

'Geoff Pegg. So, you reckon it could have been a killing? He's just a kid. I can't believe it.'

'You said yourself, drugs is big money. There must be plenty of rich customers in Cardale. Maybe it's a territory worth fighting for.' She stopped, suddenly excited. 'What if Mary and Geoff were the other gang leaders? It would make a bit more sense, then.'

Ross pursed his lips, frowning. 'Maybe. But we still come back to that question: why would you knock someone off by demolishing their house? That's a bit off the wall, even for you.'

They both laughed at his choice of words, then George walked in. He didn't look in a laughing mood.

'There's a riot going on up at the drill site. We're expecting arrests, and some of them will be coming back here for processing. We're going to have to help, so don't count on getting an early night.'

***

Jack was flat on his stomach with a knee in his back and a hand pushing his head into the damp grass. He winced as his arms were pulled back, then felt the pain as the handcuffs snapped shut.

They hauled him to his feet and started pushing him towards a police van. But where was Fliss? He jerked his head from side to side, but she was lost in a noisy crowd, now being slowly penned in by a big circle of yellow-jacketed police.

The chanting went on. 'Stop the drill: save the planet!'

Jack wasn't going without a fight. He grunted and planted his heels in the turf, but they were too strong for him.

'You're wasting your time, mate,' said one as they pushed him into the back of the van. 'Enjoy your night in the nick.'

The door slammed shut. Then a voice came from the front, laughing. 'Where to, sir?'

Jack just shook his head. They thought they'd won. But just wait till they saw the headlines tomorrow. Fliss had told him tonight's mission would get them on the front pages, and on television news. *'We won't stop the drilling yet, but we'll make sure the world rises up against it.'*

He hoped she was right. The shouts and screams were beginning to fade as the police dragged more and more protestors away.

The last time he'd seen her was when they cut through the fence. She'd led them further into the site, towards the drilling rig that seemed to shake and steam like a living monster. Always at the front, whatever the risk.

The security teams took them by surprise, their head torches piercing the darkness. They were there so quickly Jack wondered if they'd been tipped off. Fliss had shaken her head, refusing to believe it, calming him down.

She waved everyone forward, just as the coppers knocked him to the ground.

He was vaguely aware of a flash—from a camera? Maybe she was right: the media were there.

The van growled into life, and Jack bounced on the bench seat as it lurched over the field.

***

Jane watched as the first few vans drove past on their journey to stations across Greater Manchester.

Her radio was buzzing with traffic, but the message she was waiting for still hadn't arrived, which meant that Felicity Crowther had managed to evade arrest.

Aaron Barrett was already milking the situation, grimacing into TV cameras and calling on the police to 'throw the book at them'. But Jane was more interested in talking to Felicity about everything else that had been happening in Cardale. She knew she was in danger of stereotyping, but she was pretty sure a fair number of the protestors were taking drugs, and she had to explore the possibility that Keith Castle was a supplier.

She knew she was making tenuous links. She also knew that they were all she had. Simon Hopkirk had told her there was nothing to tie Castle's killing to the knife murder he'd investigated three years ago. 'Everything pointed to it being a random attack. The body was roughly buried, too, not a neat job like this one. There was no finesse to it.'

She'd gone through the files and had to agree with him.

She watched as the uniforms shepherded the remaining protestors back to their campsite. Most of the vans had gone, and the security guards were reinforcing the barriers. And still no word about Felicity.

Jane flicked her radio on to let them know she was heading back to the station. There would be dozens of arrests to process, and they'd need all the help they could get.

She drove slowly down the rough track back to the main road. Her window was down, and she savoured the cool night air.

A full moon was balanced precariously on the square bulk of St Jude's tower, and she suddenly felt there was nothing she'd like more than to get out of town. Allan had talked about it when they were making plans to get married. He'd wanted to spend his buyout on a house in a village, somewhere they could renovate, and they'd laughed, wondering how they'd cope with a garden and fresh air.

A few days later, they'd split up. But now, he wanted to try again; she could tell. She wanted to believe they could still make a go of it, but still hadn't called him.

She checked the dashboard clock. 23:10. He'd still be up. Why not now?

She pulled into a layby and pressed speed dial.

***

Ross grinned as he handed Lorry her third cup of coffee. 'It's like Glastonbury in here!'

She summoned a weak smile. 'I can't believe you're enjoying this. It's nearly midnight, and we've still got a bloody traffic jam of smelly hippies out there.'

'Don't be rude.' Ross laughed. 'We should be giving them medals, not charging them.'

Lorry snorted, just as the door opened and Alex Gledhill called out, 'Two more for the guillotine, when you're ready.'

Between them, they'd processed all charges by 3 a.m. Most were sent home with a warning, a few were formally cautioned, and three were detained overnight on assault charges.

Jane sat in her office, sipping water, too wired for sleep. The charging process had helped distract her after the phone chat with Allan. They'd talked like they'd never been apart; she'd blurted out an invitation to come round for dinner next week, and he'd instantly said yes.

As if that wasn't enough to keep her awake all night, she'd had a lightbulb moment about the case in between interviews.

What if drug use really was widespread in Cardale? They'd found cocaine in the ruins of Mary's house, and they'd assumed it was hers. But it could have been

Geoff Pegg's, whose brother was still in jail in Spain. She realised they'd been so preoccupied with events in the village they hadn't checked out the brother.

And that raised a whole new set of questions. He'd been locked up for drug offences. Could that be the source of supply? What if Geoff had been using Mary to establish a foothold in the area? Or maybe she was a willing partner?

Jane had learned to recognise key moments in an investigation. She was convinced this was one.

22.

A night in the cell had done nothing to loosen Rob Simmons' tongue, and Ross was losing patience.

'That's half an hour of my life I'm not going to get back.'

Lorry looked up from her screen and sighed. 'Look, Ross. I do care, but I've got loads to get through, so...'

'Yeah, I know. Shut up and get on with it.'

'Please.'

Ross slumped back in his chair. Something was telling him the next move could be critical, but the more he thought about it, the more he needed Rob to open up.

But how? He'd be fearing for his life if he betrayed his bosses. He wouldn't be safe in prison either. But what if Ross could convince him that the alternative could be just as bad?

He walked down the corridor and asked Jane if she could spare a minute.

'If it's about drugs and Cardale, definitely.' She rubbed her eyes, and Ross noticed how pale she looked.

'Have you been here all night, ma'am?'

She stretched and yawned, then leaned forward. 'Yes, I have. So, why don't you get us a coffee and some biscuits? Call it a working lunch...'

Ross stood and smiled. 'But it's only nine-thirty, ma'am.'

Jane drank coffee and listened as Ross told her about Rob Simmons. 'No surprise that he's not talking.'

'No, ma'am. He's scared of what'll happen to him if they find out he snitched. But what if I told him we are going to take him back to Cardale in a police car, with a couple of uniforms, and drop him off at his house. Maybe go in the house with him, all smiles and friendly, like.'

'Making it look like he's been co-operating with us.'

'Yes, ma'am. Do you think it's worth a try?'

Jane bit into a piece of ginger cake, her eyes never leaving Ross's face. Eventually, she nodded. 'It could be a waste of time. But the point is to make him worry that we might do it, and hope it persuades him to open up. He needs to be worried enough to think we'll go through with it.'

'Yes, ma'am.'

'So, one step at a time. Tell him that's what we're going to do, then let me know how he reacts.' Jane stood. 'I've been really impressed with you over the last few months. Lorry's pushed herself up to DS thanks to enthusiasm and hard work. She's on the same grade as you are now. Maybe it's time you thought about your next steps.'

Ross looked down at his notes, thinking quickly. He didn't want to tell her about his application to join the NCA. Yet. 'Thank you very much, ma'am. I will.'

Jane narrowed her eyes just enough for Ross to wonder if she'd noted his hesitation. But she just smiled. 'Good. Make sure you do. So, let's go with your plan. If anyone can spin him a yarn, Ross, it's you.'

They laughed, but Ross's smile faded as he closed the door behind him. Was that her way of telling him she'd sussed him out?

***

The Pegg family had moved to Spain in the 1980s.

A delightful family, by all accounts. They'd notched up an impressive list of petty offences, mainly theft with the occasional diversion of assault and burglary. It seemed to run in the family until Geoff—the youngest of three brothers—broke the mould. He was the only Pegg without a record.

Mum and Dad had set a fine example for their offspring. They died within months of each other, after ten years in the sun, living off their illicit proceeds.

The eldest, Michael, vanished after setting up a string of fraudulent companies that fleeced dozens of British property investors. Ronnie had kept himself busy, too, but was now unfortunate enough to be serving time in the notorious Alhaurín de la Torre Prison in Malaga for using and distributing cocaine.

Europol hadn't been able to establish a direct supply line from Ronnie to Manchester. Several gangs were working out of Spain and could easily be using one of the networks he'd set up. But he wasn't inclined to chat about it. As a weary Europol official told George: 'It is easier to drive round Paris blindfolded than to follow their supply routes.'

Jane sighed. 'The more you find out, the more you realise the drugs network is as big as the worldwide web.'

George put it more succinctly. 'Bastards.'

Jag chose not to write that down. 'What can I do to help, ma'am?'

Jane tapped her pen on the desk. 'I'm thinking there must be a connection between Ronnie Pegg and the cocaine in Ashbridge. It seems more than coincidence his brother was here...'

Jag thought for a moment. 'Geoff doesn't have a criminal record.'

Jane nodded. 'I know. Indulge me, will you?'

Jag put his serious face on. 'Can we analyse the cocaine we found at the house in Cardale to see if it matches up with the cocaine being shipped from Spain, or wherever it came from?'

'We did that, mate,' George said. 'It looks like pretty standard stuff. Quite high level. Not too much crap mixed in to bulk it out. But Ross says there is some pretty lethal pick-and-mix stuff out there.'

Jane shook her head. 'I know. Jag's right. We haven't done a direct comparison with a specific supply from a specific country. It might be worth asking Malaga if they could share any analysis with us.' She turned to Jag. 'Can you make contact, Jag? Okay, good work guys.'

She checked her watch after they'd gone. 11 a.m. She stood and felt instantly lightheaded, putting a hand on the desk to steady herself. Roy was waiting for an update, and Mum was expecting a call.

They'd have to wait. She had an urgent appointment with an all-day breakfast.

***

Jane found a table in the corner at Aunt Betty's and ordered the vegetarian breakfast and a mug of tea.

She'd lived on high pressure and very little sleep for most of her career, so why was she feeling so tired suddenly? She remembered a few months ago when she almost fainted in the corridor in front of Roy. Her mum had told her she should get a check-up, but she'd ignored the advice.

She nodded her thanks as one of the counter staff brought her tea.

Jane searched for the GP's contact details on her phone. She worked her way through all the steps on their online booking system, then cursed under her breath when she found they couldn't fit her in until next month, and even that would be a telephone appointment.

'Everything all right, dear?' An older woman on the next table smiled as Jane looked round.

'Oh yes, I'm fine, thanks.' Jane waved her phone dismissively. 'These are supposed to save time, but they're taking over, aren't they?'

The arrival of her food saved her from a conversation she didn't want, but she managed a polite wave as the woman walked to the counter to pay. The food gave her the energy boost she needed, and by the time she'd paid up and was walking back to the station, all thoughts of a doctor had disappeared.

They were replaced by thoughts about Allan. But she drove those away by phoning her mum, who got straight down to business.

'Oh, hello love! When are you coming round?'

'How about tonight? I've got some news for you...' Jane waited. 'Mum? Are you there?'

'Yes, dear. I was just working out what your news could be. Are you and Allan getting back together?'

***

Ross was feeling sorry for him again.

Rob Simmons sat slumped in his chair across the interview room table, his tea untouched, his hair a mess. White faced, apart from the dark rings under his eyes.

When he looked up, his eyes were dull. 'I don't have much choice, do I?'

'Well, yes, you do, Rob. Tell us what we need to know, and if we nail the guys who are running things, we'll make sure anything you say is between us.'

'So, I don't go to prison?'

'I can't promise anything. It all depends how much you give us.' Ross checked the recorder. 'Look, I'm going to need to change the tape. Why don't you drink your tea and think about it while I do that? Okay?'

Rob nodded, and Ross switched off. Then he leaned forward. 'Listen. Rob. The tape's not running. You've got some decisions to make. You've made a big mistake. It'll be a miracle if you don't go down. But it's your first offence. I reckon the only way you're going to get through this, and come out in one piece, is by helping us. Look at me, Rob.'

He slowly raised his head.

'Your best bet is to work with me. I promise I'll do everything to make it easier for you, put in a good word. We can ask for leniency. You'd still do a bit of time, but whoever you're afraid of wouldn't know you'd done a deal, and you'd be out in no time. The slate wiped clean.'

Rob grunted. 'They'll never let me go. They'll make me carry on, threaten my family.'

'Who's they, Rob?'

His hand trembled as he put his mug back on the table. He took a deep breath and looked into Ross's eyes. Ross crossed his fingers under the desk and waited.

'Okay. I'll tell you what I know.

***

Jane had to work hard to focus as she read through Ross's notes on the screen.

Her mum's comment had shaken her up a bit, reminded her what she was doing. Just hearing the words 'getting back together' had made it seem real. She'd kept going over it as she'd walked back to the station. Was she making a big mistake, sleepwalking into another emotional minefield, with Allan likely to explode at any time? Or had the separation made them both realise what they were missing? She'd forced herself back into DCI mode by the time she made it back to her desk, and now she was assessing the progress Ross had made.

His notes were precise.

Rob Simmons took the bait. But only limited info. He's never met the boss. They do a drop at a different location and at a different time every week. He gets a text telling him where and when to collect. He got there early once and didn't even hear the car pulling up a few yards away. All he saw was a dark coloured saloon, says he couldn't see the registration properly but thought it ended with MMN. Rob says the guy doing the drop was big, by which he means fat. He said it was the same every time. Kept mentioning the silent car. Electric, probably? We talked about the text messages, but it seems to be from a different number each time, so no chance of tracing it.

Jane pursed her lips. She'd hoped for more, but it was something. The silent car was a good place to start. It had to be electric. What better way to avoid attracting attention in a quiet rural area?

She'd never been great at touch typing but had built up speed using two fingers on each hand. The message was for Eric Sykes, copied to George and Ross.

I want a list of dark coloured electric saloon cars with M and N in their registration sold within ten miles of Ashbridge in the last six months.

Then she left a message for Ross. *Great job. Remember what I said...*

***

Phil compared the Malaga sample analysis with the cocaine they found at Cardale and confirmed there was no match.

Jane massaged her temples. 'So, another good idea bites the dust.'

Phil leaned forward. 'Are you okay?'

Jane looked up. 'I'm fine, thanks Phil. More to the point, how are you?'

'I'm doing well, or so they tell me. I'm getting sick of ECGs and blood pressure checks, but it looks like things are back to normal.'

'That's good.'

Phil raised an eyebrow. 'That sounds suspicious. What are you cooking up?'

Jane's eyes widened. 'Who, me?'

'Come on, I can take it.'

'Well, since you ask... I'd like you to take another look at all the forensics from Mary's house, Sid Marsh and Keith Castle.' She paused. 'I'm sure there's a link somewhere, but nothing is leaping out. It struck me that if you took another look...'

'I might find the missing link.'

'Exactly.'

'Well, as it's you...'

Jane smiled and walked round to open her office door. 'Thanks, Phil. And when you've done that, I'm sure I'll find something else for you to look at.'

'Oh, good.'

***

Peter Attrill spoke rather too casually.

'What did that detective woman want the other day?'

Maggie turned a page of her runners' magazine. 'Just what you'd expect. About that body they found. Nothing much *I* could say, obviously.'

He sipped his tea, noticing the emphasis she put on 'I'. 'Of course.'

'I suppose they're talking to everyone in the village.'

'Hmmm.'

'Except I know quite a few people haven't been interviewed about it. So why pick on us, do you think?'

'Please don't be disingenuous. You were the one who raised the subject. About how I knew him once.'

Maggie put her magazine down on the table next to her armchair and crossed her legs. 'So you said.'

Peter sighed. 'And what's that supposed to mean?'

'He used to work on that farm, didn't he? The one that the Marshes bought.'

Peter eyed Maggie warily as he finished his tea. 'Yes, he did. But that was years ago.' He stopped. 'Hang on, how on earth did you know? We weren't even together then.'

Maggie walked towards the French window. 'So, it's true then... But don't get uppity. I didn't know. Someone in the village mentioned it, that's all.' She turned. 'I need to do a bit of deadheading.'

Peter nodded, then pushed himself out of the chair and walked heavily up the stairs to his room.

Maggie waited till he was gone, then came back inside and flicked open the telephone directory.

***

Eric was ringing round car dealers while Ross checked the database for any references to electric cars.

'How are you getting on, Eric?'

'I've phoned a dozen dealers and got...' He glanced down at his notes. 'Twenty-three so far.'

'You're doing better than me. The nice people who peddle drugs don't do environment-friendly transport.'

Lorry snorted. 'Maybe they think the plants they make it from are green enough.'

Ross stared into space.

'Hello? Banter Central. Are you receiving me?'

Eric laughed. 'He's switched off, I think.'

Ross turned and smiled. 'All right, leave it out. I was just thinking about Rob in his tractor. He told us he did his rounds in that tractor every Saturday morning.'

Eric sat back, interested. 'Yeah?'

'Maybe he wasn't just delivering hay or straw, or whatever.'

Lorry joined in. 'You think he was delivering drugs? In a tractor?'

Eric shook his head. 'Not in a tractor, surely.'

Ross wasn't to be put off. 'It's worth thinking about. Sid Marsh admitted he was a user, and it was his tractor. Rob worked for him. Cocaine was found at the house he wrecked. I rest my case.'

Lorry walked over to him, rubbing her hands, relieved to get a break from her report on a break-in at a fashion warehouse. 'And we assumed the coke was Mary's or Geoff's.'

'Exactly, Sherlock. But what if Rob wasn't just delivering? What if he really did do it on purpose?'

Eric frowned. 'Like, you mean, planting evidence?'

'Was that a bad pun, Eric?' Lorry puffed out her cheeks. 'Hang on. That's a bit of a stretch, isn't it, Ross? He could have just shoved it through the letterbox or thrown it over the back wall.'

Ross sighed. 'Yeah, I know. But if you look at something from a different angle, you can get a completely new picture.'

'Well, I was with you up to the point where Rob did it to plant evidence. It had to have been an accident. But that doesn't mean you're wrong about the delivery round.'

Ross turned to Eric suddenly. 'Did you get a list of the places Rob delivered to that day?'

Eric flushed. 'No, sorry. It didn't seem to matter.'

Lorry smiled. 'No problem, Eric. It didn't then. But maybe it matters now. So, how about having a chat with the Marshes?'

'Don't mind if I do.' Ross jangled his car keys in Eric's face. 'Fancy a break from phone calls tomorrow, mate?'

***

Mum made shepherd's pie and talked incessantly about Allan. Jane explained that all she was doing was inviting him round for a meal, but it was no use.

'I'm so pleased you're back together. He's a lovely boy.'

'Mum—'

'I'll never understand why you didn't marry him. None of this would have happened.'

'Mum, people do get divorces. Marriages don't always last.'

'You must both come round for dinner one night. Promise me.'

Jane tried every trick in the book, but Mum fixed her with a look as she cleared the table.

'All right, Mum. I promise.'

23.

Maggie Attrill pruned at the far end of the garden, nearest the churchyard.

It was her favourite spot, especially in the early evening when the scent of the heritage roses seemed to build up next to the grey stone wall. She'd never worked out why the scent seemed heavier when the sun was shining.

She filled the trug with flower heads that turned so quickly from things of beauty to compost material.

She was sure Peter was up to something, but was it linked to that man's body? She knew he was working with that chauvinistic prig Aaron Barrett, and heaven knows what schemes they were cooking up. That might explain his preoccupation. But it was hard to escape the conclusion that the start of Peter's strange behaviour coincided with the discovery of the body.

The garden had always been her refuge, but it was so hard to switch off these days. She could hear the faint whir of a tractor. Just down the lane, someone was rhythmically clipping the hedge. The rooks were cawing from the big tree in the churchyard. The sounds of a rural village; it was all so idyllic.

Moving here with Peter was meant to be the start of a new life, away from the stress of running a business and making money. And it had been, until that tractor ran into that house.

Maggie dropped the secateurs into the trug and pulled her phone out of her jeans pocket. She scrolled down to the number she'd saved from the phone book and pressed *call*.

'Hello. Marsh Farm. Julie speaking.'

'Oh hello. My name's Maggie Attrill. I'm Peter's wife—you know, the new chair of the village association?'

'Oh, yes, hello. How can I help?'

'Well, I wondered if we could have a chat sometime?'

There was a pause. 'A chat?'

'Yes. I'm interested in village history, you see. I know this is a bit cheeky, but I know Peter used to own your farm. I've never been there, so… Well, I just wanted to see it, and meet you, too, of course.'

'Is it just me you want to see?' She sounded suspicious, and Maggie couldn't blame her.

'Well, I thought so, yes. I assumed your husband would be…'

'Yes, he's not the best of company. Well, do come over. It would be nice to talk to someone.'

'Lovely, thank you. How about tomorrow?'

'Okay, come around three and have cake.'

'I'll be there. See you then.'

Maggie disconnected and turned towards the kitchen. She looked up and saw Peter at the window, watching her.

***

Julie looked out of the window as a car drove into the yard.

'Visitors!' Sid called out from his den.

Julie sighed. 'Yes, I worked it out for myself, thanks.'

'Taxman, lawyer, police, nosey neighbour. Take your pick.'

'I've just had a nosey neighbour on the phone.'

'Well, that narrows it down then.'

Julie checked herself in the mirror, then opened the door. There were two of them, and she knew straight away what category they fell into. She'd seen one of them at the hospital. He had a self-confident look about him; the other looked young and awkward.

They held up their ID cards. 'Good afternoon, ma'am. Paul Rossiter and Eric Sykes, Ashbridge CID. Can we have a word?'

'Of course. Come in.'

She sat them at the table by the window. They turned down the offer of tea.

The confident one looked round the room. 'Lovely home.'

'More of a workplace, but, yes, thanks.'

The more idle the chatter, the more on edge she felt. They asked if Sid was around, and she called him down.

They introduced themselves, then the confident one kicked things off. Julie noticed he kept his eyes on their faces. Waiting for them to give something away, she realised.

'We're here because we have some questions about the delivery round your driver used to do on a Saturday.'

Sid looked disbelieving. 'What? Really? What's that got to do with anything?'

Julie tensed. Belligerence wasn't going to help. She put a hand on his sleeve and spoke as calmly as she could. 'Yes, my husband's right. I'm not sure how this can help, or what connection it has.'

The one called Rossiter nodded. 'Fair enough. I know we've spoken before, but can you just answer our questions, please? We're conducting a murder investigation... you know, the body in the field, on the drilling site. We are pursuing certain lines of enquiry. We are talking to lots of people. We just thought you could help, too.' He smiled. 'It's meant to be informal.'

Julie nodded. He was good. Polite, with just a subtle hint of a threat underneath.

Ross looked at Sid. 'So, Mr Marsh, could you help? We need to establish where Rob Simmons would have delivered to; on the morning of the, erm, accident, particularly.'

Sid wasn't pacified, and Julie sensed his irritation building. She intervened again. 'Oh, that's easy. You'll have to bear with us. As you know, my husband is still recovering from an, erm, accident, of his own.' She stood. 'If you'll excuse me, I'll see if I can find the right folder.'

They smiled and sat back as she left the room.

Eric tried to break the ice. 'Are you still in pain, Mr Marsh? It sounds like you had a nasty bump.'

Sid instinctively patted the side of his head. 'Not too bad now. Just the occasional headache.' He paused. 'Look, sorry I snapped at you. You're just doing your job, I know.'

Ross smiled. 'It's okay. We understand. Can I just check while your wife is out of the room; is it okay to also ask you about the drugs?'

He nodded. 'If you must. I've stayed off it since then, thanks to Julie. But, yeah, she knows all about it.' He looked at Ross for the first time. 'Thanks.'

Ross gave Eric the signal to start taking notes as Julie walked in carrying an A4 manila folder, which she placed on the table. 'Details should be in here, though what good they'll do you is a mystery.'

'Let us worry about that, Mrs Marsh. So can you list the drop-offs for us, please?'

Eric sat with his pen ready, but Julie just shrugged and pushed the folder across to him. 'You might as well have it. It's no use to us.'

Ross turned to Eric. 'Why don't you have a flick through that while we carry on?' He put on his friendly face as he looked at Sid. 'You were a user, weren't you?'

'Yes. I was...'

'Just cocaine?'

Julie hit the table with her hand. 'Is this necessary? Why can't you leave him alone?'

'Just a few more questions and we'll be gone, Mrs Marsh. Did you just take drugs, Mr Marsh, or did you deal?'

Sid clenched his fists. 'Now look—'

Ross stared him out. 'You see, it struck us it would be easy enough for you to distribute, seeing as how you are delivering all kinds of stuff round the area.'

Sid laughed. 'Oh right. So, I've been dropping off coke with the hay and the spuds, have I? Bloody hell! Are you mad?'

Ross was unperturbed. 'So that's a no, is it?'

Julie leaned in close. 'Yes. It is. Have you finished?'

'Unless there's anything else you can tell us about where your supplies came from, Mr Marsh. And who else you know who is a user.'

He sighed. 'I told you before. That man—you know, the body?—he used to bring the stuff, but then he stopped coming and someone new took over. No idea who he was. And I don't know anyone else who was, or is, a user. Okay?'

Ross nodded at Eric. They said their goodbyes and walked back to the car as Julie watched from the window.

Sid stayed at the table. 'What are they up to?'

She shook her head as the car drove away. 'I wish I knew.' Then, without turning round: 'Was that true? You don't know any other users?' She heard him shuffle in his seat. 'Okay. There's my answer.'

She turned to face him, but he couldn't look her in the eye.

***

Peter Attrill read the press release slowly, his concentration thrown by Aaron's irritating habit of constantly clearing his throat to show his impatience.

Peter wanted to tell him he'd read a lot more quickly if he could just be quiet, but he knew better than to get on the wrong side of him. Aaron had a reputation for being fiercely determined, driven. He'd made no secret of his ambition to get selected as the next parliamentary candidate, or his belief that success depended on being resolutely right-wing.

Peter finally looked up and handed the sheet back. 'It looks fine,' he said, rather lamely.

'Of course. I wrote it myself.' Aaron tutted. 'Totally rewrote a hopeless draft from our bloody useless press officer. It's time we got tough on those protestors. I mean, what are we doing, just sitting on our hands while they spread their litter in a countryside they claim to care about, leaving hard-working people to pick up the bill for the drilling delays? It's costing thousands in security alone.'

Peter nodded, but Aaron wasn't quite finished. 'Anyway, I just wanted you to know that this is just the beginning. I want the police up there, and I want them evicted. It's your land, of course, so I need to know you're onside.' He leaned forward. 'You are, aren't you?'

'Yes. I'm all in favour.'

Aaron smiled. 'Good man! Knew I could rely on you. Right, I'll get this sent out today, and we'll see what that mealy-mouthed Chief Super says when he realises he'll have to pull his finger out. What's his name again?'

'Roy Cooke, I think.'

'Yes, that's the chap. Too smooth. Can't believe he's done a hard day's work in his life.' He pressed a button on his phone. 'Ah, Mary, two coffees and tell the press office I want that release issued today without fail. And can you get Roy Cooke on the phone at some stage today? Thanks, m'dear.'

He disconnected and stared at Peter. 'Are you all right, old chap?'

'What? Oh. Yes, fine.'

'Are you quite well? You look a bit peaky.'

'Oh no. I'm fine, really. It's just Maggie.'

'Ah, say no more. Wife trouble. Know that feeling.' He stood and walked to the window. 'Not worrying about the arrangement we made, are you?'

Peter's hands were trembling slightly, but he kept them hidden and summoned a smile. 'No, it's not that. She just keeps asking me about that body.'

'Why?' Aaron laughed loudly. 'Good Lord! Don't tell me you killed him? Well, it's your land, I suppose. Prime suspect, eh!'

'I just get the feeling she thinks I had something to do with it.'

He chuckled. 'Well, did you?'

'No, of course I didn't.'

'Well, just tell her then. Problem. Solved.'

Peter started to speak. 'It's not that simple—'

But he never got the chance to explain. Aaron's PA brought the coffees on a tray and told him she'd got the chief superintendent on the phone, and he said he'd take the call now.

Peter walked down the town hall steps with the evening sun in his eyes. It felt like he was being picked out by a spotlight.

24.

Jane yawned. Another restless night. She felt twenty years older.

'Right, George. Where are we?'

'Rob Simmons has been charged, and he's worried about the effect it'll have on his mum.'

'Should have thought of that before.'

'Exactly, ma'am. Having said that, he did give us a couple of leads.'

'Has he got a solicitor now?'

'Yes, ma'am.'

Jane rolled her eyes. 'George, I keep telling you. It's Jane. I'm not the chief super anymore, all right?'

'Old habits...'

'I know. I called Roy Cooke 'Charles' the other day. He didn't approve. Anyway, did Rob's info get us anywhere?'

'Eric's trawled through the electric car registrations and come up with a couple in Cardale.'

'Well, fancy that. Names?'

'You're going to like this... One was registered to Mr Peter Attrill. Dark-coloured Toyota. And he's still the owner.'

Jane wanted to punch the air but kept herself in check. 'Anything else?'

'The other was registered to someone called Barrett.'

'What? Aaron Barrett, the council leader?'

George frowned. 'Can't say, sorry. I'll get Eric to check.'

Jane frowned. 'Okay, do that. Might be nothing but seems an odd coincidence. And you know what I think of coincidences.'

'Yes, I do. Oh, yes, and Ross and Eric went to see the Marshes about the delivery round Simmons used to do for them.'

'And?'

'Ross wondered if he was using the round as cover to drop off drugs. Simmons claimed he only started doing the drugs when Marsh sacked him after the accident.'

'Ross is doing well. That's good thinking. Outside the box.'

'It certainly is. It seems a big stretch to me, but anyway, they got details of the drops he made, and now they're going to pay visits and cross-check names with known drug offenders.'

Jane sat quietly after George went. She still couldn't see the big picture, but she was more optimistic that the pieces were sliding slowly into place.

***

Fliss lay back, her head resting on Jack's chest.

The sun was warm through the van window, and she felt drowsy. Their clothes were strewn across the floor, and they'd got so carried away they'd forgotten they'd left the door open. She'd never worked out why, but they always felt randy in the mornings; by the time the light was fading, they were too.

Jack's regular breathing told her he was still out cold, but she could feel her adrenaline slowly returning.

She'd never been able to stay still for long. She smiled, remembering how she would spring up straight after tea and run outside to play. It used to drive her mum wild. 'Sit still and let your food go down!' she'd yell.

Her mum had died five years ago, and there was no one to call her daft anymore. Obsessed, yes. Crazy, maybe. It took her till her early teens to find a way to channel her energy into something that mattered: spreading the word about the catastrophe that was befalling planet Earth.

She did the research and was horrified. It was mur-der—worse than murder: destruction on an obscene scale. The oceans fouled with oil and waste and plas-tics; wildlife decimated by farming, logging and raging fire; ice melting; and mighty machines boring through the planet's skin to suck up its precious resources—all justified by the blind, misguided pursuit of economic growth. It could become sensible, sustainable growth by working with nature, not against it. The circular economy was a model that worked, but she soon real-ised there were too many vested interests determined to ignore the facts.

She eased Jack's arm off her chest and sat on the floor, quickly pulled on her vest and denim shorts, then tiptoed outside.

She hadn't told Jack yet, but she was going to end the protest. They'd got nowhere. Breaking through the barrier had caused a stir, but it had been reinforced now, and they'd never get past security again. News coverage was drying up, too. She'd talked it through with a mate in Greenpeace, and he'd said the best way to make a point was to go extreme. 'That means spending money. Lots of it,' he'd said over a crackly phone call.

The more she listened, the more she thought about the environmental impact of their protests, including the fuel they burned as they travelled the country. Greenpeace had the budget to buy things—like a ship to harass whaling fleets—so they could afford extreme, but they were burning fossil fuels to make their point, and something had to change.

She'd agreed with him on one level, though. For most pressure groups, the most effective action is through social media. 'Use all the channels,' he said. 'You'll be reaching millions of people, and your influence will grow. Plus, you can do it all from home—wherever that is. And it costs peanuts.'

Fliss sat on the step, nodding and smiling as campers walked by. They were chatting happily. They enjoyed the occasion, but if it wasn't achieving anything, what was the point? If they wanted a good time, they could go to a festival.

She'd have to think carefully about how to handle the exit, otherwise Barrett would claim it as a victory. But she'd take great pleasure in rubbing his nose in it by coming back with an even more effective social media campaign.

She stepped back inside and sat on the bench seat opposite Jack. He was snoring gently. She had a fair idea how he'd react if she told him she was setting up a permanent base somewhere. It would be the end of their relationship. He lived off the buzz. He wouldn't last five minutes sitting in an office at a computer screen. But she could live with that. Nothing mattered more than the cause.

She checked the bank statement on her phone. There was more than enough. It wouldn't cost that much to rent a place and get a broadband connection. She might even be able to persuade a few followers to stump up some cash and to help spread the online gospel.

She smiled. *The Gospel according to St Fliss.*

Then it hit her. The perfect solution. Strawberry Fields Forever would set up its new HQ in Ashbridge. Right on Barrett's doorstep.

***

Allan spread the page proofs for this week's *Free Press* across his desk and stood up so he could get an overview of the layout. His old editor used to say, *'Don't look at the words yet. Just look at the shapes.'*

Jenny had done a good job. There was a nice balance of pictures and text, and not too many boxes and awkward column widths either. It looked professional yet accessible: just the feel he wanted, and the opposite of the rabid redtop approach the *Ashbridge Times* was taking to win back the readers the *Free Press* was taking off them.

Satisfied, he sat down and began to skim through the stories. She'd led with a piece on the drill site protest: *BREAKTHROUGH! Protestors smash down barriers in a bid to halt drilling.*

He read the words and shook his head. It was a nice play on words, but it clearly wasn't a breakthrough. The story quoted Universal Energy saying the protest had caused minor damage to the fence, and Aaron Barrett confirming that drilling had not been interrupted.

He circled the headline in red and scribbled a reminder on his pad to get Jenny to change it.

There was a gentle tap on his door, and Ruby stepped in. 'Sorry to disturb, but Aaron Barrett is on the line. Do you want to speak to him?'

Allan sighed. 'To be honest, Ruby, no. Can you ask him if he'll be around in half an hour? I'll call him back then. He'll probably shout at you, sorry, but just explain we're on deadline day for the *Free Press*.'

He happily accepted the offer of coffee and settled back down to the proofs.

Then his mind began to wander. Why was Barrett calling him and not Jenny? He checked his watch. They still had four hours before the paper went to print. If Barrett did have some big story to tell, Jenny might have a bit of reworking to do.

He called him back on loudspeaker after coffee, and Ruby sat with him to take notes.

'Allan! Good! Got some news for you. Haven't shared with anyone else yet, but I'm calling on the police to end the drilling protest immediately.'

Allan raised an eyebrow at Ruby. 'Okay. How do you propose to do that, though?'

'It's simple enough, surely. They're trespassing on someone's land. That's illegal, so I—we—are saying that if they won't move, they should be arrested.'

'Right. I see. Okay, yes, that will make us a story, and we've just got time to get it in this week's—'

'That's why I'm calling. Thought you might like the tip-off. Always keen to work with the local media, you know.'

This time, Allan raised both eyebrows, and Ruby stifled a laugh.

Allan was enjoying this. It was like going back to his days as a reporter. He winked at Ruby. 'That's appreciated. I'll get Jenny to give you a call with follow-up questions. Do the police know yet? Obviously, we'll need to talk to them.'

'I've sent them a copy of the release and emailed their chief super, whatever his name is.'

Allan passed on the info to Jenny. She jumped even higher up his list of favourite people by relishing the challenge of changing the front page at the last minute.

'While you're looking into it, Jenny, find out who does own the land, will you? We've not even looked at that angle.'

'Aye, you're right there, boss. I will.'

He put the phone down. He was willing to bet spineless Cooke would talk it through with Jane before he did anything. Jane always said he would do anything to avoid taking responsibility.

He stopped. The inside page proofs were still waiting, but he was thinking about Jane. Was she thinking about him? He checked his phone calendar and felt a nervous bubble forming in his stomach.

Only two nights to go until he sat down to eat dinner with her. In the house they used to share.

***

Ross kicked his front tyre in frustration. 'Waste of time.'

'At least we tried.'

Ross paused, mid-kick. 'Your trouble, Eric, is you're too nice. You should be telling me not to be a prat and get on with the job.'

Eric grinned. 'All right. Stop being—'

'That'll do. Stop.'

They got in the car and drove out of Cardale after a long and fruitless morning being scowled at by farmers and people with Range Rovers pretending to be. All of them used to get a hay delivery from Marsh Farm. Perhaps understandably, they were all bad-tempered.

Eric summed it up as Ross drove off at speed. 'I can imagine all of them overdosing on cider, but not on cocaine.'

'Cider? Champagne, more like. But there must be some people in that bloody village who are druggies. It wouldn't be worth Castle coming out here, or Rob taking over, otherwise.'

'Would Rob help us? You know, pay a few visits, with us watching?'

'Look, mate, if Rob was being that co-operative, we wouldn't be wasting our time on a bloody farm tour, would we? He's prepared to talk, but only up to a point.' Ross sighed. 'Sorry. I'm just impatient. We can crack this; I know we can. Trouble is, I don't trust any of them. I bet they all look after one another. We need to find another way. Smoke them out.'

Eric laughed. 'If that's the right expression.'

Ross smiled, then accelerated to get past a tractor, so fast it pushed Eric back in his seat.

They drove in silence up to the T-junction, then took a left turn onto the dual carriageway towards Ashbridge. A few minutes later, Eric clung to his seat as Ross suddenly swerved into a garage.

He switched the engine off and smacked the steering wheel. 'Electric car!'

Eric was mystified. 'What?'

Ross opened the door. 'Come on, let's get a brew and I'll tell you. They do a good takeaway here.'

They leaned on the bonnet, sipping from paper cups, Eric waiting patiently for an explanation but enjoying the sun on his face and the traffic noise. He wasn't a big fan of the countryside.

Eventually, Ross enlightened him. 'We've been looking at the delivery round Rob used to do, right?' Eric nodded. 'So, what other kinds of deliveries do people get out here?'

'No idea. Oh, yeah—online shopping.'

'Yeah, but not every day, or every week. They get milk from the milkman, don't they?'

'Do they? We don't.'

Ross gave an exaggerated sigh. 'You need to use your eyes, mate. Every place we went to had empty milk bottles on the step.'

Eric scratched his head. 'Okay, but how does this help us?'

'Milkmen travel in electric vans, don't they?'

Eric was tempted to laugh but resisted. 'So, you think we're looking for a milkman who delivers cocaine as well?'

'No. But that's what set me thinking. You know how difficult it is to find some of these remote houses, don't you? You need local knowledge. So, our dealer is a local man who knows the area, maybe because he does deliveries. Or used to. And Rob is terrified because he's getting his supplies from someone he knows very well. And I bet all his customers know him well. A local man they don't want to upset, see?'

Eric sipped his coffee and tried without success to understand Ross's thought process. 'Oh, right.'

***

Julie Marsh was a very attractive woman. Maggie admired the natural blonde hair, blue eyes and slim figure. It could have been her, a few years ago.

Maggie also noticed the frown lines and the way she held herself. She didn't look happy. So, at least they had something in common.

Julie was chatty enough, though, as she gave her the tour of the house and the outbuildings. Maggie felt bad about her deception and was so preoccupied about Peter that she wasn't taking in the information she had pretended to be so interested in.

Julie stopped and leaned on a galvanised steel gate. She smiled and looked years younger. 'Sorry, I'm not letting you get a word in. It's been a while since we had a visitor, apart from the police, of course. Sid always says I talk too much.'

Maggie took her opportunity. 'They're asking lots of questions, aren't they?'

The breeze caught Julie's hair and she swept it to one side. 'Have they been to see you too, then?'

'Oh yes, a few times.'

Julie laughed, without much humour. 'Oh well, I'm glad it's not just us. Gets a bit wearing, doesn't it?' She looked at Maggie and put a hand on her arm. 'Oh, I'm sorry. I haven't even offered you a cup of tea. Would you like one? We'll be all right in the house now. Sid will be upstairs in his room.'

Maggie smiled, relaxing. 'Yes, please. Peter spends a lot of time in his room, too.'

'It's a man thing. I wonder what they get up to.'

'I'm not sure I want to know.'

Maggie pondered on that as Julie left her alone while she made tea. What were they up to? What if both their husbands were involved in that man's death? She didn't know anyone else in the village who'd had more than one visit from the police since Mary died.

She heard Julie opening the door. The cups rattled gently as she walked from the kitchen.

Maggie took a deep breath. She needed to know what questions the police were asking the Marshes. She hoped Julie would see her as an ally, but she had no idea how she was going to broach the subject.

Julie did it for her. She put the tray on the long oak coffee table between them and smiled nervously. 'Do you mind me asking, what questions were the police asking you?'

'I don't mind at all. In fact, I was about to ask you the same question.'

They both laughed, and Julie began arranging the cups and saucers.

Maggie thought for a moment. 'Peter's been behaving oddly, and I'm worried. The police keep saying they are investigating the murder, but I don't understand why they keep coming back to us. No one else in the village seems to be under suspicion. I'm left with the awful feeling that Peter's hiding something.'

Julie rolled her eyes. 'I know. Tell me about it. Milk and sugar?'

'Just a little milk, please. So, what are they quizzing you about?'

Julie hesitated, then looked up. She took a breath, poured the tea, then sat up straight as if her mind was made up. 'I don't know if it's common knowledge, though I suppose it's bound to be in this village, but Sid has—had—a drug habit.'

Maggie listened, forgetting about her tea, then realised Julie had stopped talking. She sipped her tea and talked slowly. 'They wanted to find out if Peter knew the man who died. I happened to know that he used to work on one of his farms, a few years ago—this one, actually—so I was surprised when Peter made it seem that he didn't know him. And he has been behaving oddly for a few weeks now, as if he is ill—shaky hands, hot flushes, that sort of thing.'

Julie opened her mouth to speak, then stopped herself.

'What is it?'

Julie put her cup and saucer back on the tray and lowered her voice. 'I was just going to say, that's what Sid was like when he stopped taking the drugs. He was on cocaine. He still suffers occasionally, but he's a lot better now.' She twisted her hair in her fingers. 'So that man used to work here?'

Maggie suddenly felt numb. She wanted to speak, but the words wouldn't come. Julie came round to sit next to her. Instinctively, they reached out and held hands.

Julie's voice was soft. 'I'm sorry. I shouldn't have said that about the drugs. I didn't mean to worry you. It's probably something else...'

Maggie felt off balance. The closeness, the physical contact... all the things she longed for but had learned to live without. She tried to speak but patted Julie's hand instead.

It felt as if the fog inside was clearing. Peter's erratic behaviour. His occasional strange moods that evaporated as if by magic. She turned to face Julie, but avoided looking into her eyes.

'You said Sid got his drugs from the man who died.'

Julie nodded. 'Keith Castle, yes. But then another supplier took over.'

Maggie stood quickly. 'Thank you so much. Sorry, but I've got to get back. I must talk to him.' She walked towards the door, blurting out the words. They must have sounded so brusque.

She saw Julie wave from the window as she drove away. Maggie's breath was coming in short gasps, and she was driving so fast she only just had time to swerve onto a grass verge to avoid crashing into a cyclist.

She sat in the car with the engine running.

Peter used to own the farm where Keith Castle worked, so he knew him. He was showing all the signs of addiction. Castle must have been his supplier. He knew the police would eventually make the connection, so he'd given up drugs and was suffering withdrawals.

Maggie switched the engine off. Her hand was shaking. The time had come. Peter needed to start being honest with her.

25.

Peter stood at the kitchen sink and gulped down a glass of water.

Maggie was out and he wasn't sure where. She'd been looking at him strangely off and on for days, ever since the police came round with their questions. She suspected something; that was obvious.

They'd always been able to talk, but it was superficial stuff. He'd never understood why women seemed to want to know what you were thinking, why you felt like that. Why couldn't she just take things as they were? Life was complicated enough without constantly having to explain your inner self.

But this was different. The look in her eyes was cautious, nervous. She knew something was going on, but why couldn't they just carry on? Why did she have to know everything? He didn't ask her where she was going, or what she was doing. For all he knew, she could be having a mad passionate fling with a farmer's lad.

He jumped as the phone rang, and snatched the receiver up almost angrily.

'Peter Attrill.'

'Oh hello, Mr Attrill, it's Jenny Jones, *Ashbridge Free Press*.'

Just what he needed. What now? 'Hello. Yes?'

'We're running a story about the protestors at the drill site. Did you know the council has demanded their arrest?'

Peter felt the tension lift. He was on safe ground. 'Well, I didn't know that, but I am very pleased to hear it. It's time they left them to get on with the job.'

'Would it be fair to say that you have a vested interest in that happening, Mr Attrill?'

'What?'

'Well, you do own the land, don't you?'

Peter sat down heavily on the kitchen chair. He couldn't speak. How did they know?

Jenny's voice was calm. 'Hello, Mr Attrill. Can you give me your response, please? We are holding the presses now. I just need your confirmation, please.'

The pressure in his chest turned into sharp pain. His breath came in short gasps. Sweat ran down his face.

He talked to himself, as the doctor had taught him. 'Calm down, it doesn't matter. Breathe deeply.'

'Mr Attrill? Are you alright?'

Peter pulled himself together. 'Yes. Thank you.' He took another deep breath. 'Sorry. Yes, I do own the land. It's not a secret. I inherited a lot of land round here. My family ran a few farms.'

'Okay, thanks. Well, it does matter in a way. You are the new chair of the village association, which has come out in favour of drilling, and you are a close ally of Aaron Barrett. Would it be fair to assume that you are making a nice fat sum out of this environmental damage, Mr Attrill?'

Peter stared into space. He snapped, 'No comment' and put the phone down.

Then Maggie walked in.

***

The letter from Gloria MacDonald was succinct.

My solicitors have advised me to pursue a case against Sidney Marsh for causing death by negligence. Those proceedings have now begun, and we are in contact with his representatives with a view to reaching a settlement.

I know money won't bring Mary back, but the lack of any explanation for her death is causing me much stress.

Can you give me any updates on the investigation before I decide what to do next?

Yours, Gloria.

Chief Superintendent Roy Cooke adjusted a gold cufflink. 'So, what's the latest on the investigation?'

Jane ran through the lines of enquiry. It was only when she mentioned cocaine that he seemed to show interest.

'What, you mean drugs are at the root of all this? Seriously? Two people die in the wreckage of a house and we're saying it's a drugs-related crime?'

Jane rested her notebook on her lap and looked up. It would help if he listened. 'No, what I said was that drugs are a connection linking that apparent accident with the body that was found. That man was a dealer, probably low level, who operated in the Cardale area. As you know, we found cocaine in what was left of Mary's house. And the young man who drove the tractor has just been arrested for supplying drugs in the car park of the local pub. So, you can see the way it's leading.'

Roy nodded but Jane could tell he was losing the thread. She wasn't surprised. She wondered if she was, too.

He cleared his throat loudly. 'So, are you telling me that Gloria's daughter was a drug user?'

'No, I'm not. We didn't find traces on her. We did find them on the man she was in bed with at the time, though.'

'So where is all this going, Jane? It's been—what—over a month since Mary died, and we still can't give her mother any closure on what everyone is saying was a tragic accident, can we?'

Jane sighed. 'I think we can say that what happened to Mary was accidental. It was caused by human error rather than a deliberate act. What I can't say is whether the guy who was driving the tractor was under the influence of any illegal substance. We breathalysed him but didn't test for drugs.'

'Okay, we can be forgiven for that.'

Jane stared. 'I hope so, sir.'

'But if you're right, then the Marshes would have a good defence against Mrs MacDonald's claim.'

'True enough. But—'

'Right. Well, we need to reply to this letter. I'll tell her we can say that Mary's death was not the result of a deliberate act but that we are still investigating the circumstances that led up to that event. I also want to say that you will keep her updated from now on. Okay?'

Jane nodded. 'Sir.' She thought for a minute. 'I could phone her, if you prefer?'

Roy tapped his keyboard and glanced at the screen. 'No, I don't think so. Let's keep it formal and on the record. All right, thanks Jane. I've got a call to make to Aaron Barrett now, so...'

Jane smiled. 'Deep breath, sir.'

He frowned. 'What? Ah yes, right! And Jane, let's get this case off the books, shall we? I know it's murder, but let's not be afraid to say we can't make progress. Let's be honest, we're talking about a low-level drug dealer, more than likely knocked off by a rival gang.

Which means we have a low probability of catching anyone. But we keep the case open. We do have other things to do. Such as—'

'Tackling the spate of house burglaries in suburbia?' Jane kept her voice level, though she was boiling inside. 'Yes, I know. They must miss their flat-screen tellies so much...'

He looked up sharply.

'Sorry, sir. I've got Lorry looking into those. I just need more time. It's complicated. I don't care who the victim is, and the minute we start saying someone doesn't matter is the time I pack it in.'

As Roy tried to interrupt, she held a hand up, feeling her anger spill out. 'I can't—sorry, I won't—shelve a murder inquiry, not until we've explored every angle. We owe it to the victim. And if that counts as insubordination, well, frankly, I'll pay the price.'

She stopped before she completely lost it.

He sat in silence. After what felt like an age, he spoke. And the minute she saw the look on his face, she could have predicted his response word for word.

He sighed and shook his head as if in sympathy. 'Well, okay, Jane. But on your head be it.'

***

Ross sat on the bench in Rob's cell and waited for him to calm down.

'Come on. Just sit down and we'll talk.'

Rob looked close to tears. 'I've already told you too much. I can't say any more.'

'Okay, let me talk then. But sit down, will you? I'm cricking my neck looking up at you.'

Rob grimaced and sat stiffly.

'Good, thanks. So, let me tell you what I think, and you can just listen, and nod or shake your head...'

He nodded.

'Good start. Right. The man who is running the drugs racket in Ashbridge and Cardale lives in, or near, Cardale. He drives an electric car. Okay so far?'

Rob nodded.

'And I think I know who it is.'

Rob looked up, his eyes wide.

'Don't worry. Just listen. We found someone in the village who drives an electric car. This person is a farmer or was a farmer. He's very well known to everyone. I'm going to write his name in my notebook and show you. All you have to do is nod or shake your head.'

He quickly wrote it down and showed it to Rob. Rob stared, then slowly gave the slightest of nods and whispered something.

Ross leaned in closer. 'What was that?'

Rob shook his head.

'Okay, anyway, thanks, Rob. You've done yourself a big favour, and I promise you I will make sure you are looked after. No one's going to hurt you. Has your mum been to see you yet?'

A tear ran down Rob's cheek and he roughly wiped it away. 'Yes, every day. When can I get out?'

Ross spoke softly. 'Soon, mate. But let's keep you here a bit longer, where you're safe. We just need to wrap up this case and then we can get you sorted. All right?'

'Will I still have to go to court? Go to prison?'

'You'll go to court, mate. Prison is the thing we're working on. Like I said, the more you help us, the more we can help you.' He tapped on the door to be let out and patted Rob on the shoulder. 'It's going to be fine, Rob. You're doing the right thing.'

'Promise?'

'Yeah. Promise.'

'All right. I'll tell you what I said when you showed me his name...'

***

They sat on opposite sides of the big kitchen table. Peter attempted a smile, but Maggie just raised her eyebrows, and he lost his nerve.

He'd known something was coming the minute she walked in. He'd told her he had some admin to catch up on, and she'd turned on him. She'd kept her cool, but he sensed she was likely to explode.

'Sit down, please,' she'd said. 'We need to talk.'

'What's this about, Maggie? Why are you looking at me like that? Say something.'

She looked into his eyes before she spoke, and his stomach lurched. 'All right, Peter. I'll say something. I believe you're a drug taker. I believe you've lied to, or at least misled the police. I believe you knew Keith Castle very well and that he was supplying your drugs. I don't believe you killed him because, frankly, you haven't got the guts. But I do believe you know what happened to him, and that's why you're so terrified of the police finding out.' She paused and leaned back in her chair. 'Any comment, or would you like to consult your good friend Aaron Barrett?'

Peter tried to speak, but nothing came. He knew he should be telling her she was talking rubbish, but he couldn't find the strength to fight back. He slumped forward in his chair, his chin almost touching his chest.

Maggie jumped up. 'Peter! Are you alright?' She nudged his shoulder and knelt so she could look into his eyes. He was crying. 'Oh God, Peter. What have you done?'

He swivelled and put his head on her shoulder, sobbing. She cradled him and felt the tears running down her face and onto the back of his head.

'Come on. Let's talk now... I'll make tea, all right?'

He nodded and she handed him a sheet of kitchen roll. He blew his nose noisily. She filled the kettle, put a teabag in the pot and reached for two mugs from the wall cupboard. She used the time to compose herself, telling herself over and over that whatever he'd done, she would support him.

Looking out, she could see the heritage roses in the far border. They were beginning to fade now.

She filled the teapot and turned to put the tray on the table.

Peter's eyes were red. 'I'm ready to talk.'

***

Forensic Phil was back on form. Jane noticed the twinkle in his eye, and on closer inspection, it looked like he was starting to put on weight. George, on the other hand, couldn't afford to.

Jane mused on the lottery that was life. Phil had always looked after himself, hardly touched alcohol, followed the Mediterranean diet, never smoked, and went on walking holidays. He'd ended up having heart surgery.

George had a belly the size of a beach ball and chewed wine gums constantly when he wasn't eating bacon butties and knocking back a beer. His idea of exercise was reaching for the remote control when football was on TV. And he'd never had a day off sick in his life.

And then there was Charles Aston, the former chief super at Ashbridge, who'd promoted Jane to DCI, given her self-belief and the confidence to thrive in what was then a misogynistic environment. He'd been even bigger than George and so full of life—until he was struck down by a cancer that came from nowhere, faded to frailty and died in a hospice.

Phil was apologetic as he explained he couldn't offer any more forensic detail.

George was unimpressed. 'Bloody useless, you are.'

'I know,' Phil replied. 'Everyone needs a hobby, though, don't they?'

Jane grinned. 'Now, now. Break it up. So, George, stop slagging Phil off and impress me.'

George scraped a hand over his stubble and sighed. 'I wish I could. Ross is the star of the show on this one. He's done a lot of digging around the drugs connection, and he's got a tasty lead from young Rob, who has more or less confirmed that Peter Attrill was his supplier.'

'What?' Jane paused. 'Wait. More or less?'

'He wouldn't actually say the words, but when Ross wrote down the man's name, he nodded.'

Phil closed his notebook with a snap. 'I'd say that was categoric enough.'

Jane leaned back, smiling. 'Let's bring Attrill in.'

George heaved himself out of the chair with a grunt. 'There's something else. Rob said Attrill's known as The Milkman.'

Phil snorted. 'The Milkman? Really? Two pints and a line of coke, please.'

'Yes, very good... It's just his codename. Ross is checking it out with the National Crime Agency to see whether it's come up on their records.'

'Well, well. It all fits. The Milkman... He used to be a farmer, didn't he? I like it.' Jane couldn't stop smiling.

'So go and get him. But no fuss, okay? We want to catch him off guard. Tell him we have some more questions. He's not under arrest. Yet.'

26.

Fliss had half expected a riot when she told them she was calling off the protest.

Jack had been sulking for hours. He wanted his revenge after being locked up in a cell for a night. She wasn't worried. He could always take out his aggression on the rugby field next weekend.

But she was disappointed at the lack of reaction as she'd gathered the group leaders round, sheltering from the wind behind her VW. She'd expected more resistance. But it convinced her she was doing the right thing.

Her message was clear enough: 'We need to rethink the way we do things. Think about the fuel we burn, think about the impact we've had on the environment, not to mention the damage the police and security have caused simply by us being here.'

There were no complaints, and a few hands were raised when she'd asked if anyone would like to help with a new social media campaign.

She sat on the van step sipping peppermint tea, nursing the mug with both hands, feeling the warmth of the sun on her face.

Jack was doing his daily fifty press-ups round the back. He'd soon be off on his run. They'd hardly spoken since she broke the news. He'd probably look for another cause to latch on to—one that gave him the opportunity to use his muscle.

She blew on the tea to cool it. She didn't owe him anything, and she didn't expect anything back. It had been good while it lasted. The sex had been energetic rather than soulful, and she could certainly survive without it. They both knew he was more like a bodyguard than a soulmate. He'd gone quiet because he knew she wouldn't need him anymore.

She thought back to earlier in the day, when the *Free Press* reporter had told her Barrett was calling for the police to evict them. It was no surprise to learn the land they were drilling on was owned by a mate of his. That was the clincher. Wealthy and influential mates lining each other's pockets. It was all the motivation she needed to refocus the campaign, and setting up a new base right on their doorstep in Ashbridge might even wipe the smiles off their smug faces.

She smiled. It was doubly satisfying to imagine their shock when they turned up to kick the protestors out, only to find they'd already gone.

She went inside and opened the laptop. She'd bookmarked an office to rent. Perfect position, right above a tearoom, and just far enough away from the town centre to be affordable. The Strawberry Fields trustees had given their backing after she negotiated the deal. Only three months' rent up front, and a discount for not-for-profit organisations.

She waved as Jack tapped on the window and set off on his run with one of the girls from the camp, then clicked into her email account and tapped out her acceptance.

***

Ross felt embarrassed when Jane called him in to thank him for his work on the drugs angle, but readily accepted the invitation to join her for the first interview with Attrill.

He walked to the canteen, knowing it was empty in the late afternoon, and sat nursing a paper cup of coffee. Its only redeeming feature was that it was hot, but he sipped it gratefully, enjoying a moment of quiet.

The more he got involved in the drugs scene, the more he wanted to specialise. But Jane was encouraging him to go for promotion to detective inspector, which would put him on the same rank as George.

He knew that if he got a job at the NCA, he'd be starting at the bottom. But if he got the promotion at Ashbridge, what then? George had been talking about retirement, so there was a chance he could take his place. Was that the right move, though? He'd put down roots here, but he was still only twenty-eight, and joining the NCA would open a new world. There was more to life than Ashbridge, but...

He drank the last of the coffee, just as Lorry walked in.

'Hello, you.'

She sat down opposite. 'Hello yourself. Penny for them?'

Ross sighed. 'Between us, okay?' Lorry nodded. 'Jane's telling me I should go for promotion, but I've been checking out the NCA. They're up against it and they're looking for recruits. I really got a taste for it from working on this case, so...'

'Are you going to apply?'

He smiled. She always got stuck straight in. 'That's the problem. I don't know. What would you do?'

She thought for a moment, her eyes flicking round the room. Then she leaned forward. 'I'd go for the promotion. Then you could find out if you like the responsibility, and the money. Then, if you still want the NCA, you'd be in a much stronger position with that on your CV. And if you change your mind, you'd be all set to apply to another force anywhere you like, wouldn't you?'

Ross expertly tossed his paper cup into the bin near the door. 'You're a star. You're right as well. Seems so obvious, now you say it.'

Lorry smiled. 'It's easy when it's not your own life.' She paused and put her hand on his. 'Ross, I've got a decision to make too. It's your turn to advise me, okay?'

***

Peter Attrill looked up as a woman with brown hair tied back walked in, followed by a young man he thought he recognised.

He found it difficult to process the situation he was in. Neither of them looked like his preconception of detectives. She was slim and rather pretty. He looked like a college student, with tousled hair and a slightly bored expression.

The uniformed officers they'd sent round to bring him in had been very polite. It was just routine questioning, they said. Maggie wanted to come with him, but they said it might take a while and she'd just be sitting around, so why not stay at home. They even said they'd drive him back after.

And so here he was, in a padded chair in a small conference room, with a cup of tea and a plate of biscuits.

So far, so civilised. But when the man closed the door and they sat down opposite him with a scrape of chairs, he felt the atmosphere change.

The woman smiled, but she clearly meant business. 'I'm DCI Jane Birchfield, and this is DS Paul Rossiter. Can you confirm your name and address, please?'

'Yes, of course. Peter Attrill, Church Cottage, Cardale.'

'Thanks. You are here voluntarily, Mr Attrill, and you are free to leave at any time. We simply want to ask you some questions concerning the death of Keith Castle, whose body was discovered on the drilling site near your home. Do you understand?'

He nodded, and she turned to the man sitting next to her, who wrote something in his notebook before speaking.

'Did you know him, Mr Attrill?'

'Erm... who? The man?'

'Yes. Keith Castle.'

'Well, yes, a long time ago.'

The woman smiled again. 'You seem on edge, Mr Attrill. How did you know him?'

'I... He... worked for me. Once.'

She sat back and crossed her legs. He tried not to look. 'You were a farmer, weren't you? Owned a lot of land.'

'Yes. My family did. I just inherited some farms. Got rid of them now.'

The man spoke this time. They weren't giving him much time to think, and he was starting to sweat. 'So, Mr Castle... he worked for you, doing what?'

'Farm labour, driving, that sort of thing.'

'Deliveries?'

'Yes. He would have done, I suppose. Can't really remember.'

The woman leaned forward. She had brown eyes and her lipstick was a light shade of pink. 'Why didn't you tell us this when I came to see you, Mr Attrill? You surely can't have forgotten him? Well, you obviously haven't because you clearly remember him today. You can see how it looks, can't you? He was murdered, and we are investigating a murder. You deliberately withheld information...'

Peter clasped his hands tightly to stop them shaking. 'I'm sorry. I just wasn't thinking straight. I knew how it would look and I just panicked, I suppose—'

'Do you, or have you ever, taken drugs, Mr Attrill?'

He stared at her, then nodded. He reached for his tea, but his hand was shaking too much.

She spoke softly. 'Can I make a suggestion, Mr Attrill? Or can I call you The Milkman?'

His eyes widened in shock and his hand covered his mouth in slow motion. Was this really happening?

The woman opposite just nodded. Her voice seemed far away.

'Tell us everything. If you hold anything back, I promise you it will come back to haunt you. Would you like a few moments alone to think about it?'

Peter forced himself to sit up straight, remembering how he'd managed to make peace with Maggie by owning up. 'No, thank you. I'll take your advice.'

***

Jane gave Ross a fist bump as they walked into CID. Her mood was lifted even further by the sight of Jag chatting with Lorry. Just like old times. She cleared her throat, and they spun round guiltily.

'Thanks to Ross, we have a breakthrough. Attrill has admitted his role as The Milkman. He's been supplying drugs in the Cardale area for years. We've charged him, but he's a low-level operator—and a user, by the way, though he says he's off it now.'

She smiled as she looked round. It was good to have them all back together again. 'We talked about connections, didn't we? Well, here's one for you. Attrill says Geoff Pegg recruited him.'

George was first to react. 'Blood and sand! The guy in the wrecked house, with Mary what's-her-name?'

'The very same, George. We found cocaine in the wreckage, you remember. Now we have an explanation. And more significantly, a possible link with the Keith Castle killing.'

Phil put down his mug of tea. 'How so, ma'am?'

'Think about it. Geoff Pegg was the main man in a drugs outfit operating on that side of Ashbridge. And he worked for Universal Energy, who are drilling up at Cardale.'

George again. 'Which is where Castle was found.'

Ross took his chance. 'Castle remains... Could become a tourist attraction.'

Lorry tutted. 'Bad taste, Ross, even for you.'

He grinned, annoyingly. 'Sorry, Lorry.'

Jane raised her voice. 'So, as I was saying, there's a new connection, right there. And there's every chance that if Attrill worked for Pegg, Castle did too.'

Ross thought for a moment. 'Yes, ma'am, that's right. And we also have Sid Marsh, who was a user. He had what we thought was an accident, but maybe he knew too much about Attrill and Pegg...'

'Good, Ross, yes. So, come on, let's dig deeper. Phil, I need you to look again at prints on that cocaine packet we found at Mary's house. And Claire, can you double check the forensics at the scene of Sid Marsh's so-called accident?'

Claire nodded, her red hair catching the light. She was sitting next to Eric. Jane wondered briefly if that was significant.

'Lorry, I'm taking you off burglaries for a while, you'll be gutted to know.' She laughed at Lorry's whoop of delight. 'I want you to take a fresh look at Geoff Pegg's background. We need a new pair of eyes on it, okay? Ross, keep doing what you're doing. We need as much intelligence as we can get on the drugs operation.

'Jag, please keep monitoring the Marshes. And George... Attrill is a close ally of Aaron Barrett, who in turn is very pally with Universal Energy. You can see where this is going. And not only was he supplying drugs in his spare time, but his brother is still doing time in Spain for drug pedalling.'

'Nice people.'

'So, did he have any contact with Aaron Barrett, who just happens to live in Cardale? And if so, what form of contact was it?'

Ross leaned back with his hands behind his head. 'Bloody hell! Imagine the headlines!'

Jane already was. 'George, see what you can find.'

She looked round the room. She could sense their excitement. The case had just moved to a different level.

***

Julie put the phone down and walked out into the wildflower meadow.

The flowers were fading but their beauty was enhanced as the late afternoon sun began its imperceptible fall towards the horizon.

She remembered being fascinated by the horizon line when she was a girl. She was an only child in a big house and spent lots of time on her own. She used to wonder how long it would take to get there; if the sun was bigger there; was it like the edge of a cliff?

After the call from Maggie, it was more tempting than ever to start running towards it.

She said Peter had confessed to being a user, and he'd also told the police he was a supplier. Now he was locked up for the night.

Maggie said she'd only wanted him to tell her the truth. She could forgive him if he was honest with her.

Julie leaned back against the gate. Honesty had been in short supply, but more than anything, she was tired of being the strong one. She'd taken on the farm with Sid against her better judgement, then witnessed his slow decline. It had taken a long time to realise he was killing himself with drink and, much later, drugs. He was surviving without them now, but for how long?

Meanwhile, the court case was rumbling on. Sid was convinced they'd settle out of court, but where would that leave them? Homeless? What a reward that would be for everything she'd done.

She felt the warmth leaching away as the sun touched the hill behind the church. The clouds were already tinged red, gaining colour as the fields lost theirs.

Julie wiped the tears from her cheek. She'd done everything—given everything—for Sid. Tried to put things right. And for what? Maggie and Peter had been through hell too, but they were closer together because of it. She felt totally alone. They had little, if any, physical contact. Their sex life had been non-existent for months.

Hugging herself against the chill, she walked slowly back to the house.

***

'You all right, Lorry?'

'Yeah, fine, George. A bit tired, that's all.'

'You look a bit pale...'

'I'm fine, honestly!'

'Okay, okay, keep your hair on!'

Lorry looked up from her screen. 'Sorry, boss.'

George smiled and threw her a wine gum. 'That's okay. I'm used to being shouted at.'

Lorry laughed and turned back to Eric's notes from his house-to-house enquiries, and particularly the gossip about Geoff Pegg. His affair with Mary was common knowledge, and a few people had concluded he'd only been interested because she was the association chair. Having said that, it looked like his lobbying for the drilling had worked: just about everyone was in favour. Apart from the Marshes.

Lorry was struggling to concentrate, and the nausea was making her irritable. The nurse had warned her that morning sickness could hit her at any time of the day. She seemed to get it worst when she lay in bed.

Her fear was that it would affect her work. She'd only just stepped up as a DS and she was terrified of letting the team down. Snapping at George wouldn't exactly help.

Ross had told her she should come out, just as he had, not too long ago. '*I worried about what people would think, and you lot told me you knew anyway.*' He'd laughed. '*Maybe they already know you're up the tub.*'

The dilemma she was facing was whether the baby would spell the end of her career, and Ross had been typically blunt about that, too. '*Why should it? You can do what you like these days. Why shouldn't Mark give his up instead? Doesn't have to be down to you, does it?*

And anyway, you're both working, so you could afford childcare, couldn't you?'

She'd nodded, but he was missing the point. It wasn't just about the practicalities. She didn't know how she'd feel, holding a baby in her arms for the first time. Would work suddenly become irrelevant because she wanted to devote her life to their new child?

She didn't have any answers, and her preoccupation meant she was finding it harder to concentrate on the job at hand.

She frowned at the screen, remembering she'd spotted an angle in Eric's notes but had already forgotten it. Where was it?

She scrolled back. There it was. *Apart from the Marshes.*

Lorry frowned. What had struck her just a moment ago? She forced herself to think again.

Sid was found in a ditch, but that was after Pegg had died, so that wasn't down to him. Pegg was lobbying for the drilling, and Sid was opposed. Pegg was further up the drug supply chain that Sid was using. Could Sid have known? Could Pegg have warned the gang about Sid before he died?

Lorry began typing.

What if Sid's injury wasn't an accident? What if Keith Castle had been bumped off because he had become a security risk, too? Pegg could have dealt with Castle, but not Marsh. Check Pegg/Castle links. Attrill took over drugs supplies from Pegg after his death. Could he have attacked Marsh because he didn't want to be exposed?

***

Jane put a flag on Lorry's note and sent a message to Claire, asking her to check for any signs of Attrill at the scene of Sid's 'accident', and another to Ross to alert him.

Her phone pinged. *Still on for tomorrow? Looking forward to it! A x*

She began tapping out a reply, then stopped. She couldn't decide what to say. *Can't wait*, was putting it too strong. *Yeah, see you then*, was too cool. She settled for: *Me too. C u at 7 x*, and pressed send.

Then she opened Jag's latest email.

Mrs MacDonald and the Marshes have reached an out of court settlement of around £1 million. The Marshes have proposed to sell their farm and pay this amount from the proceeds of the sale. Mrs MacDonald has agreed although her solicitors have insisted on a 12-month time limit, after which the money will have to be paid, whether the house is sold or not. I understand this will be confirmed by letter tomorrow. The court officer I spoke to says that Mr Pegg's brother is his only living relative and that he has no interest in making a claim.

Jane sent Jag her thanks and logged out.

She wondered how Julie Marsh would be feeling. She'd be glad to get rid of the farm, but would this be the end of their marriage? They'd been under strain for a long time, and she seemed to be suffering.

It was hard to work her out. She projected a tough image, and could turn on the charm, but there was an edge to her.

Jane sighed as she packed case papers into her bag. Maybe Julie was becoming a preoccupation because Jane identified with her problems. She and Allan had come within an inch of getting married. It had fallen apart in a moment of madness, brought on by the stresses they were both under.

It felt weird, imagining sitting down at the kitchen table with him again tomorrow night. She wanted to believe they could make a go of it.

She wished she could sit down with Charles Aston in his office one more time. They used to spend the last fifteen minutes of every working day talking things over. He could read her like a book, and he knew the right thing to say. He'd become like a father—a big, fat, cuddly dad—and she still welled up when she thought about how much strength he'd given her.

She snapped her briefcase shut, closed her office door, walked slowly down the concrete steps, pushed the heavy fire door open and stepped out into the drizzle.

27.

Allan got the round in, and they clinked their glasses.

The Wheatsheaf was busy, but then it usually was on a Thursday teatime, for some reason. Allan asked Jenny if that was because it was payday.

'I think the days of people being handed wee packets full of five-pound notes have gone, boss.'

He laughed, but it was another reminder of the gap between them. Jenny was young enough to be his daughter, and Mike Brook was only just out of college. They tolerated him because he was the boss, and he bought the drinks at their weekly publication-day bonding session.

He could tell they'd enjoyed the buzz of making late changes to the front page. The headline was attention grabbing...

Exclusive!

DRILL PROTEST ENDS
but secret council land deal exposed

Environmental campaigners ended their protest over gas drilling on land at Cardale today – to the delight of Council Leader Aaron Barrett.

But his joy was short-lived. The Free Press can reveal that the land was acquired by the council from Barrett's close friend Peter Attrill in a behind-closed-doors deal that could have netted Mr Attrill a six-figure sum.

Now Opposition councillors, and environmental campaigners, are demanding to know when and how the decision to line Mr Attrill's pockets was taken, and how much public money was involved.

'Well, cheers, team!'

Allan savoured his pint. Jenny downed her vodka and lime in one. Mike was sipping orange juice.

Jenny smacked her lips. 'Cheers, boss, and nice work, Michael.'

Mike smiled. 'So, what's next? Keep digging?'

'Aye, definitely.'

Allan nodded and finished his drink. He was eager to get away. He knew Jenny was all set to drink everyone under the table, but he wanted to chill tonight ahead of a big night tomorrow.

He put a ten-pound note on the table. 'Get yourselves another drink and I'll catch up with you tomorrow.' He stood. 'Yes, Mike, you did a good job—you both did, and we want to keep it going. We need to find out how much was spent, and how the decision was taken, and by whom. And don't forget the Strawberry Fields lot. Find out where they are now and what plans they have. I find it hard to believe they've just given up.'

Jenny nodded. 'Aye, that's right. Ye'll nae mind chatting up that blondie again, will you Michael?'

Allan laughed and left them to it. God, he felt old! Leaving a pub after one pint? What was that about?

***

Alistair Grant's tone was icy.

'Good morning, Mr Barrett. We need to talk, do we not?'

Aaron attempted upbeat. 'Morning, Alistair. Yes, of course. What can I do for you?'

'Shall we start by discussing how my company became embroiled in a contractual relationship with a drug dealer?'

'You mean Peter Attrill?'

'Why, how many others do you know? Come, come. You must know you have placed me in a totally unacceptable position. My people are already fielding calls from shareholders. I'm disappointed you didn't think to alert me.'

'I—'

'Please don't waste my time with excuses. This project was a lifelong ambition, as you know. A chance to give something back to the place that made me who I am. Now, I'm faced with a very difficult decision.'

'What do you mean?'

'Give me one good reason why I shouldn't immediately pull out.'

Aaron made a slight choking sound, but swiftly recovered. 'I can give you more than one good reason. How many do you want?'

'It's been nice talking to you, Aaron. I will expect your response in writing within the hour. Email will be perfectly acceptable. You will have my decision soon after that. Good morning.'

Aaron heard the click that ended the call, and realised he'd been gripping the receiver so fiercely his hand was aching. He put the phone down and walked over to the window looking out over the town square. It was the usual crowd out there: layabouts smoking roll-ups on the town hall steps, a disinterested street cleaner, college kids giggling, smartly dressed women with bags for life.

All of them in their own little worlds, uninterested in the massive decisions taken every day by the council. He'd never understood why only about a third of eligible adults bothered to vote in local elections.

He turned away and checked his computer. His diary was crammed, but he needed time to think. He jabbed a finger at the desk phone and told his PA to give him thirty minutes free from interruption.

If Universal pulled out, no one else would touch it. The company would claw back the £400k they'd already paid, of which Attrill had generously agreed to take just twenty-five per cent. Losing £300k from the cash balance would make a big hole in this year's council budget, but the damage to its reputation would be massive. If not terminal. And what about his own future? He'd staked everything on it. He'd even been getting mentions in Parliament for standing up against rabid environmentalists.

Aaron sat down heavily. Just yesterday, he'd been celebrating with cabinet colleagues after a poll showed most locals were in favour of the drilling. They could see the financial benefits. And the new local energy supply made them feel secure and virtuous. How would they feel about it being snatched away?

His political opponents would have a field day. So would Felicity Crowther. He'd be slaughtered by the media. He'd be finished.

He was back at the window. He felt the sweat begin to trickle down his face.

It was all going to come out. His life was unravelling. And he felt completely helpless.

***

Peter managed a few spoonfuls of watery porridge, then sat in his metal chair, gazing at the small rectangle of light from a window way over his head.

He was hungry, but they'd be coming for him soon, and he was dreading the next round of questions. He'd been allowed to phone Maggie last night, but he hadn't said anything because he started crying as soon as he heard her voice.

She'd told him not to worry. 'Just tell the truth.'

They'd told him he could have legal representation, but he was too ashamed to call the family firm, and too proud to make do with the duty solicitor.

Ironically, he'd had his best night's sleep for months. Maybe there was something to be said for being locked away. But now, he had to think hard about what to say. The truth, the whole truth, or just a bit of it?

The lock slid open loudly, echoing off the grey, shiny walls. The heavy steel door seemed to groan as it swung open. A large man walked in, smiling. He smelled of sweets and coffee.

'Morning, Mr Attrill. I'm George. Blimey! Fancy leaving all that porridge. You'll need your energy today. Still,

I'm sure we can find you some biscuits... Right, come on, let's go and have a little chat upstairs, shall we?'

Jane, the detective in charge, was waiting for him. She smiled, too, but if it was supposed to make him relax, it was having the opposite effect. Why were they being so friendly?

He sat down, and George sat next to Jane on the other side of the table. There was a jug of water and three glasses. Jane asked if he'd like one, and he nodded.

She had a nice voice, quite soft with a hint of a Manchester accent. George sounded more like a Yorkshire miner, if there was such a thing anymore.

George shuffled some papers and spoke, as Jane poured the water. 'Right, Peter, I'm going to switch the tape on so we can record our conversation. You all right with that?' As soon as Peter nodded, George pressed a switch and spoke again. 'Interview on Thursday, September twenty-second at eight thirty-five a.m. with Peter Attrill, DCI Jane Birchfield with DI George Creasey.'

Jane leaned forward. 'Peter. Thanks for the information you gave us yesterday. You confirmed you've used cocaine yourself for years, but you also told us you recently became a supplier. You realise you have admitted criminal offences, and you understand that this is now a formal interview, that you have waived your right to legal representation, and that you remain under the caution we gave you last night?'

Peter nodded.

George smiled. 'Please confirm for the tape.'

'Yes, I understand.'

'Thank you. You can, of course, change your mind about legal representation at any time.' Jane paused. He seemed reluctant to look her in the eye. Was that shame, or because he was trying not to be distracted from his rehearsed speech? Give someone a night in the cell, and you give them loads of thinking time. She'd lost count of the number of times villains had changed their stories.

Jane had warned George she didn't want to mess about. 'So, Peter. Tell us about Keith Castle. Why do you think he was killed?'

He looked shocked. 'I don't know! I didn't do it. That's all I can say.'

'All you can say, or all you want to say? Is there more you could say if you weren't so scared?'

'No! I just don't know. That's all. I've admitted supplying drugs and using them myself. What more do you want? I did know Keith Castle once, a long time ago, but—'

'But for some strange reason, even though he was a drug supplier too, in the same area, you don't know anything about him, and you never had any contact with him over, say, the past year. Is that what you're telling us?'

Peter paused, still looking down at the table. 'Well, I did hear he was still operating in the area...'

'Who from?'

'That would have been Mr Pegg.'

'For the tape, you mean Geoffrey Pegg, of Universal Energy, whose body was found at Mary MacDonald's house?'

'Yes.'

'And he was the man who recruited you?'

'Yes.'

'Go on... what did he say, exactly?'

Peter looked up. He reminded George of a frightened rabbit. Yet he was successful in business and chaired the village association. Was this all part of his act?

George grunted. 'Come on, Peter. You must be able to remember.'

'Well… he just said Castle was back and he was working for another… erm… organisation, and to let him know if I came across him.'

Jane sat back. 'And did you? Come across him?'

Peter nodded. 'Yes, I didn't remember before, but I did see him in his car near the pub.'

'The pub in Cardale?'

'Yes.'

'And what was he doing?'

'He was standing at the back of his car with the boot open. There were a few people with him.'

Jane smiled. 'That's good, Peter. Did you recognise any of those people?'

Peter frowned. 'I—erm…'

Jane sighed. 'You do see where this is going, don't you? Who had motive to kill Mr Castle? A rival drug dealer? A customer who didn't want to be exposed? As it stands, you're the main suspect.' She rapped the table with her knuckles. He looked up. 'Come on, prove us wrong. If it wasn't you, Peter, help us find who did it.'

Peter sighed heavily. 'All right.'

***

George came back with the coffees, munched a custard cream and made himself comfortable while Jane scrolled through messages.

She spoke without taking her eyes off the screen. 'So, comments?'

'Barrett's got a lot of questions to answer.'

'Yeah, but do you believe Attrill? Is Barrett really going to stand in a line next to a drug dealer's car, in full view of people he wants to vote for him? I can't see it myself.'

'But why would he lie?'

'The usual reasons. To throw us off the trail. To get his own back on Barrett for something he did. And if he is lying, he's probably thinking he's fooled us. Which also means we may have got our man.'

'Fair enough. But we're talking about Peter here. He was like a frightened rabbit.'

'He's made a fortune, so he's not stupid. And he had all last night to come up with something...' Jane swivelled in her chair and reached for the coffee mug. 'It could be a pack of lies for all we know. Anyway, get Eric to check out the other names, and we'll save Barrett for later. Did we get anything interesting off Peter's mobile phone?'

'Zero. He's been on the phone to Barrett a lot, and a few calls to local farms.'

'That's it?'

'Yep. He could have another one stashed away.'

'Yes, and Eric's checking the home phone, though I can't imagine he'd be that stupid.'

'Search warrant?'

'Do it, George.'

He scribbled a note, then looked up. 'I can't see Barrett knifing Castle, even if he is a user.'

Jane shook her head. 'No. Neither can I. Anything from Claire or Phil?'

'Claire said something about the knife wound. She wondered if we'd ruled out a woman having done it.'

'Oh?'

'Yeah. She said it could have been someone smaller, and the fact that the blade was long made her think maybe it was someone weaker.' George picked up another biscuit and gazed at it.

Jane frowned. 'She's right. But why didn't Phil give us that? Maybe we're not asking the right questions. Anything else?'

'I've just got a feeling we've got our man.'

'The frightened rabbit?'

'People are capable of anything when they're scared. And he had a lot to lose if Pegg, or Castle, or Barrett, exposed him.'

'It's not looking good for him, no. Electric car, self-confessed dealer, a user, and he knew Castle from way back.'

'Motive is obvious, and he must have had opportunity.'

Jane sipped her coffee slowly. Something was nagging at her. She thought back to the beginning. There was something about the people involved... a connection she'd seen but since forgotten.

George watched and waited. Jane looked as if she'd switched off, but he wasn't fooled.

She slammed her coffee mug on the desk. 'Hang on a minute.'

She logged in to the case file and attacked the keyboard, then looked up. 'We're looking in the wrong direction, George.'

28.

Phil bit into an apple and yearned for unhealthy fast food. He was taking so many tablets to thin his blood and blitz cholesterol, surely the occasional bacon sarnie wouldn't do any harm?

He'd resisted the temptation, despite Claire's daily provocation. She was sitting in the corner with today's temptation: fish and chips out of the paper. At least she had the decency to sit with her back to him, but the smell was too much.

'Spare me a chip?'

She turned and smiled. 'Well, maybe just one...'

'That's all I ask.' Phil picked the fattest chip out of the tray and savoured the hot salty taste. He walked back to his desk, wiping grease off his fingers with a tissue. 'What's on your to-do list, Claire?'

Claire stopped eating as her computer pinged. 'Have you seen this? Jane wants us to revisit the Cardale forensics.'

'What? Again? What is it this time?'

'She wants us to look for anything that would suggest a female perp.'

Phil ran a hand over the grey stubble on his head. 'We surely would have picked up on that, wouldn't we?'

'I don't know... Jane says "we appear to have become fixated on this being a man's work. Let's put that out of our minds and start from a different perspective."'

'Okay, well, far be it from me to question Jane's judgement. You start with Sid Marsh; I'll do Castle, then we'll swap, okay?'

'Okay, boss.'

'But first, give me another chip. And that's an order.'

***

Ross took a deep breath and tapped on Jane's door. He'd been re-reading a letter from the NCA this morning, inviting him for an interview, and he was desperate to share the news with someone. Then Jane had asked to see him.

Should I tell her? If not now, when? Does she want to see me because the NCA asked her about me?

The green light came on. *Enter.*

Jane was standing, pouring coffee. She turned and smiled. 'Want one?'

Ross breathed again. *She doesn't know...* 'Not for me, thanks. I'm overdosing at the minute.'

'Good choice of words. We need to talk about drugs.'

'Yes, ma'am?'

'I've belatedly concluded that the three separate Cardale incidents—Mary, Sid and Keith Castle—are all connected by two factors. And one of them is drugs.'

Ross nodded as she settled back in her chair. It looked like she just wanted to talk through ideas, and he began to relax.

'I think that's true, ma'am. It's more than coincidence.'

'Yes, but is it?' Jane was fizzing with energy, even though she sat perfectly still.

Ross frowned. 'Ma'am?'

She spoke quickly. 'What if it is coincidence? So, we find cocaine in the wreckage of Mary's house. Sid Marsh is a user, and he's found in a ditch with a head wound soon after. And Keith Castle, a known dealer, is found dead in a hole in the ground soon after that. We've fallen into the trap of linking them together. That's the way we work, isn't it? Making connections? We always want neat solutions. And no wonder; it's easier to try to pin things on one person.'

'So, are we saying there's no connection?'

She sipped coffee. 'Drugs is a connection, but there's something else at play. It was something that struck me right back at the beginning. It's just taken me a while to reassemble everything.'

She was maintaining eye contact, waiting for a response. Ross was flattered to be invited to share ideas, but he felt tongue tied and decided to admit it.

'Sorry, ma'am. I don't know what to say. Have I missed something?'

Jane laughed. 'Not at all, Ross. You have been—to quote George—the star of the show. You've done a fantastic job of proving the drugs connection, and I need you to keep working on it.'

Ross found himself gagging for the revelation he sensed was coming. 'But you said it wasn't the only connection, ma'am.'

'I did. It's all about women, Ross. What's that thing a lot of men say about women?' She laughed at Ross's obvious discomfort. 'Okay, don't worry, I'll save you the embarrassment. The stereotypical male response is that women make all the decisions. You know, how to decorate the house, what to buy, jobs that need doing. Men give the impression they're the passive partners.'

Ross nodded. 'Yeah, I get that. My lodger tells me we're getting like a married couple. I'm her landlord, and she's already running the place.'

'Exactly. So that's where I'm going with this, and I just wanted you to know, first, that you need to keep following up on your work, and second, to shift focus slightly. All the intel you have gathered is about male involvement, correct?' Ross nodded. 'Okay, so go back, and look for women of any age operating at any level.'

'Yes, right. Thanks, ma'am.'

'And report straight back to me, Ross. I've cleared this with George. From now on, you are my number two on these cases. I need George to focus on a few others that have been gathering dust, okay?'

'Yes, ma'am! Thank you.'

'Thanks Ross.' She stood and shook his hand. 'That's it for now.'

Ross walked straight to the gents and locked himself in a cubicle. He read the NCA letter again and shook his head.

Jane was talking about coincidences. Was it a coincidence that she wanted him reporting directly to her on the same day he got invited to an interview? It had to be. How could she have known so soon? Instinct told him the NCA hadn't tipped her off yet. But how long could he put off telling her when she'd been so good to him?

She was brilliant to work for. And she'd just handed him an opportunity to work more closely with her. But he'd have to be single-minded if the NCA offered him a job. After all, trying to advance your career wasn't a crime, was it?

***

Maggie's hair was wet, and she smelled fragrant.

'Hope you don't mind the bathrobe, Julie. I've just washed off a six-k run. Come in!'

They sat at the big kitchen table, waiting for the coffee to percolate. Maggie's husband was in a cell, but she looked carefree. Julie decided to be direct.

'How do you do it, Maggie? I came round thinking you'd need a bit of support, but...'

'I'm a hard-faced cow, that's how I do it.' She laughed and slid the jug out of the coffee machine. 'It's kind of you, but I'm okay. I meant what I said... I just wanted to know the truth, now I know what I'm dealing with.'

Julie accepted the porcelain mug and grimaced. 'I know what you mean. I tried hard not to acknowledge the truth, hoping it would go away.'

Maggie put a hand on her shoulder. Her touch was gentle, reassuring. 'But it doesn't, does it? I was always impatient with people in business, the ones who spin you a line, take advantage because you're a woman.'

Julie nodded. 'Yeah, Sid was like that.'

'Was? He's changed then?'

'Well, I bloody hope so. He'd better have! Still, I think we can cope either way. Women do, don't they?'

They laughed and Maggie guided Julie to the two-seater sofa. There wasn't much room, and their hips and shoulders were touching. Julie found the physical contact comforting.

Maggie leaned back and sighed. 'I'm glad you came round.' She turned as Julie sank back into the cushion. 'I bet our husbands wouldn't approve. Meeting up with-out them? Gossiping about God knows?'

Julie laughed. 'How dare they? Sid would probably be jealous. How sad is that?'

'Yeah, but they're not here, are they? It's just us, and God knows we need each other.'

Maggie held out her hand. Julie slowly held onto it and pressed it against her cheek...

Next thing she knew, she was opening her eyes and Maggie was sitting at the kitchen table with a cup of tea.

'Oh God, what time is it? How long have I been asleep? Maggie, I'm so sorry!'

Maggie smiled. 'Don't worry. You looked peaceful; I didn't dare disturb you. It's only four o'clock, and it's not as if I've got any plans for the rest of the day.' She poured a cup and handed it to her.

Julie sat up. She held on to the teacup and sipped slowly.

'God, Maggie, I can't believe I did that.'

'I'm flattered you felt comfortable enough to do it. To be honest, it looked like you needed a nap. Is everything okay? Anything you want to tell me?'

'No, I'm fine. It's just Sid. Well, you know the story, and you've got far greater issues with Peter. That's why I feel so bad about it. I wish I was as strong as you.'

Maggie walked to the window and opened the curtains. 'You work on a farm. You look strong enough to me. I don't feel strong. Just resigned, I suppose. And hopeful, you know? Thinking maybe it's true that you must reach rock bottom before you can climb back.' She laughed briefly as she rinsed out her cup. 'You can't beat a cliché to get you through the day.'

Julie laughed. 'Women are the stronger sex. And you're right about the farm. I'm the one who's been doing the heavy work, even before Sid got hurt.'

'I'm not surprised. Anyway, do you have to rush back, or can I show off my garden before the light fades?'

Julie didn't stop to think. 'I'd love to see it.'

***

Jane waited at the traffic lights and tweaked the dial to get a better signal.

She'd missed the national headlines, but the local stuff was always on straight after.

"... confirmed that the drilling at Cardale has been suspended. Universal Energy boss Alistair Grant apologised and said it was due to unforeseen circumstances. Council leader Aaron Barrett said it was the company's decision and that the council was now reviewing its options. The news was welcomed by Strawberry Fields Forever leader Felicity Crowther, who said it showed the power of protest. More news as it comes in. More shops in Manchester are running out of stock as—"

Jane switched off and inched through the rush-hour traffic. Cardale, it seemed, was never out of the news. At least it stopped her overthinking tonight's reunion with Allan.

She'd decided to keep it low key. A meal for two from the posh supermarket, a couple of bottles of his favourite beer, and a box of Malbec.

Her mum was horrified when she rang on her way to the car. 'You mean you're not cooking him a meal? Jane!'

'Mum... you know I'm a hopeless cook. At least this way, he gets a decent dinner and I'm spared the stress of messing up. Anyway, I'm in the middle of a complicated case. I don't want any hassle.'

'Well, I hope it works out all right for you both. I like Allan.'

'Yes, I know. You keep telling me...'

'Don't be cheeky. I'm still your mother. Let me know how you get on.'

Jane promised to call her tomorrow. Were they ready to get back together, or would it spell the end?

Would it just be a loose '*let's keep in touch, let's be friends*' kind of outcome?

The car clock flicked to 18:11. Just over an hour to go.

29.

'I enjoyed that, thanks.'

'All my own work, of course. Do you want pudding?'

'Do fish swim? What's on the sweet trolley?'

'Toffee sponge and custard.'

'That's a yes from me, thanks.' Allan stood. 'Shall I clear away?'

'No, relax. Help yourself to a drink.'

Allan poured himself a Malbec and looked round the room that had once been so familiar. Jane had moved the table in from the kitchen for some reason. But everything else was the same: the old gas fire loyally fizzing and burbling in the marble fireplace, the grey carpet that had been there when they first moved in, the big squashy sofa they'd bought from the Red Cross charity shop, the ancient brass wall lights that looked like something out of a Dickens novel... and the old telly, about two feet deep and ten minutes to warm up.

He sat down at the table and sipped wine. They were getting on well enough. But there was a slight edge, as if they were tiptoeing round each other, like hotel guests forced to share a table with strangers.

It was impossible to gauge what Jane was thinking. She was being friendly. They'd laughed about a few things, talked about work a lot—as usual—and he was guessing they'd be fine until the meal was over. That would be the moment the pressure built, wondering who would be first to broach the subject. *Where did we go wrong? Could we make it work? Should we try again?*

He heard the ping of the microwave and the clatter of dishes. He checked his phone—no messages. He was trying hard not to think about the end of the evening. They'd lived together for years, and yet here he was, fretting like a schoolboy about whether he'd end up staying the night.

He looked at the wine in his glass. One more and he'd be over the limit.

Jane pushed the door with her foot and hurried through carrying two bowls, one bigger than the other. 'There you go, sir. Extra helping for you.'

'Well, if you insist. Excellent service, if I may say so.'

Jane curtsied. 'Why thank you, sir. Will that be all, sir?'

Allan laughed and picked up his spoon. 'Seriously, thanks. You've spoiled me. I know you must be rushed off your feet with this Cardale case.'

'True. But that was always our problem, wasn't it? Too busy at work. Too busy to make time for each other.'

Allan put his spoon down, frowning. Jane recognised the expression: the one that had first told her he was genuine, that he cared, had feelings. It was part of the formula that had brought them together.

He sighed. 'I know. I've been trying to work out what I'd say to you tonight, and I couldn't find the right words. But I think—I know—I made a stupid mistake, walking out like that. I've regretted it ever since.'

He paused, then slowly looked up, and met her gaze. He took her hand by instinct. It felt natural, and she didn't try to move it away.

'I've never stopped loving you, Jane. Can you forgive me? Can we try again?'

Jane's mouth felt dry. She nodded. 'We need to forgive each other. We both messed up. And yes, I would like to try again.' She saw tears in his eyes. 'If you're going to cry, Allan Gary Askew, so am I.'

He sniffed and smiled. 'Happy tears?'

'Course they are.' She stood up and held her arms out. 'Now, are you ever going to stand up and kiss me?'

***

Alistair Grant placed his elbows on the desk and steepled his fingers.

He'd risen to the top by staying several steps ahead. He was always telling his friends that life was a game of chess, and you were in control if you anticipated the next moves.

The financial loss at Cardale was inconsequential. Profits throughout the business were soaring, and even the media exposure hadn't had the slightest impact on share price.

He knew Aaron Barrett would be seeking to save face by taking legal action and/or securing a drilling contract with another company. He was equally certain he would fail. No one would want to touch that place after the drugs headlines. On the contrary, Ashbridge Council would soon be writing him a cheque for compensation, and he would be certain to let the press know when it was done.

The real issue for him, the one he had stupidly allowed to be made known, was that the Cardale scheme had symbolic meaning. It was personal. It was meant to be his gift to Manchester. And now it had been taken away because a sordid little man had developed a drug habit. Attrill was wealthy, by all accounts, living in a desirable location. Hardly a stereotypical drug user...

Alistair sipped his tea. As he gently inhaled its aromatic steam, an idea began to take shape.

Maybe there was another way to leave a legacy.

He smiled to himself and picked up the phone as his beloved nineteenth-century French ormolu grandfather clock chimed ten o'clock.

***

Jane sat on the loo, worrying whether to invite Allan to stay the night.

He'd had more than enough to drink, so driving home was out of the question.

Everything had gone so well. He'd been thoughtful, careful, sincere, funny. She'd fallen for him all over again.

She flushed the loo even though she hadn't used it, and laughed at herself for the deception. Looking in the mirror, she saw a light in her eyes that had been missing for some time. She knew what she wanted.

'Right, Allan, get your coat.'

He stood up quickly, avoiding eye contact. She kissed his cheek and whispered, 'Don't look so shocked. I'll drive you home, and I thought we could stay at your place tonight. I'll drive you back here to get your car in the morning. What do you think?'

He kissed her hair and hugged her. 'I think you're a bloody tease. I'll get my coat.'

30.

Two squad cars arrived about half an hour after Julie had gone home. The light was fading, and the flashing blue lights were guaranteed to get the whole village's attention.

They showed Maggie the search warrant, and she walked away to the summer house, leaving the front door open for them.

'Help yourselves. Let me know when you've finished.'

She flicked through a magazine and watched from the window as they carried boxes up and down the front path. One of them had Peter's big computer base unit, another carried a stack of ring binders. She wondered if Julie was going to get the same treatment. From the way she was behaving, Maggie wouldn't be surprised.

Julie was nice, but something was wrong, Maggie could tell. She was holding things back.

The young one tapped on the sliding door and held out his card.

'Thank you, ma'am. We're almost done. Please call me if you have any questions. DC Eric Sykes.'

'I trust you found what you were looking for?'

'I can't say, ma'am.' He stepped inside so quickly she had to move to one side. 'I'm sorry to disturb you but I just need to check in here.'

Maggie stepped to one side and waved him in. 'Please do... You're welcome to borrow any books.'

She watched as he picked books off the shelves at random, then dropped to the floor to look under the cane sofa and the table.

He smiled apologetically as he brushed his trouser knees and reached into his pocket. 'That's it, ma'am. Thanks for your co-operation. Could you sign here, please?'

For the first time in her life, she signed a form without reading it.

The blue lights were switched off as they drove away, and Cardale was dark and silent once more.

Maggie looked up into the clear evening sky. It was too early for bright stars, but the moon shone like a question mark over the church.

She walked back into the house, took out the phone she'd found in one of Peter's jackets and switched it on.

***

Phil gulped down the last tablet of the day and put the kettle on.

He'd watched yet another episode of *The Detectorists* on catch-up. For once, its gentle humour had failed to cheer him. Now a banal presenter was droning away on Radio 2 when all he wanted was to listen to music.

Time seemed to be dragging—a sure sign the black dog was making another appearance.

He knew why. He'd failed to cover all angles in the Cardale forensics reports. Jane's comment about him ignoring the possibility of a female perpetrator kept coming back to mind.

She was too supportive to call him out, but he had to admit that he'd fouled up. He hadn't been thorough. It was his first offence in a long career, but that was no consolation.

He'd been trying to dismiss the negative thoughts all day, hiding them from Claire, burying the sense of shame so he could concentrate and maybe somehow redeem himself. But he'd bottled it up too well and now it wouldn't go away.

He whisked the chocolate powder into the hot water and checked the kitchen clock. Ten fifteen. It was bed-time, but he knew sleep wouldn't come.

He put the mug down on the kitchen table and flipped the laptop screen up.

He gave himself a pep talk: 'Come on Phil. It's not a setback. It's an opportunity. Stay positive.' He'd never been too shy to admit that he talked to himself. Almost everyone in the hospital ward who lived alone said they did it too.

Moggie, the ginger cat he'd adopted from the RSPCA shelter, pushed through the flap and jumped onto his lap. She purred as he stroked her, and he was instantly soothed. 'You're just in time, Moggie. Now, let's see if we can spot anything. Ready?'

He tapped the keyboard and picked out a picture of Keith Castle's body when it had first been discovered. He magnified the image and leaned in closer.

***

Jane eased out of bed and pulled on a T-shirt that was hanging off the back of a chair. Allan turned over onto his stomach. The clock on his docking station glowed blue: 06:16.

Jane opened the bedroom door gently and tiptoed across the hall, then helped herself to a banana from the glass bowl on the kitchen worktop.

It had struck her last night how tidy everything was, like a show home. Allan had showed off about the way he could control the heating, lighting and security cameras with his phone. But Jane had been blown away by how new it all looked.

She'd never expected to be swayed by glossy white kitchens and contemporary furniture, but she was seriously impressed.

Allan had just shrugged. *'It should be good; it costs me enough.'* He told her he missed their house, how he felt comfortable there and how this felt like he was an intruder. She'd laughed and told him how ironic it was that she was jealous of his place when he was so fond of the old terraced house.

Jane walked to the window and pressed a button to open the floor-to-ceiling blinds. The view almost made her step back. It felt as if she was on the edge of a cliff. The thin ribbon of the Manchester Ship Canal glittered far below.

'Admiring the view?' Allan stood behind her and wrapped his arms round her.

She leaned into him. 'Hang on to me, in case I fall.'

He laughed. 'You won't. I've got you.' He kissed the back of her neck and she felt goosebumps all over her body.

She squirmed free. 'Don't start that again, Askew. What's for brekkie? No, don't tell me: you just push a button on the wall and a full English appears.'

''Fraid not. I've got to make it all by myself. So, what do you fancy? A toasted bacon muffin? Fruit with Greek yoghurt?'

'All of the above. I'm starving.'

'Hang on! You're not a veggie anymore?'

'Not a hundred per cent, no. I've cut right down on meat, but...'

They talked about work as they ate and drank tea from white porcelain mugs.

'Have you cracked the Cardale thing yet?'

Jane mopped up some stray brown sauce with the remains of her muffin. 'Getting there. Very slowly. You know what? I think I'm losing my touch. It's taken ages to get a handle on it.' She stopped and put a hand on Allan's arm. 'You remember Phil?' He nodded. 'Well, I'm seriously worried about him.'

'Why?'

'He's missed things that normally he'd be the first to spot.'

'Yeah, but you just said you thought you were losing your touch. Maybe he's just temporarily lost his. Having a bad time for some reason.' He smiled ruefully. 'It happens.'

'Yeah, I suppose. He deserves the benefit of the doubt. Anyway, it's down to me if things get missed.' She checked her watch and sighed.

'It's okay. I know. Time to go. I've got to be in Sheffield by half nine. Best get a move on.' He stood and pulled her up. 'But first... May I say, ma'am, how sexy you look in my T-shirt.'

She moved in close. 'Which is now my frock.'

They kissed, and she trembled as his hand slid up under the T-shirt. Her soft moan produced an instant reaction. She pushed away, breathing hard.

'Woah. Let's save it for later.'

He put a sulky face on. 'Okay. I'll try to hang on. But only because I like the sound of seeing you later.'

Jane smiled. She felt more alive than she'd done for months. 'Come on, you. I've got to drive you back home, remember.'

Her phone pinged.

It was Phil: *I think I've found what you were looking for.*

***

Sid Marsh walked down the gravel path to check the postbox, breathing in through his nose, out through his mouth, relishing the fresh air and the movement.

The hospital had signed him off yesterday. No permanent damage, no sign of any aftereffects. And they'd told him to stop taking two of his tablets. His head felt clearer, and his appetite was returning. Things were still tense with Julie, but they always would be. Still, it felt like a new start.

There was a handful of mail, including the one he'd been waiting for.

Julie was defrosting a loaf from the freezer, and a couple of eggs were bouncing gently off each other in a pan of boiling water.

She set the microwave timer and sat at the table with him as he waved the letter in the air. 'Go on, put me out of my misery. Is it sorted?'

Sid nodded. 'Yes, settled out of court. One million.'

'And nothing else? No small print?'

'Just the time limit.' Sid smiled. 'Mrs MacDonald is prepared to wait for a year.'

'What? A year? I thought we'd only get six months.'

Sid sat back, stretched, yawning. 'So did I. She must have taken pity on us, or something. Anyway, it means we've got time to plan.'

'Bugger that! Get it on the market. Our last valuation was one-point-five million. Let's get on with it.'

Sid leaned across to kiss her on the cheek, but she turned to one side. 'I know. Don't fret. I only meant time to plan what we do next.'

As the microwave pinged, Julie jumped up and made herself busy with breakfast. She'd already made her plans. She called over her shoulder as she sliced the bread. 'The estate agent has all the details. She's just waiting for our call. We need to get it on the market now.'

'What about the planning permission? We can't just let that go.'

'Now we know where we stand, why don't you get a formal valuation on that piece of land? I don't know why you've been holding back. Permission for housing round here? It'll be worth at least as much as the house. You do that, and I'll deal with the estate agent, okay?'

She saw him nodding, but the look on his face told her he had no intention of letting that land go. It was so easy to read him these days.

Julie had told herself every morning for the last month that it was time to move on. Sid could do what he liked, but nothing was going to hold her back, not after what she'd been through.

***

'How's it going, Phil?'

'Not bad, Ross, thank you. And you?'

'Yeah, good. Busy looking into the drugs scene. Did you know the papers have started calling it *Cokedale*?'

'The headline writers are annoyingly clever some-times.'

Ross sat across the table and stirred his tea. Phil took quick sips of the scalding coffee. He wanted to be at his desk when Jane arrived, not chatting in the canteen, but it seemed Ross was keen to talk.

'Jane asked me to be her number two on the case. I wanted to ask you if you'd had any luck with dou-ble-checking the forensics.'

'Oh. Right. Well, Jane's asked to see me first thing, so I'd better...'

'Oh, yeah, sure. Wasn't trying to butt in. Just inter-ested.' Ross brushed his hair out of his eyes. 'It's just this angle that the killer could be a woman... I've been digging around through drug cases and there are loads of women involved, most of them are the runners, or the ones providing storage at home, that kind of thing.'

Phil nodded. 'Go on.'

'But I couldn't find any operating round Cardale way. So, I'm kind of worried that Jane...'

'... is barking up the wrong tree?'

'How do you think she'd take it? She's convinced it is a woman, isn't she?'

Phil finished his coffee and stood up. 'Why don't you join me for my meeting with Jane?'

***

Jane opened the air vent and turned the fan up a couple of notches.

She could still feel Allan's presence in the car, still taste his kisses, still catch the subtle scent of his cologne. But he was on his way to Sheffield now, and she was ten minutes late for her meeting with Phil.

Last night had been perfect. There was no awkwardness. They both knew they'd messed up; they both wanted to make amends. And the sex had left her glowing.

She stopped at the lights and quickly checked her face in the rear-view mirror. Was it her imagination or did she look younger?

Jane tapped the steering wheel with the flat of her hands, willing herself to get into work mode. It sounded like Phil had made a breakthrough, and if that was the case, it meant he'd found something that confirmed that a woman, or women, was at the centre of it all.

As the line of traffic edged along Manchester Road, she went through the sequence again...

A tractor demolishes a house, killing two people; drugs found at the scene; tractor driver confesses to becoming a dealer; Sid Marsh—a user—found in a ditch with serious head injuries; Sid a lone voice opposing drilling at the village; Keith Castle—a drug dealer—found buried at the drilling site...

She indicated left and turned into the station car park. Was today the day she would finally make sense of it all?

31.

Maggie put the phone back in Peter's tweed jacket pocket. She hadn't known he had a spare phone. It was an old Nokia, and Julie Marsh's number was stored on it.

She could understand him storing the Marsh Farm landline—he had numbers for just about every farm in the area. But this was her mobile number. And the only one listed against a first name.

She'd stopped trusting Peter a long time ago. And now this... what was going on? Was Julie playing some sort of game with her? She'd been friendly—perhaps too friendly, looking back—but there was an edge to her.

She couldn't believe they were having an affair, though anything was possible in Cardale, as Mary Mac-Donald had proved with her procession of unlikely lovers. The word was she'd favoured older men, the ones with influence. Peter just about fell into that category since he'd taken over leadership of the village association, but... Julie? Really?

But if not an affair, then what? That detective had told her the case was complicated because there seemed to be so many connections. What could possibly connect Peter and Julie—apart from drugs? They were the reason he was in a cell, after all.

Maggie stood at the window, searching for the beginnings of an idea, any theory that made sense. It was there, but frustratingly elusive: something Julie had said about the farm, about Sid.

She felt inside the wardrobe, feeling pockets, but they were empty. She stopped. Of course they were. The police had searched the house. Maybe they'd found something and taken it away as evidence.

Maggie sat on the bed, but she was too wired to rest. Thoughts and what-ifs were competing. She looked outside. It was a sharp, clear morning with a hint of mist on the hills and the first touch of sun on the tops of the pines. A perfect time for a run.

And if her route happened to take her near Marsh Farm, so much the better.

***

'Right, Phil. Let's have the good news.'

Jane clicked her pen as Phil took his time finding the right page in his notebook. She'd learned that he was not to be rushed, but he was taking noticeably longer to get his brain into gear lately. She tried not to smile as she glanced to her right and saw Ross also fidgeting with his pen.

Phil smoothed down the page and looked up.

'Grovelling apology is in order. We've been looking again at all the forensics, as you asked. And you were right, because we've found something. Originally, we found marks on Keith Castle's clothes which we put down simply to the fact that he had soil thrown over him.

'But we—sorry, I—should have paid more attention. Hidden among the dirty marks was faint staining, which we have now identified as eye makeup.'

Jane punched the air. 'Yes! So, can we identify it?'

Phil was playing it cool. 'I think so. Claire's taking samples to see if we can pin down the shade and, hopefully, the make.'

Ross leaned forward. 'Blimey, Phil. Good luck with that. There must be thousands on the market.' He paused, smiling sheepishly. 'Not that I'm an expert.'

Phil wasn't to be distracted. He kept his eyes on Jane as he sipped water. Then he sat back. 'There's something else. This is down to Claire, who I must say has been doing a fantastic job.'

Jane nodded. 'Agreed. Go on, Phil.'

'Well, we—sorry, Claire—has done more work on the stab wound. You remember we described it as penetration from a long, thin blade. So, after you asked us to rethink, we looked at it again, and there is a chance that it may not have been a knife, but a fork...'

Ross looked at Jane with a bemused expression. Jane held up a hand to stop him speaking. 'A fork, Phil?'

'Sorry, that was a cheap play on words. Having looked again, I think the wound is sufficiently deep to suggest a thrust with something like a hay fork—you know, long handle, two prongs.'

Jane looked over Phil's shoulder. 'Which would explain the depth of penetration if a smaller, weaker person had done it.'

Phil nodded. 'You wanted to know if a woman could have done it, and we think the answer is yes.'

Jane spoke quietly, as if to herself. 'You wouldn't choose to carry that around as a murder weapon. Not exactly inconspicuous...' She turned to Ross. 'Which suggests?'

Ross came back quickly. 'It just happened to be there. It wasn't premeditated, ma'am?'

'Precisely.' She leaned forward. 'Okay, thanks, Phil. So, we're looking at a murder carried out on impulse, on a farm, not too far from where the body was found. There's still no proof the killer was a woman, but it remains a strong possibility…

'Right, Ross, let's draw up a list of farms near the drill site, starting with the closest and working out from there. And let's hope whoever did this is still using that hay fork.'

32.

Julie came in from the yard and wrestled her wellies off.

'I'm back. It's looking good out there.'

No reply. She swore under her breath. She'd been out for an hour, feeding the chickens, digging out the last of the potatoes. And there was Sid, still in his dressing gown, elbows on the table, head in his hands, staring at a sheet of paper.

He looked up, grinning. 'This is amazing! I genuinely do not believe it. Alistair Grant is offering us two million for that piece of land—you know, the one with planning permission. He wants to use it to create, and I quote, "a model development showcasing sustainable, environmentally friendly and affordable housing".'

Julie lifted a bucket of potatoes onto the worktop. 'And don't tell me, you're going to bite his hand off, right?'

Sid looked wounded. 'Oh, come on. Yes, I am! Two million? That's at least half a mill more than it's worth. Solves all our problems, doesn't it? We pay off the compensation and keep the house. Result.'

'So much for principles, eh? Let me get this straight. You are going to sell land to a multi-billionaire who was your sworn enemy. The man who was going to drill for gas in Cardale. You, the only man in the village who opposed it?'

'He's obviously got the message, though, darling.' She flinched as she recognised the patronising tone of his voice. 'He's going to use local traders, fit solar panels, water harvesting, ground heat pumps, recycled sewage that feeds the gardens—the full works.'

Julie felt months of pent-up anger rising and spun round to stand over him, almost spitting the words in his face. 'Oh, that's fine. Have you seen the state of that drill site? So much for his environmental credentials...' She banged her fist on the table. 'Take the bloody money! Go on! You take it, enjoy spending it. You never know, he might give you a seat on the board as well. You know what? You make me sick!'

She leaned back against the worktop, breathing hard, realising that was the closest she'd come to hitting him.

Sid didn't move. He spoke quietly. 'It's our big opportunity, Julie...'

'Oh, shut up!' He recoiled as she yelled at the top of her voice. 'I've had enough. Tell you what, take his bloody money. Just give me half and I'll get out of your hair. You can keep the bloody house.' She walked away. 'I can't do this anymore. Our relationship is a bad joke. What's the point? Let's get it over with for both our sakes.'

There was no sound as she went up to their room. It was almost laughable. After everything she'd done for him, he hadn't even tried to talk her out of it.

She sat on the cane chair by the window and let the anger drain away. She took a few deep breaths and closed her eyes.

When she opened them, she realised Sid was right: it was a big opportunity. It was all coming together.

The scrunch of footsteps on gravel broke into her thoughts. It was Maggie, jogging up to the door in skin-tight leggings and a yellow top. Julie hurried down the stairs and out into the yard. Sid had disappeared.

Julie checked her hair in the mirror, practised a smile, and opened the door. 'Maggie! Gosh, you look so fit and well!'

'Oh shucks, thanks. Anyway, what are you doing out in your socks?'

Julie looked down. 'Ah, senior moment. Oops! Fancy a cup of something?'

Maggie shook her head and Julie immediately sensed a change of atmosphere. 'Can we talk?'

They sat at the big table. Maggie didn't waste time. 'Why has my husband got your mobile number?'

'He owned this farm. So what?'

Maggie met her gaze. 'But why did he have it on a spare mobile that he kept hidden from me?'

'I don't know. Why don't you ask him?'

'I can't. He's in a cell.'

Julie smiled briefly. 'Oops again. Sorry.'

'Please don't play games with me. I like you, but there's clearly something going on, and I want to know what it is.'

Julie laughed, disbelieving. 'You mean... You do, don't you? You think I'm having a mad fling with... with Peter? My God! Are you mad?'

'No, I don't think that for a moment. But there's something else, isn't there, Julie? You're very nice but you're hiding something. I can see it in your eyes.'

'Oh, so you're a psychoanalyst as well, are you?'

'I've been in business a long time. I know when someone is lying. Come on, I can see you're struggling. You try to hide it but you're under a lot of strain. Why not just tell me what's going on and get it off your chest.'

Julie looked up. Maggie looked sincere enough, but was she? Was she as innocent as she made out? It was impossible to judge whether she'd always known what Peter had been up to. Or even if she was the brains behind it all.

She heard Sid coming down the stairs and decided to go for broke. He needed to hear this, and it would be perfect to study their reaction.

She waited till Sid was standing next to her and put on a smile. 'Hello, darling. You've joined us at just the right time. Tell me, Sid. Tell me, Maggie. How long have the pair of you been running the drugs operation in Ashbridge?'

'Are you out of your mind?' Maggie laughed, but Sid was silent, expressionless.

Maggie pointed at him, still laughing. 'I have no idea where that came from. Did you know we were drug dealers?'

Sid spoke slowly, carefully, looking at Maggie all the time. 'Don't know what she's talking about.'

Maggie nodded and stood up. Julie pushed Sid out of the way and confronted her. 'You put on a good act, Maggie, I'll give you that. But Sid wasn't quite convincing enough, was he? Let's see what the police make of it, shall we? Now get out of my house!'

Maggie made a point of adjusting her headband before walking slowly to the door. She turned. 'You're bonkers. You do know that don't you? If I were you, Sid, I'd get her a doctor.'

She slammed the door, and the noise acted like a detonator. Julie walked up to Sid, her fists clenched. He flinched as she picked up a cup and hurled it against the wall. She turned to face him, her voice low, threatening.

'You're a stupid, spineless, weak man. I can't believe I've put up with it for so long. Anyway, I'm leaving. Right now. I'm sure you and Maggie will be fine together. Such a good team, eh?' He sat down abruptly as she leaned in closer. 'Oh, by the way, I've already instructed the agent to accept an offer we've had for this dump.'

Sid looked up, his eyes widening. 'What? But—'

'Oh dear. Didn't you know? Didn't I tell you? Now you know what it feels like. So...' She pulled a manila folder out of a drawer and sat next to him. 'Here's the agreement for you to sign. It's been drawn up by my solicitor. Sign it there and print your name there.'

He rapidly scanned the document, then signed and dated it. When he turned to face her, he'd recovered, and his eyes were as cold as his voice. 'My, you have been a busy bee.'

'Haven't I just? Just think, if you'd paid any attention to me lately, you might even have noticed. Anyway, that's all done, which means the house is mine and I'll get the cash when it's sold. Leaving you with all that cash from your grubby little land deal. Two mil for you, one for me. I think that's a good deal, don't you? The only question now is whether I let you stay here, or not. What do you think?'

His voice was calm. 'You're not really thinking of kicking me out, are you, Julie? You're better than that.'

She couldn't keep the contempt out of her voice. 'My God, you're a real case. A devious, cowardly crook. I wasn't going to kick you out, if you must know, but now I'm sorely tempted.' She paused. 'Ah, but I don't want to sink to your level. So, here's the deal: you like doing deals don't you, Sid? I'll let you stay until contracts are exchanged, which, bearing in mind the buyers have got nothing to sell, should be six weeks max. How does that sound?'

Sid moved slowly to the window, turned and smiled. 'Fine. Call me if you need help with your bags.'

***

Lorry grunted and arched her back.

'Okay, Lorry?'

'Yeah, fine. It's just... you know...'

Ross nodded and lowered his voice, even though they had the office to themselves. Eric was out knocking on doors in Cardale. George was with Phil, and Jag was on one of his two days off a week. 'Maybe you should tell everyone.'

'Yeah. Maybe.'

'You don't want to?'

'I do. It's just...'

'What?'

'Well, they'll start treating me differently.' She put on a mumsy-type voice. 'Oooh, poor little Lorry. Don't give her too much to do. Think of the baby.'

Ross scoffed. 'Yeah, right. Somehow, I can't quite see George being like that. He'll just tell you to shut up and get on with your work.'

Lorry smiled. 'Hope so. But, you know, he'll start to think I'll be leaving soon, and so will the others. That's what I mean. It'll be... different.'

Ross leaned back in his chair. 'Yeah, I suppose... But, I mean, what do you want? Would you come back to work after?'

Lorry sighed. 'I don't know, Ross. I keep turning it over. My mum says I won't know until I've got the baby at home. She says I shouldn't commit either way.'

Ross nodded. 'Good advice. You'll be a great mum, though, I bet.'

'Awww, stop it. I can't bear it when you're nice to me.'

'Sorry, mate. Think about it, though. You're going to have to say something soon. Best to get it over with.'

'I know. I'll do it. Promise.'

'When?'

'Today.'

'Really?'

'All right. Tomorrow.'

'Want me to hold your hand?'

'Get lost. They might get the wrong idea. Anyway, what about you?'

'What about me?'

'The NCA, idiot. Any news?'

'Oh, yeah. They offered me an interview.'

'What? That's fab! Well done, mate... So, when is it?'

'I've got to phone them.'

'Well, phone them then! Like, now!'

'I don't know, Lorry. I don't want to let Jane down on this Cardale thing. And if you're going to go off on maternity leave...'

Lorry banged the desk. 'That's just what I meant. As soon as you mention a baby, everything bloody changes. Christ, Ross! You can't let me having a baby stop you taking a big opportunity. How do you think that would make me feel? Get on the bloody phone and stop making me the excuse.'

Ross held up his hands in surrender. 'All right. I'll call them today, promise.'

Lorry walked over to stand behind him and put her arms round his neck. 'Oh God, Ross. Everything's changing. I can't bear the thought of not working with you anymore.'

He made a choking sound. 'If you don't loosen your grip, that might happen sooner than you think.'

***

Roy Cooke looked relieved. 'So, we're closing in, Jane, is that what you're telling me? How long before an arrest?'

'I can't say yet. We've reviewed the forensics in the light of new information, and like I said, it's thrown up the probability that Castle's killer was a woman, and that the murder took place on a farm.'

'Well, that narrows it down.'

Jane ignored the sarcasm. She made a point of consulting her notes, extending the silence so he could start worrying whether he'd offended her. It worked.

Roy cleared his throat. 'So, what's next?'

'We're getting a sample of the eye makeup analysed, and Phil is also getting a DNA test on it.'

'Really? Why?'

'He thinks it may be mixed with tears, in which case—'

Roy snorted. 'How the hell does he work that out? Bit far-fetched, even for Phil.'

Jane kept her tone even and looked him in the eye. 'Phil doesn't do far-fetched. He's the best forensics guy in the region, if not the country. I'm quite happy to follow up on his suggestion. However, if you want to call this line of enquiry off...'

Roy frowned and held his hand up like he was stopping traffic. 'No, hang on. Don't bite my head off for adding a note of caution.' He paused. 'And please don't disrespect me with spurious challenges like that. At the risk of annoying you again, what do you mean by reviewing forensics? That suggests to me they weren't done properly in the first place.'

Jane nodded. 'Sorry, sir. I'm out of order. And you're right about Phil. It shouldn't be happening, and I'm worried about him. We've been together a long time.'

'Understood. So, what do we do? We can't jeopardise this inquiry. If Phil is no longer up to it, I'm sorry but we need to move him out of the way.'

'I don't think we're at that stage yet. It hasn't knocked us back that much. He's overlooked a couple of things, but—'

'—you're cutting him some slack. I wish my boss was so forgiving… But, come on, you know it can't happen again. I'll trust you to handle it, but no more covering up for him, okay? Anyway, let's move on. You said you had another request?'

'Yes. You're really going to like this—not. We need to interview Aaron Barrett on suspicion of illegal use of drugs.'

Roy looked incredulous. 'What? The leader of the council? Come off it! On what evidence?'

Jane tapped the screen and turned her tablet round. 'Here's a picture, supplied by a man now in custody. It clearly shows Mr Barrett among a small group of people gathering round the car of a known supplier. The building to the left that you can just see is the village pub in Cardale.'

Roy sat back with such force the seat rocked. 'Wow! Can't argue with that… Okay. Good work, Jane. Bring him in.' He held out a hand to stop her as she began to pack up. 'First, not a word of this to anyone outside CID. They are sworn to secrecy, and if this gets out to the media, there will be hell to pay, and I mean it. Second, you handle it personally. Take one other member of the team with you. Third, this must be done exactly by the book. No clever tricks. And finally…'

'Yes, sir?'

He smiled. 'Bloody well done.'

'Thanks. I'm thinking we don't need to rush into it, though. The murder is priority. So shall we hold off until we've sorted that?'

'Makes sense. May be useful to have someone stacking up the evidence so we have unbreakable proof. We need more than a photo.'

Jane nodded. He was starting to sound like a real copper. 'Yep. I was going to put George the Rottweiler on that.'

'Good. Well, I can't pretend I'm over the moon about it, but Barrett will get what he deserves. It's proving to be quite a case, isn't it? A house gets knocked down in Cardale and causes a bloody tsunami.'

'It's made me feel like I'm drowning, that's for sure.'

Roy grinned. 'Sounds like you're nearly there, though. So, yeah, keep going. And if you need a change for an hour, I've got an invite to an Ashbridge Business Club working breakfast tomorrow. Fancy going with me?'

'Sorry, sir, but I think you know the answer. Not my scene.'

He nodded. 'Can't say I blame you. I used to think I enjoyed networking, as they call it, but now...'

32.

Jane sat at her computer, listening to the distant sound of banter from the night team. She'd seen the rota on Alex Gledhill's whiteboard, so she knew there were at least three female PCs on tonight's shift, but the men were making all the noise. As usual.

She remembered the knot in her stomach as she'd walked into a locker room full of loud lads on her first day. The memory had stayed with her, which was why she'd always made time to talk to new women recruits, uniformed or not. Most of them tried too hard to be like the men, but Jane always advised against it. She told them that a high percentage of men act like sexist morons because they are desperate to fit in, too.

'So, don't play it their way. Be yourself. And if they cross the line, look them in the eye and tell them. One or two will always be prats, but most will respect you for it.'

The banter died down. No doubt Alex was giving them a briefing.

Jane finished her email to Phil:

It's likely the murder was committed on a farm, and the body moved to that field. Can you double check soil and debris on the victim's shoes and clothing to see if we can pin the location down?

She switched off the computer and tapped out a text to Allan:

Hey. I'm leaving in 10. Your place or mine? xx

And another to Mum:

Hi mum. I'm seeing Allan tonight. Shall I come round for tea tomorrow? All ok. Hope you are too. Janey x

***

The tyres rumbled as Ross drove slowly along the cobbled street. He parked up a few yards from the Feathers and stared at his phone.

All he had to do was make the call, fix a date for the interview, and maybe change his life. But something was holding him back.

He'd been thinking about it on the way here to pick Amy up at the end of her shift. It wasn't the fear of change. He'd always thrived on it. It was something Lorry had said, about making the most of being Jane's number two on the Cardale case.

He got out and leaned against the passenger door, pulling up his collar against the fine drizzle, and nodded at an ancient Feathers regular who was dragging on a cigarette as if it was life support.

What was it Lorry had said? Something about how things change when people think you're leaving—yes, that was it. He wanted to see the Cardale thing through, if only to show his experience on drugs cases. Going for an interview at the peak of the investigation would send the wrong signal to Jane, and maybe the NCA.

And the last thing he wanted was to let Jane down.

He put the phone back in his inside pocket just as Amy opened the door. She walked up to the car, her heels clicking loudly on the rough flagstones, now gleaming in the glow from streetlamps. 'Hi, landlord!'

'Good evening, tenant. Ready to go?'

Amy put a hand on his arm. 'The boss has asked if I could do an extra half hour, just to cover because someone's running late.' Ross groaned. 'But... he says there's a free pint in it for you.'

Ross pushed himself upright. 'Come on then. Let's not waste any more time.'

***

'My turn to do the catering.'

Jane put her bag on a black leather chair and watched Allan unwrap a ready meal.

'I can't believe how neat and tidy your kitchen is.'

'It's easy to keep it clean when you never do any messy cooking. I live off food made in factories by complete strangers, and I can't remember the last time I washed the pots.'

Jane stood beside him. 'Prawn linguine. I like your style.'

'Because we're worth it.'

'Yeah, right.' She sat down and sipped water. 'How was your day?'

Allan set the microwave timer and put plates in the warming drawer. 'Uneventful. But improving by the minute. You?'

'The opposite. We're close to cracking the case. I think.'

Allan sat down and unscrewed a bottle of Pinot. 'Cardale?'

Jane nodded as he poured the wine. 'Yeah. I'm convinced a woman did it. But I can't prove it; I'm not sure which woman, and there's the small matter of working out why.'

'But apart from that...?'

Jane laughed.

'No obvious motive, then?'

'Well, the victim was a dealer, so the most obvious reason is that he was on someone else's turf.'

'Yeah, I can see that. We know from our contact with the police that drugs are a big issue now. Jenny, the editor of the Ashbridge paper, did a piece a couple of weeks ago saying that they reckon about half of all murders and a third of robberies and burglaries are drugs related. Scary stuff.'

Jane sipped her wine. It was already helping her relax. 'Yeah, it's grim. But come on, let's talk about us. What's the plan?'

Allan frowned and rubbed his hands together. She'd always had that ability to put him on the spot, needing to come up with the right answer. 'Oh. Well, I reckon you know how I feel. Erm... I'd like us to get back together again.'

She stroked his hand. 'I worked that bit out. Me too. But where? Do you want us to live here? I wouldn't complain, but it might not be quite so neat and tidy by the time I've moved in.'

He laughed and jumped up to turn off the microwave. 'I've got this on a rolling six-month contract, so we could live here. But to be honest, I miss our place. It's a proper house—a proper home, know what I mean? We could use this as a retreat until the contract runs out, couldn't we?'

Jane winked. 'Love that idea. Our posh weekend retreat... But that terraced house is a bit basic for a company director with a swanky car.'

'Rude.' Allan dished up the meal. 'Anyway, now you mention it, a posh place like this is a bit above DCI level, isn't it?'

'Even ruder. So, come on, do you want to move back in with me?'

He put his fork down. 'I'd like that more than anything in the world.'

'Final answer?'

'Final answer.'

Jane leaned in and kissed him so quickly he didn't have time to react. 'I've missed you.'

'I've missed you too, lots. And I promise I won't mess up this time.'

Jane shook her head. 'What matters is that if we mess up, we're strong enough to get through it. I think that was our problem. We expected too much. We should be able to mess up and it's not the end of the world.' She smiled wistfully. 'That's something Charles Aston told me once.'

Allan reached out to take her hand. 'He was right... I sometimes think I'm like that at work. Demanding perfection. Expecting everyone to be spot on all the time.'

'Me too. And then when I get it wrong, I can't understand why people don't cut me any slack.' She stopped, lost in thought.

'What is it?'

'What? Oh, it's nothing. Something you said, just struck a chord...'

Allan took their empty plates to the dishwasher. 'So, it made you remember something?'

'Yeah. Something that occurred to me right back at the beginning.'

'Now you've lost me. You mean Cardale?'

'Yes. It's been a nightmare of a case. So many angles, connections, you know?' Allan mumbled something unintelligible as he topped up the dishwasher salt. Jane carried on, oblivious. 'Maybe it's not that complicated after all...'

***

Phil bagged the last of the soil samples and handed the padded envelope to the courier, who was travelling incognito with the help of a hoodie over a baseball cap.

'Thanks for waiting. Quick as you can, please.'

He sat at his desk and blinked a few times. His eyes felt raw, his back ached, and he was desperate for sleep. He'd got the job done, but it should have been done already. He'd been worrying all day. He'd never had to be told to be thorough before. Was he finally losing it?

He checked his Casio watch. 21:35.

That watch had been on his wrist since he was a teenager. He remembered his mum taking him to a jeweller's shop on the high street and telling him he could choose one for his birthday.

It struck him that he could remember events from so long ago but forget to do the basics at work. He'd read up on short-term memory loss and knew it was usually just a sign of ageing, lack of sleep and stress. He'd almost laughed as he realised he could tick all those boxes. But it could also be a sign of dementia.

Phil stood to stretch his back, but the sudden movement left him lightheaded, and he tottered back against the wall. He breathed deeply, trying to shake it off, but it felt as if the room was moving.

He put out a hand to steady himself on the desk, but he missed and lost his balance.

He remembered the sensation of falling, and then there was only darkness.

33.

The wind was gusting at fifty mph and the first drops of rain tapped loudly on the window. According to the *Edinburgh Evening News*, it was going to be like this for the next couple of days.

Gloria MacDonald drew the heavy floral curtains closed and turned up the gas fire.

She'd always loved Scotland, but it was wearing a bit thin. As if the weather wasn't bad enough, the SNP seemed to be going to war with everything English. The poisonous atmosphere was engulfing everyone, polarising opinion, splintering families. Gloria had little respect for the prime minister, and not much more for the first minister. Her view was that Scottish politicians were as bad as any in Westminster, and she was yet to be convinced that achieving independence would benefit anyone, except perhaps the English.

She hated conflict. She'd always shied away from it, and she put that down to her clever husband and the equally voluble Mary, who seemed to disagree enthusiastically about everything. They were so quick-witted, too.

She put the newspaper on the sofa and picked up the letter. The compensation was settled at last. It was just a question of when the money would come through.

The prospect of becoming a millionaire meant nothing. She had a strong sense of guilt that not only did Mary's life have an arbitrary value attached to it, but that she was accepting it.

The initial anger had been fierce enough to obliterate other emotions. The grief only took hold after the celebration service in Cardale, but it reached another level when she watched Mary being lowered into the ground at the funeral in Edinburgh.

That was when the anger turned to sorrow. She was sorry for herself because she'd lost a daughter, and for the farmer whose one moment of negligence was responsible. Ever since, she'd been preoccupied by the randomness of it all—that so much can change because of one moment.

Another blast of air rattled the window and she shivered.

Mary's death had changed her. She told a friend that she felt like a stranger in her own home, let alone in Edinburgh—like she didn't belong anymore. More accurately, like she didn't *want* to belong.

She'd thought about investing the money in something meaningful: a donation to charity, perhaps. Mary had always been an animal lover and there were so many abandoned pets these days. But she knew what Mary would say. In fact, she could hear her saying it in her loud, laughter-infused voice: '*Oh, Mum! Grab the dosh. Make the most of it!*'

Gloria leaned back against the squashy cushion to rest her head, and let the memories wash over her: Mary sitting close on the sofa, like she did after school, clutching a glass of milk in her little dimpled hand; skipping beside her all the way to the park; trying not to cry when she fell off her bike… They'd always been so close.

Gloria opened her eyes.

She switched on her tablet and tapped out a search: *property for sale Cardale.*

***

Jane was leaning back against Allan's chest, her eyes closed while he stroked her hair. Then the call came through.

Minutes later, Allan was driving her to hospital. They hurried down the corridor, pulling face masks on, to find Phil sitting up in bed with a cup of tea, looking perfectly relaxed.

'Oh! Nice to see you both. Not seen you for a while, Allan.'

Jane couldn't decide whether to hit him or hug him. Instead, she gave him a reproachful look. 'You scared the life out of me, Phil.'

'I know. I'm sorry. I don't know what happened. But I'm okay now.'

Jane turned to look at the nurse, who was updating his notes on a clipboard.

She smiled. 'He's doing fine, but we're keeping him in for observation.'

Jane took Allan to one side. 'Can you sit with him for a minute while I have a word?'

She walked to the nurses' station at the other end of the ward. 'What happened, do we know?'

'His blood pressure was extremely low, and we want to do more tests.' The nurse checked the records on her screen. 'His blood oxygen level is down, and he's got all the signs of being under-nourished.' She looked up. 'He lives alone, I take it?'

Jane nodded. 'Is he going to be all right?'

'I'm sorry, but the consultant will have to review him tomorrow, and we'll take it from there. All I can say is that he's stable and we'll put him on a feed line to try and build up his strength.' Her eyes crinkled as she smiled. 'Leave him with us, love. We'll look after him.'

Jane tried to keep her voice steady. 'I know you will, thank you.'

***

Sid watched from the upstairs window as Julie put two big suitcases in the boot and slammed the lid down.

She stretched her back and zapped the remote, then walked slowly to the field gate and stood with her back to the house.

Sid turned back to his desk. According to the solicitor, the house sale would be completed in less than a month. All he had to do was sign the land sale paperwork and he'd have a couple of million in his pocket.

He read through it again, searching for any clues that might suggest a stitch-up. He knew from his days at the bank how easy it was to manipulate the wording just enough to give yourself a loophole. Then you could cheerfully tear up the agreement and walk away.

No way was Alistair Grant going to do that to him. Sid started reading again, then stopped. A car was pulling up outside. He looked out.

It was a police car. But where was Julie? Her car was still there. She must have seen it coming.

He hurried downstairs as the doorbell chimed. A young guy in a suit held up a badge that was impossible to read. 'Good morning, sir. DC Eric Sykes, Ashbridge Police. We have a warrant to search the farm. Would you mind staying in the property with my colleague?'

He waved over a uniform who looked about fifteen. Sid nodded, and DC Sykes continued. 'Thank you, sir. It won't take long. We'll just take a look at the farm buildings first.'

The schoolboy in a uniform nodded at him to go back inside.

Eric tiptoed carefully round the muddy yard and leaned back to heave open a barn door that was at least eight-foot high. He blinked to adjust to the darkness and saw faint streaks of light coming through the gaps in the corrugated walls.

In one corner, a few bales of hay had been stacked up. To his left, what looked like a vintage tractor and an assortment of metal barrels and big plastic containers.

Then a woman's voice: 'Looking for something, officer?'

He didn't see her at first. She was standing in the opposite corner, almost camouflaged against some rolls of dark sheeting.

Eric took a few steps towards her and saw a rack of farm implements to her left. There was a rake, a scythe, various spades and shovels, an axe. And a hay fork.

Eric felt his heart beat a little faster but kept his voice calm. 'Can I ask you to wait for me outside, ma'am? I have a search warrant.'

She moved towards him. 'What on earth for?'

'I'd be grateful if you could go to the farmhouse and wait there for me. Thank you. It won't take long.'

He watched her all the way into the house, then jogged over to the hay fork, wrapped it in plastic from his backpack, then phoned in.

George didn't hesitate. 'Well done, young man. Bring them both in, right now.'

Back at the house, he asked if someone could open the car that was parked outside. Julie unlocked it and watched as he opened the boot.

'Are you going away, ma'am?'

'Yes. I'm leaving my husband, if you must know.'

Eric tried to look sympathetic. 'Sorry, but you and your husband need to come to the station with us, please.'

34.

'Could someone just tell me what this is about?'

Ross held up a hand. 'Just bear with us, Mr Marsh. We need to talk to you in connection with an item we found on our search today.'

Sid looked at Julie. 'What the hell is he talking about? Do you know?'

Julie tried to shut him up with a look, but that didn't work so she shook her head, then stopped as Jane walked into the room.

Jane nodded as she sat down. 'I need to inform you that this is an investigation into the murder of Keith Castle. We found an item at your farm today, and we'd like to question you in relation to—'

'Are we under arrest, or what?'

'Not yet, Mr Marsh. You are helping us with our enquiries, but—well, let's put it this way: if you decide not to help us, I may have to change my mind. So, are you happy to answer some questions at this stage?'

Julie nodded as she glared at Sid. 'Yes, of course we are.'

Jane noted the contrast between them. Sid, indignant, but giving the impression he had no idea what was going on. Julie, outwardly calm, but holding herself rigidly. She produced a photograph from her folder.

'Recognise this?'

Julie reacted first. 'Well, yes. I do believe it's a hay fork.'

Jane smiled. She welcomed the sarcasm. Any response was a win at this stage. 'We found it in your barn today, behind some sheets of landscape fabric. Bit unusual, hiding it away like that.'

Julie sighed. 'Right. What is this about? Why would you even think we were hiding a hay fork? What possible reason—'

She stopped and looked at Sid.

Jane spoke quietly. 'Go on, Julie. Why do you think the hay fork might be important to us?'

Julie shook her head and spoke under her breath. 'You stupid, stupid...'

'Who's stupid, Julie?'

Sid clapped his hands in mock applause. 'She means me. She always was a great performer. What she's trying to do is make you think I hid the fork because I'm guilty.'

'Guilty of what, Mr Marsh?'

'Killing Keith Castle. That's what you're getting at, right? One of us killed him with that hay fork.'

Jane turned to Ross and raised her eyebrows. 'I've heard enough already. Sidney and Julie Marsh, I am arresting you on suspicion of the murder of Keith Castle.' Neither of them met her eye as she gave them the caution, then advised them of their right to legal representation and told them they would be interviewed separately.

She stopped on her way out, as Ross held the door open.

'Can I remind you this is a murder investigation and both of you are under caution? I recommend that you tell us everything. One of our officers will take you to separate rooms now. You can make a phone call. We'll give you time to think about what you want to say. Please use it wisely.'

Back in her office, Jane drank from her water bottle as Ross went off to make coffee.

Julie's behaviour was puzzling her. It seemed unnatural, staged. She was stiff with tension, her shoulders hunched. On the other hand, Sid's anger seemed genuine: righteous indignation, as her mum would call it. Their reactions to the hay fork suggested both were involved in some way, but were they in it together, or was one of them—or both—innocent?

She finished off the water—that was her one litre a day ticked off. It helped keep her head clear. She had the feeling she was going to need it.

Ross tapped on the door, and Claire followed him in.

'Oh, hi Claire, thanks for coming. Ross, could you give us a minute?' He nodded and closed the door gently. 'Sit down, Claire. This isn't easy. You know about Phil?' Claire nodded, trying to stay composed. 'Well, he's doing okay, but he's not coming back for a while. So, how would you feel about stepping up?'

Claire put a hand up to her mouth, her eyes widening. 'Oh! Lead the team, you mean?'

Jane nodded. 'I know it's hard. You want to be loyal to Phil, and so do I, believe me, but we're at a critical stage in the investigation now. You've been close to it from the start, involved in every key incident. Plus, I trust you. We all do. It's temporary, till Phil comes back, so you don't need to feel even a tiny bit guilty.'

Claire took a deep breath and cleared her throat. She smiled. 'Thank you so much. I don't know what to say. But, yes, please! I'd love to have a go at it.'

'Good. You'll be great. But if you're unsure at any time, just talk to me. I'm always here for you.' She winked. 'And to be honest, I rather like the idea of another woman in charge of a team. So, any questions?'

'I was thinking about Marsh Farm. Now we've got them in custody, shall I go out and do a forensic search? Soil samples, too?'

Jane nodded. 'Yes—don't go alone, though; take Jag with you, okay? You've already got someone looking at the hay fork?'

'Yes, ma'am. Bloods, prints, residues, the lot. We should have something by the end of the day.'

'What about the eye makeup? We have a female suspect a few doors away, so easy enough to check for a match.'

Claire twisted her fingers together. 'Erm... would it be okay to check what she has in the house first? She could always say she'd been using a tester or something.'

'That's why you're running the team, Claire. I'll do the paperwork and sort out the salary right now, okay?'

Jane showed her to the door and watched her walk away. She moved like a model, her long red hair catching the light: very much a star in the making.

Jane sat at her desk, closed her eyes and whispered an apology to Phil, not that he could have heard it from his hospital bed three miles away: 'Sorry, Phil, but it's only till you get back.'

When she opened her eyes, she realised she'd instinctively crossed her fingers.

She gathered up her papers and headed off to talk interview tactics with Ross.

***

Peter Attrill lifted his head as the guard came in, smelling of mints. 'You've got a visitor, Peter. Come on.'

Maggie's first thought was that they must be feeding him well. She'd prepared herself for the shock of seeing him pale and gaunt. But as he walked into the visiting room, he looked like he'd been on holiday.

'You're looking well, Peter.'

'Not so bad. You look tired. Are you okay?'

'Oh, I'm fine. Just wanted to have a catch-up, you know.'

He smiled sardonically. 'I'm afraid I haven't got any news. Though, that's not quite true; I watch BBC News 24 all day.'

Maggie leaned forward, then sat back when she got a warning cough and a look from the young officer in the far corner. She spoke in a loud whisper. 'I wondered if you could tell me all about your secret mobile phone, and why Julie Marsh's number is on there.'

He kept still but his eyes were looking everywhere. She smiled, but it only made him more uncomfortable. 'Come on, Peter, I was sure you'd have an instant explanation. After all, you're quite good at hiding things from me, aren't you?'

'Maggie, I...'

She nodded and waited. 'Yes, dear?'

There was no mistaking the tone of her voice, and Peter was so taken by surprise he couldn't find words.

'Let me help you. Don't bother confirming or denying anything until I've finished.' Maggie spoke slowly, her voice growing louder. 'You and Julie have been working together on this drugs thing. She's your partner, isn't she? Knowing you, she's been doing the dirty work—getting the supplies, doing the deliveries—while you sat in your little headquarters upstairs, counting the money. All right so far?'

Peter gulped and bowed his head.

'I'll take that as a yes. That's all I needed to know.'

He looked up quickly as she pushed her chair back. 'Where are you going? What are you going to do?'

'I'm leaving you, of course. Don't think for a minute that I will stand by you after the way you've deceived me.' She stood over him, flicked a glance at the guard, who was staring at a blank wall, and shouted, 'I don't know what story you've spun, Peter, but I'm going to tell them what you've been up to. The truth. Have you ever heard of it?'

It felt like a release.

Peter shook his head, disbelieving. 'But—'

'But what? There are no buts. I made the mistake of believing you, but not anymore.'

The guard was paying full attention now. He moved nearer. She nodded an apology and started walking away, then turned.

'Goodbye, Peter. Keep watching the news. You might be on it soon.'

35.

Ross scribbled a note and looked into Sid Marsh's eyes. He'd interviewed lots of suspects and liked to think he had an instinct for sniffing out the guilty ones.

But Sid Marsh... He was different. Difficult to work out. He'd been an investment banker, and that suggested he could fix things, manipulate figures, play games. But he was coming over as an ordinary, genuine bloke.

He could be a great actor, but he didn't seem like your average killer. It wasn't just the way he was handling the questions; he looked too weedy to go around ramming hay forks into people.

The tape was off, and they both needed a break. Ross flicked back through his notes while Sid finished his tea.

Last saw Castle a couple of months ago. Drugs handover for cash at the pub. First met when he worked at the farm. A bit slow-witted but took a shine to Sid. Went for a pint a couple of times, Cardale; talk about London and drugs scene. Sid was occasional user. Everyone he worked with was. Castle became supplier, then prices went up. Sid complained. New supplier. Wife probably suspected but never said anything, till after fall/attack.

Julie mad as hell. She's strong enough to have done it, but reckons another druggie bumped him off.

Ross tapped on the paper. That was it, right there: was he trying to incriminate her to save himself?

Ross frowned. He'd been on a train of thought just then. It felt like a light had been switched on. Something that made sense. But the moment had gone. He told himself to trust that it would come back to mind. That's what his grandad used to say, anyway: '*We never really forget anything. It all gets stored up top for when you need it.*'

He leaned to his right and recited the time as he flicked the recorder back on. 'Right, Sid. We need to go into a bit more detail. You seem to be saying your wife could have done it...'

***

Jane had never enjoyed chess, but it felt like she was in the middle of a game.

Julie took an age to answer the simplest of questions, her eyes fixed on the table. Jane couldn't decide if it was natural caution or a deliberate attempt to wind down the clock and gain control. Allan used to shout at football teams that took their time over corner kicks or rolled around screaming after innocuous tackles. She now understood why they did it. It was all about disrupting the other team's rhythm.

Jane decided on a change of approach.

'When I look at you and Sid, it's obvious who's the strong one.'

Julie sat back and tried to look bored. 'Really.'

'It's not unusual. Men make all the noise, but women are the organisers, the decision-makers.'

'And your point is...?'

'No point. I just wonder if you agree with me.'

'Oh right. And I'm supposed to say 'yeah, you're right' and you come back at me accusing me of leading him on.'

Jane sat back. She'd taken the bait. 'Interesting you should say that. You weren't supposed to say anything, Julie, but now you mention it...' She sat up, hands clasped in front of her, waiting.

It was Julie's turn to be unnerved by the silence. She crossed her legs and turned in her seat to face the window. She was picking at the skin around a thumbnail.

Then she broke the silence. She looked close to tears, but she was fighting to keep control. 'Actually, you're wrong. Sid's the boss, always has been.'

Jane nodded. 'Go on, Julie. Tell me about him.'

'He's weak, devious...' She laughed harshly, then the words spilled out with barely a space between them. 'Why did I end up with him? God knows. He was alright once, back when he could turn on the charm, or the little boy act—anything to get what he wants.'

Jane interrupted. 'And he wanted you.'

Julie looked into her eyes for the first time. 'Oh yes. I was a looker.' She held out her hands. 'Hard to believe now—hands like a builder, and you should see my muscles... He loved showing me off at company events. Spent a fortune on me, and I enjoyed it. And then he had this idea of escaping to the countryside. It had always been a dream, he said. I didn't want to go, leave all my friends behind, but he was persuasive. We'd just set off on honeymoon and he told me he'd found a farm we could buy.

'It was our honeymoon, but he was on the phone all the time, fixing it, making the deal as he called it. It sounded exciting, and I gave in.'

'But it didn't quite work out.'

'You're damn right. It was a disaster. Everything that could go wrong did go wrong: the weather was bad, the fertiliser we used was wrong, he paid way over the odds for the farm, crops failed, you name it. And who do you think was doing all the hard work while he was sitting in his nice, warm upstairs room playing with spreadsheets?'

'Must have been tough.' Jane shook her head. 'And then you found out he was taking cocaine.'

Julie just nodded and sipped water. The torrent of words had dried up, for now.

Jane spoke for the tape: 'Interview suspended at fourteen thirty-five.' She stood. 'We'll take a short break. I'll be checking what Sid has been saying. When I come back, you need to tell me the whole story, Julie. This isn't going to end until you do; you know that, don't you?'

Julie turned away. Her voice was flat. 'Give my love to Sid. A cup of tea would be nice, thank you.'

***

Jane took her time on her way back to the office. She wanted to compare notes with Ross before planning the next round of questioning, but she felt sure they could make a breakthrough today.

Sid would bend under questioning from Ross. He could get anyone talking. The issue was how far they'd go to protect or blame each other. It was a great way to muddy the water. Their stories could have been carefully rehearsed. Either way, it would be difficult to get to the truth.

But something told her they held the key to everything that had happened in Cardale.

She stopped at the dispenser outside CID and gulped a cupful of ice-cold water. Ross jogged up the corridor, slightly out of breath.

'Mrs Attrill has just turned up at the front desk, ma'am. Says she knows who killed Keith Castle, and why.'

36.

Maggie paced round the interview room with growing impatience. They'd told her she might have to wait, but she'd been stuck there nearly half an hour. There wasn't even a window to look out of, the coffee was like stewed bitumen, and the room was only four paces by four.

She'd had so much time to think about what she wanted to say, but it was getting blurred as the implications sank in. And all this waiting was jangling her nerves, as if she hadn't been through enough...

The soles of her trainers squeaked on the vinyl floor as she walked, trying to regulate her breathing, trying to hold on to the central point, the reason she was doing this: it was the right thing to do.

She stopped and turned as the door opened.

'DCI Jane Birchfield. Hello, Maggie.'

'Finally...'

'Yes, sorry. Please, sit down. You have some information, I'm told.'

***

Jane thanked Ross as he handed her a coffee, then leaned back in her chair and stretched. She ached from sitting in uncomfortable plastic chairs, but Ross looked fresh as always.

'Okay, Ross, let's review where we are. You first. What's your thinking based on what you've heard from Sid, and now Maggie?'

'I don't believe either of them, ma'am, though I'd be more inclined to accept what Sid says, to be honest.'

'Okay... go on.'

'I can't see him killing anyone. With all due respect, he's a bit of a weed, you know what I mean?'

Jane choked slightly on her coffee and put the mug down. 'Was that a drug reference?'

'It wasn't, no.' Ross smiled apologetically. 'It just makes me more likely to believe him when he says he knows nothing about it. But he was dropping big hints about how strong his wife is. Planting ideas in my mind... Maybe he suspects her but is frightened to come out and say it. He did say that she probably suspected he was taking drugs but hadn't said anything till he was in hospital. I reckon she did know.'

He stopped and sipped coffee. 'Listening to Maggie Attrill, it made me wonder what she's trying to do. Why try to stitch her own husband up? She's got no evidence that he killed Castle. I reckon she's just paying him back for having it off with Julie Marsh.'

Jane held up a hand. 'That sounds reasonable, Ross. But we have no evidence they were even in a relationship. So, what's your theory?'

Ross puffed out his cheeks. 'Julie did it.'

'Okay, why?'

'She was mad as hell because her life was being ruined by Sid's drug habit. She blamed Castle. Castle came to the farm to meet Sid, and she killed him.'

Jane checked her computer screen. 'Claire says soil samples taken from his shoes suggest that Castle may have died at Marsh Farm, but it's not conclusive. Soil composition is uniform round there. Julie's prints on the hay fork, of course, but you'd expect that, and no trace of blood, so no luck there.'

Ross shook his head. 'She did it. She's the only one with the guts to do it. She's strong, and she had motive.'

'Hmm. What about Maggie? What if all that is a smokescreen? What if she knew early on what Attrill was up to? Castle could have destroyed their lives if he'd grassed on Peter. They're pillars of the Cardale community, so they had plenty to lose.'

'Yes, ma'am. But that would mean premeditation. And we reckon it was a spur-of-the-moment killing. The hay fork just happened to be there. I can't see Maggie leaving anything to chance if she was going to bump someone off.'

Jane felt the adrenaline kicking in. Ross was the perfect partner for a brainstorm, and she loved feeding off his energy.

She started writing as she spoke: 'Could Maggie have been following him or were they working together? Peter's a big bloke, so he could easily have moved Castle a few hundred yards. He owned the drill site, didn't he? Castle was buried on his land.'

'But Sid or Julie would have known, if this happened on their farm.'

'Not if they collared Castle before he got there. Attrill would surely have known who he was flogging coke to, and when.'

Jane picked up her coffee, then froze. Ross waited. He watched her; her eyes were bright and unblinking.

'What is it, ma'am?'

'What are we missing, Ross?'

***

Peter Attrill waited till George had opened his note-book.

'Thank you for coming so quickly.'

'That's okay. I love it here. And it's a nice change from unsolved burglaries and shoplifting. So, you said you wanted to make a statement?'

Peter nodded. 'Yes, I wanted to confess.'

George looked up. 'What to?'

'It was me who assaulted Sid Marsh that night.'

***

Jane got George's text just before she went into the interview room to face Sid and Julie Marsh. She held out her phone so Ross could read it.

He grinned. 'Hellfire! Who'd have guessed.'

Jane moved a few paces away from the door and lowered her voice. 'So now we know he's capable of violence...'

Ross leaned against the wall. Jane envied his ability to stay relaxed under pressure. 'Yes, but I can't see it—can you, ma'am?'

'Come on, let's see what the happy couple have got for us.'

They were sitting together on the same side of the table, but they could have been strangers. Julie, legs crossed, arms folded, staring straight ahead. Sid, slouching, turned slightly away from her.

Jane sat opposite Julie. Ross waited for her signal before switching on the recorder.

The room was so quiet Jane could hear Sid's sharp, shallow breathing.

She took her time, looking through her notes, before signalling Ross she was about to start.

'You remain under caution. You are being questioned in connection with the murder of Keith Castle. You have the right to legal representation at any time. Just say the word and we will pause the interview.'

Julie stared. 'I thought we were being interviewed separately.'

'We thought it might help to reunite you. You don't object, do you?'

Julie kept looking over Jane's shoulder, but Sid shuffled in his seat. Jane and Ross exchanged glances.

'Okay, so tell me when you found out that Sid was a drug addict?'

Sid sat up straighter but kept his eyes on the table. Julie shook her head. 'I don't know. I didn't make a note in my diary.' She sounded like an insolent child.

'I remember the first time I came round to see you both, after the tractor accident. I could hear you both arguing from outside. You were both clearly under stress back then. I reckon you'd known he was taking it for quite some time, hadn't you, Julie?'

She shrugged. 'Maybe.'

'But you never spoke about it, did you, Sid?'

He shook his head.

'For the tape, please.'

'No. I wasn't particularly proud of myself.'

'You were scared of what she might do, weren't you?'

'I knew she'd be upset. That's obvious, isn't it? Not rocket science.'

Ross sighed. 'Just answer the question and save the smart remarks, Sid. Were you scared?'

'Yes. A bit.'

Jane checked her notes. 'A bit, right. So, you thought you were keeping it a secret. Meanwhile, Julie was keeping a secret from you—weren't you, Julie?'

'What the hell are you talking about?'

'You complained about all the time Sid was in his room upstairs. But it was convenient for you because it meant you were free to come and go as you pleased. But you weren't always hard at work on the farm, were you?'

Julie rolled her eyes. 'Oh no, I must have gone shopping a few times... I confess, okay? Come on, just make your point, will you? This is getting tedious.'

'Sorry you find being a suspect in a murder case boring. Still, moving on... It's interesting that your name was the only first name on Peter Attrill's spare mobile phone: the one he has admitted he used to organise his little drug empire. It's quite a list of contacts, too. Amazing how many villagers were users. Going to keep us busy for a while. So...' Jane paused, holding Julie's gaze. 'Did you tell Sid you were a runner for Peter Attrill, or was that your little secret?'

Sid jerked into life as if he'd been electrocuted. He turned to face her. 'What? Julie?'

Ross took over. 'So, Sid, are you telling us you didn't know that some of the cocaine you were taking had been delivered to Castle and the others in Attrill's little network by your own wife?'

Sid looked numb. His shoulders slumped again. Julie was expressionless.

Ross carried on. 'It was all very cosy in Cardale, wasn't it, Julie? You even started delivering to young Rob Simmons, your one-time tractor driver. His life had been wrecked by the accident. He was a vulnerable young man, living with his mum, but you and Peter saw an opportunity to rope him in. Looks like pretty much the whole village was getting dependent on the pair of you. You were quite a team.'

Jane leaned forward. 'By the way, Rob is in the nick awaiting sentence, so well done for destroying him again. And do feel free to stop us any time if you think we're wrong, won't you...?' She waited, but Julie maintained a defiant stare.

Jane nodded at Ross: 'Looks like we're on the right lines, DS Rossiter.' Ross grinned, and Jane continued. 'Keith Castle saw how well it was all going. He wanted a bit more of the action... God knows how much money you were raking in. He wanted more, didn't he? And so—'

'All right! Shut up!' Julie's shout made all three of them jump. 'Just... leave it, will you?' She sat upright and scraped the hair off her face. 'Okay, I'll tell you.'

37.

The old boys were lined up at the bar, but the dining room at the Frog and Firkin was empty as usual, apart from the table by the little bay window.

Gloria MacDonald smiled and held out her hand. 'Nice to see you again. May I call you Jane?'

'Of course. Thanks for the invitation. I didn't expect to see you again. You said on the phone you were having a house built in the village?'

Gloria nodded. 'Yes, close to where Mary's house was. It felt... right, somehow. I didn't feel I belonged in Edinburgh anymore.' She laughed. 'The people in the village think it's a spooky thing to do, coming here.'

Jane nodded. 'I expect they do. But they're not the best judges, are they?'

Gloria gave her a sad smile. 'Not really. From what I've been reading in the press, they think it should be called Cokedale, don't they?'

Jane waited as Gloria poured white wine into her glass. 'Yes, but that will pass, don't worry. You'll be fine. We've broken up the network, and we're keeping a close eye on the place. No drug dealer is going to want to touch Cardale.'

Gloria sipped wine. 'There are people in Edinburgh who hand it round as cheerfully as if it was a box of Quality Street.'

They laughed and Jane leaned back in her chair, grateful for the chance to relax for an hour.

Gloria was chatty. 'I took the liberty of ordering salads. The landlord tells me it's all local farm produce. But while we're waiting, I wanted to thank you. You promised me you'd find out what happened to Mary, and you did.'

'The Marshes admitted liability. It was their negligence that caused the tractor to veer into the house.'

Gloria dabbed her lips with a napkin. 'I know. So cruel that it should happen at that moment. If it had just run into a field or something...'

'I know. None of this would have happened. I'm so sorry...' Gloria turned to look out of the window. Jane felt it was her turn to talk. 'But then we had a murder to solve... It was all about drugs in the end, though it was hard to believe, somewhere like Cardale. The victim was a dealer who wanted more of a cut. The next person up in the chain wasn't having it.'

'Peter Attrill. I met him, in here. I found him unnerving.'

'Yes. It got complicated. He wanted to keep himself clean by using someone else to do his dirty work.'

'That would be that good-looking woman who lived at Marsh Farm: Julie?'

'Yes.'

'I was astonished. I remember you talking about connections, but I never thought the Marshes would be involved in both events.' She sipped wine, just as a girl arrived with their salads. 'After we've eaten, you must tell me how you worked it all out.'

***

The official statement was that Julie Marsh had confessed to the murder of Keith Castle, and that she did it because his drug dealing was ruining Sid's life, and their marriage. Greater Manchester wanted to keep Attrill out of it for now because the NCA was still hoping they could use him to lead them to the next link in the supply chain.

George had persuaded Jane to talk as he and Ross sat in her office after Julie confessed. He'd passed round the wine gums, then popped the question: 'How did you work it out, boss?'

She'd told them: 'It's been a bit like playing a board game for the first time. Everyone else is playing better. They know what they're doing. You've read the rules, over and over, but it doesn't help. Then, without thinking too hard, you understand. You see why that person made that move or made that choice. You can't explain why, but something just clicks.'

She went through it again with Allan that night. Too wired to sleep, she was at his flat, talking into the early hours. It felt like a kind of therapy.

She kicked off her shoes and leaned back on the G Plan sofa. Allan massaged her feet.

'Mmm... That feels good. It's all thanks to you, you know.'

He looked dubious. 'Come off it. How?'

'Remember when we chatted after dinner that night, talking about changing our ways? You said you were always demanding perfection, expecting everyone to be spot on all the time.'

'Yeah, that sounds like me.'

'I said I'm the same, and yet when I get it wrong, I can never understand why people don't cut me any slack.'

Allan looked puzzled. 'Yeah, so?'

'It struck a chord when I remembered the first time I met Sid and Julie, and it came back to me when I was interviewing them for the final time. Sid had fouled up big time – the farm project was a disaster, and he was under pressure, so he revived his coke habit. Julie was clearly the organiser—the perfectionist—and couldn't cut him any slack. It ate into her, so much that she couldn't let it go.

'I felt from the start that everything that had happened in Cardale was connected. There were so many strong women involved; it had to be something to do with them. The forensics confirmed it.'

Allan still looked puzzled. 'So, it was just a feeling?'

'An instinct. I was thrown off track when we found out that Julie was secretly working for Peter. It was a stupid thing to do, but she was trying to keep the cash coming in: Marsh Farm was losing money big time.

'Then Peter confessed to assaulting Sid. He thought if he owned up to that it might send us off down a blind alley. But Claire rechecked all the forensics and is a hundred per cent certain Sid just fell in that ditch under the influence of drink and drugs.'

'Sounds like a pretty naff attempt to mislead you.'

Jane smiled. 'Yeah. He's made a pile of money, so he's no fool. I think he got too smug, thought he was immune.'

'But you're saying he was the brains behind the murder of Castle.'

'Yes, he knew Castle had been stirring things up. Usual discontent, thinking he's doing all the hard graft while Attrill takes the biggest share of the cash. Attrill wasn't having anyone muscling in, and he manipulated Julie.'

'How?'

'Something like this: "Castle is not only feeding your husband's drug habit, but he also wants a bigger share of the pot, which will mean less for you, dear Julie." The straw that broke the camel's back came in the hay barn at Marsh Farm...'

Allan groaned. 'Jane, it's two in the morning. I can't cope with bad jokes.'

'Sorry... Above all else, Julie was raging inside about Sid ruining his own life, and hers. She admitted it had been building up for months. Then she heard him arguing with Castle in the barn. Castle was trying to blackmail Sid into helping him force Peter Attrill to give them a bigger cut of the cash. He said he'd expose Sid if he didn't help.

'Much to her disgust, Sid rolled over and said he'd do it, and they decided to confront Attrill. Sid walked away to get the car out of the garage. He had to drive because Castle kept fit by running everywhere.'

Allan laughed. 'The original drug runner...'

'Ha! Yeah. And while Sid was out of the way, Julie— with Attrill's words fresh in her mind—went into the barn, grabbed the nearest weapon she could find—'

'The hay fork.'

'—and killed Castle from behind. She claims she completely lost it, but she had the presence of mind to drag the body into the hay to hide it. Sid comes back. No sign of Castle. Assumes he changed his mind. Goes to the house.'

'But Sid was arrested too. Why, if he had nothing to do with it?'

'I told you it was complicated... Later that night, he's in his office upstairs. Hears the door shut. Thinks Julie must have gone out. He looks out of the window.'

'No! He saw her moving the body!'

'Yes, bang on. He watched her push it out of the yard in a wheelbarrow, arms and legs hanging out.'

'My God... So, he kept quiet, and that was his offence.'

'You could say that. But get this...' Jane swung her legs round so she could sit up straight. 'He never told Julie he'd seen her.'

'What? I'm getting lost here. So, she didn't know he knew? Wow! That is just... I mean—what kind of a marriage did they have?'

Jane reached for his hand. 'They kept things buried.'

'Was that another joke in poor taste?' Allan gave her one of his endearingly mournful looks. 'How could they even stay together, after all that? How could they live a normal life? The atmosphere must have been poisonous.'

Jane sighed. Her eyes were stinging with tiredness now. She reached for a glass of water. 'It certainly was. Julie left him once, soon after. She said she wanted to get away for a few days after the tractor accident, but that was bollocks. She'd built up a nice bank balance thanks to her part-time job as a drug runner. She intended to leave him for good. She had friends in Islington. She was hoping to disappear completely, start a new life.

'She only came back because we called her and told her Sid was in hospital. She didn't dare keep away because of the message that would send out. She had to go on playing the poor wife for a bit longer. She was very good at playacting, but the strain of hiding the truth eventually broke her. I wonder if we'd ever have nailed her if she'd stayed in London.'

She leaned back, lost in thought. 'I wonder if we'd have got her to confess at all if she hadn't been totally worn down by the deception. You could see the pain, even at the start. It was there, written all over her, only I couldn't see it at first. Sid's confession that he knew she'd done it just about finished her off. They were both wrecks by the end of the interview.'

Allan held her hand. 'They'll never get over it. What's that expression? *Oh, what a tangled web we weave, when first we practice to deceive*... Anyway, supersleuth, you're being too modest, as usual. She owned up because she knew you'd worked it out. Your amazing intuition has done it again.'

'Well, maybe, but only up to a point. Ross and I had got it in our heads that she was acting alone. We never thought for a minute that Attrill was behind it.' Jane shook her head. 'God, what a bloody mess.'

Allan yawned and slumped back on the sofa. 'Can we go to bed now, miss?'

Jane laughed and shuffled across to lean on him. She rested her head on his chest. He stroked her hair, and her eyes began to feel heavy.

38.

'Ross! I didn't know you cared.'

'Shut it and drink.'

Lorry winked and sipped her coffee as Ross did a slow circuit carrying over-filled mugs on a tray that was too small.

'There you go, Eric... Jag... George.'

George raised his mug. 'Here's to us, boys and girls. I propose a toast, to the top team.'

They stood and echoed the toast, and Ross gave Lorry an encouraging smile.

She nodded and cleared her throat. 'Okay, guys. I've been putting this off, but I've got some news for you.'

George spoke through a mouthful of ginger biscuit. 'It's all right, Lorry, don't look so bloody nervous. When's it due?'

Ross laughed. 'Told you.'

Lorry sat down heavily. 'How long have you known?'

'It's been obvious for a while, luv. Congratulations.'

Eric hesitantly put a small parcel on her desk, blushing slightly. 'Yeah, well done—I mean, congratulations Loretta.'

'Oh, Eric...! You shouldn't have.'

'No, you shouldn't have,' George grumbled. 'Showing us up.' He winked at Lorry. 'My gift is in the post, honest.'

Lorry looked across the room. Jag was staring into space. 'You okay, Jag?'

'Oh yes, yes. I was thinking how nice it is to be back. Then I started remembering how I felt when Aarav was due. We were so happy.' He cleared his throat. 'I am happy for you and Mark. But also sad, wondering what you will do. Will you be leaving us?'

Lorry shook her head, showing a certainty she didn't feel. 'No way. I'll be back as soon as I can.'

***

Jane forced herself to drink the cup of Darjeeling that Roy Cooke put in front of her.

He was in high spirits, and Jane was suspicious. He'd bragged at length about winning the police squash tournament at the weekend, but she was sure there was something else.

'Well, Jane, what can I say about Cardale? You've done it again. Congratulations.'

'Thanks, Roy. It's always a team effort, and I'm grateful to you.'

'What for?'

'Giving me the time and freedom to work on it. I need that space to get my brain into gear. I'm always liable to take a wrong turn if I'm in a rush.'

'Bit like my driving, then.'

She smiled. 'Anyway, you know... thanks.'

Roy leaned back and steepled his fingers. It made him look like a teacher, and it always annoyed her. 'I bumped into the boss earlier.'

She sipped the last of the tea and put the cup back in its saucer gratefully.

'He was asking about you. Mentioned he'd promised to get in touch when an opportunity came up at HQ.'

Jane sat up straighter. 'Sir?'

He smiled. 'He wants you to go and see him tomorrow, ten o'clock.'

***

Rob Simmons looked ten years older, but he greeted Ross cheerfully enough, walking him through the narrow hall to the small kitchen at the back.

The enamel sink was half full of sudsy water, and clean dishes were stacked on the wooden worktop. Outside, Ross could see a washing line bending under the weight of a long row of jeans, skirts and shirts.

He accepted the invitation to sit at the old table. 'Your mum keeping you busy then?'

Rob nodded. 'Yeah. She's upstairs, having her afternoon nap.'

'My grandad used to have naps. As he got older, they got longer. Is she okay?'

'The doctor comes round now and again to check her over. He says I can't expect her to go on much longer.'

'Sorry, mate. So, what about you. Not easy for you, is it?

'No, I'm all right. Just glad I listened to you. Cleared up all the stupid stuff.'

'And that suspended sentence means you've got to be squeaky clean. Good motivation.'

Rob waited for the kettle to boil then poured the water into a big brown teapot. He grabbed biscuits from a glass jar and put the plate down between them with a smile. 'I know how much you like these.'

Ross gave him a thumbs up. 'Shortbread? Excellent choice.'

'Do you think I'll get any grief because I talked?'

'Not a chance. We've got uniforms all over the place, and the National Crime Agency are working their magic on that slimeball Attrill. Word is he's already naming names. So, if anyone is feeling nervous, it's going to be him. You can relax.'

Rob poured the tea and glanced nervously at Ross. 'You remember I told you his nickname, The Milkman?'

'Yeah. That was a big help.'

'Well, I was thinking of starting a round in Cardale. I know a farmer with a herd of Jerseys, and he's put me onto the processing plant in Ashbridge. I just need to find a vehicle. What do you think?'

'Brilliant move... You should do it. And don't forget to put me on your list when you branch out into Ashbridge, okay?'

***

Ross drove slowly for once.

The NCA job interview was scheduled for next week, but Jane was still pushing him to go for the rank of DI. It was so tempting, and flattering, too.

Ashbridge CID wouldn't be the same without Lorry. He was willing to bet she wouldn't come back to work after maternity leave. And what about George? He was the DI. No way would Roy Cooke pay for two of them on the same level. But Jane was encouraging him to go for the promotion. Was she expecting George to retire? He'd been threatening it for long enough...

He stopped the car at the viewpoint—better known locally as Lovers Layby—and looked across the valley.

Cardale looked so perfect from here, with its church tower, thatched roofs and the spirals of smoke from garden bonfires.

***

Allan was at the door, bearing gifts. He shook the rain off his coat and put the carrier bag on the doormat in the front porch.

'You've been shopping? On a Friday? Are you mad?'

'Now, don't be like that. I bring fine wine and smelly cheese.'

'You'd better come in then.'

They were on the second glass of Pinot Noir and Jane was enthusiastically devouring Saint Agur on wheat crackers, when Allan said, 'So, I was thinking...'

'Oh, don't do that.'

'No, this is serious. This is a celebration of you cracking the Cardale case—'

'C, c, c...'

'Yes, very good, señora. And getting that promotion you've deserved for so long.'

'Allan... I haven't accepted it yet.'

'But you will, won't you?'

Jane stacked the plates in the sink. 'Come on, let's get the fire on and chill out.'

'Right. Interesting use of words.'

Jane elbowed him. 'Oh, stop being a journalist. Sit down and listen.'

She sat next to him and put a hand on his knee. 'I've decided I won't accept the promotion if it is going to make life harder for us. I know how you used to hate being here on your own so much, and there's every chance I'll be out more: travelling to meetings, late nights, you know what it's like.' She took his hand in hers and held it to her cheek. 'You mean too much to me. I don't want anything to come between us, Allan.'

Allan put his wine glass down. 'I promise you on my life that nothing will come between us again. I'm older and a tiny bit wiser now. Anyway, I've got far more commitments than I ever had, so I'm busy, too. What I mean is that I want you to take the promotion, if you want it. Take it, without any worries, because we'll be okay, whatever happens.'

He leaned in tentatively and kissed her gently, slowly, on the lips. 'I love you, Jane.'

39.

Sid Marsh hit 'send' and pushed back into his reclining desk chair.

He was on bail for what his solicitor described as a wish list of offences, including use of illegal drugs, wilful obstruction and failure to report a crime. She'd reassured him, 'They're covering all their bases because they don't know what to do. They need you as a witness to make the case against Julie stick. So, sit tight and leave it with us.'

Sitting tight was easy enough. He hadn't left the house for a week. He couldn't come to terms with the fact that he and Julie had deceived each other for so long: her earning drugs money on the side, him carrying on after he saw her pushing that man's body into the field.

She'd called him a coward and she was right. He'd spent his life as a yes-man, too uptight to question dubious orders at the bank, too easily sucked into the cocaine circuit, and too frightened of losing Julie to confront her.

Now, she was in a cell, and he couldn't even bring himself to go and visit her.

He opened his Sent folder and read his last message again. The sale of the land to Alistair Grant had gone through. He'd achieved his dream of becoming a millionaire, but it meant nothing. He just wanted to give it away.

The email was to Felicity Crowther, confirming a donation of £100,000 to support the work of Strawberry Fields Forever. She'd told him they wanted to use the money to set up a community hub running workshops on environmental issues for adults and children, and that, despite everything, there would always be a place for him on the board of trustees.

She wrote: *Yours was the lone voice opposing the drilling at Cardale, and we would be delighted to welcome you.*

Sid wrote back to tell her he was happy to donate the money but that she didn't need that kind of publicity.

Cardale was certainly in the news. He'd just heard on the radio that Aaron Barrett had resigned as council leader after an inquiry was launched into the Universal Energy deal, and he'd also been bailed on drugs charges. Attrill was still locked away, and the local papers quoted the police as saying that there will be more arrests.

Sid heard a car door slam and looked out of the window. It was grey and misty and raining steadily. Someone in a high-vis jacket was tapping a 'sold' sign on the estate agent's board. Julie had been right. It was a quick sale, and they wanted to complete within a month.

It was time to move on. Sid poured himself another whisky and wondered whether he had the strength to do it.

***

Jane made lunch: scrambled eggs, a few scraps of smoked salmon she'd found in her mum's fridge and a couple of rounds of toast each.

Her mum was in good spirits, buoyed up by the news that she and Allan were getting back together. It was all she wanted to talk about. It felt like rapid fire on a rifle range.

'I knew you'd be all right. He's a good man. When are you bringing him round? Are you staying in that house? It's not too late to start a family...'

'Mum! We're not even living together yet.'

'Are you going to live at his place? Sounds lovely there. You must take me to see him. Better than your little terraced...'

Jane escaped to the kitchen and smiled as she slowly stirred the eggs, waiting for that key moment when they turned from mushy to marshmallow—another of her mum's little catchphrases she'd never be able to forget.

Allan loved her, that was clear. Told her she should be thankful she and her mum were so close again. He often got worked up about older people: 'It's easy to write them off, just because they're old. It's criminal the way we do that. All the experiences they've had, the struggles, the successes—when did we decide that old people should be pushed to one side?'

Jane put the slices in the toaster and thought about Mary's mother, Gloria, still glamorous in her early sixties, and still brave enough to leave Edinburgh to make a new start in Cardale. She'd already made friends with Maggie Attrill, according to Eric Sykes.

Brought together by mutual need... Was that what getting together with Allan was all about?

Jane spooned the eggs onto the toast and carried the plates into the dining room. Her mum nodded approvingly. 'Just right, dear, thank you.'

'You're welcome, Mum.'

They ate in silence. Jane sat back and dabbed her lips with a paper towel and decided to share her news.

'I've got an interview this afternoon, Mum.'

'A new job? Oh, that's lovely—you're not...?'

'No, it's only in Manchester. Assistant chief constable.'

'That sounds posh. What does it mean?'

Jane laughed. 'Good question. I'll find out at the interview.'

Mum frowned. 'I suppose it's more money and longer hours. You will be careful, won't you?'

'Careful?'

'Yes. Don't take on too much. Think about home life: Allan, children...'

'Mum, I'll be fine. I've talked about it with Allan, and he's happy. We'll make it work. We're both busy, but it's fine. It's what we both want. Anyway, I haven't got the job yet, so...'

Her mum patted her hand. 'Sorry, dear. I don't mean to be a wet blanket. I worry about you.'

***

Driving into Manchester, Jane suddenly felt nervous. The promotion had been on the cards for so long, she'd thought she'd got used to the idea.

She remembered her mum saying that life can be turned upside down by one event. In her case, it was meeting Dad and falling for him. She gave up her job to become a wife and mother.

It felt like the whole of Cardale changed forever when the Marshes' tractor crashed into Mary's house. It was a seemingly random act, but it had a cause— Sid's dependence on drugs—and many effects. In one moment, so many lives had been lost and broken.

Jane parked the car, shouldered her bag and walked slowly up the steps into Greater Manchester Regional HQ.

The big glass doors slid shut behind her.

She took a deep breath and smiled as the receptionist handed her an ID lanyard.

'They're ready for you, ma'am.'

40.

One month later...

Julie Marsh has admitted all charges and remains in custody.

Sid has moved into a flat in Ashbridge and is receiving support for alcohol addiction. He was offered a suspended sentence in return for appearing as a prosecution witness in Julie's trial but has told his solicitors he would rather take his punishment. Discussions are continuing.

Twenty-six Cardale residents are facing court appearances for drug offences.

Alistair Grant has submitted a revised application for the housing development at Marsh Farm. It will consist entirely of affordable homes, powered by sustainable energy. An office in the community facility at the centre of the development has been reserved for Strawberry Fields Forever.

A retired colonel has been elected chair of the renamed Cardale Association for Residents, which is almost united in its opposition to the housing development on the grounds it will make the village less desirable.

Maggie Attrill and Gloria MacDonald have become friends and jogging companions. They support the revised application and want to form a rival village group.

Rob Simmons's new enterprise is going well. He decided that calling it The Milkman could send out the wrong message. His electric van bears the sign 'Just Milk'. He wants to expand into Ashbridge and has advertised for another driver.

Ross turned down a job with the National Crime Agency. He was promoted to the rank of detective inspector at Ashbridge and is now leading the CID team. His first act was to promote Eric Sykes to acting detective sergeant.

George announced his retirement but agreed to work two months' notice to support Ross, on the grounds that 'It'll be better than watching Antiques Road Trip'.

He held a joint celebration with Forensic Phil, who has retired on medical advice and moved to northwest London to take up a part-time post as a lecturer in forensic investigation at Hendon Police College.

Claire has been appointed to head up the Ashbridge forensics team on a permanent basis.

Loretta Irons is on maternity leave. Her husband Mark has taken paternity leave. They have decided to call their baby daughter Laura Jane. Lorry has not decided whether she'll go back to work. She told Ross she wants to find out how she takes to motherhood first.

Jag has been signed off by his consultant and returned to full-time work. He has gained some vision in his damaged eye and is busy co-ordinating evidence in the Cardale drugs cases.

Jane has been appointed Assistant Chief Constable of Greater Manchester, with special responsibility for changing the culture of the force, and co-ordinating major investigations that cut across divisional boundaries, including the battle against drug gangs.

Roy Cooke is covering Jane's role as detective chief superintendent at Ashbridge, while they wait for a replacement. He and Ross play squash together, and he has acquired a taste for English Breakfast tea.

Jane has put her house in Ashbridge on the market and is living with Allan at his apartment. They are in the process of buying a cottage with a large garden on the outskirts of Ashbridge. It has an annexe, and Jane's mum has accepted their invitation to move in.

THE END

AUTHOR PROFILE

I've loved writing since I was a schoolboy and feel very privileged to still be making up stories many years later! It's easy to find inspiration and space to write here on the Isle of Wight, but the Jane Birchfield series—of which this is the fourth book—is very much grounded in Manchester, where I lived up to my early twenties.

I've also written several plays and a collection of short stories.

My career has included newspaper and magazine journalism, private and public sector communications, and freelance consultancy work.

When I'm not glued to my desk, I love walking the dogs, living with an overgrown garden and reading.

***

WHAT DID YOU THINK OF BENEATH THE SURFACE?

A big thank you for purchasing this book. It means a lot that you chose this book specifically from such a wide range on offer. I do hope you enjoyed it.

Book reviews are incredibly important for an author. All feedback helps them improve their writing for future projects and for developing this edition. If you are able to spare a few minutes to post a review on Amazon, that would be much appreciated.

PUBLISHER INFORMATION

Rowanvale Books provides publishing services to independent authors, writers and poets all over the globe. We deliver a personal, honest and efficient service that allows authors to see their work published, while remaining in control of the process and retaining their creativity. By making publishing services available to authors in a cost-effective and ethical way, we at Rowanvale Books hope to ensure that the local, national and international community benefits from a steady stream of good quality literature.

For more information about us, our authors or our publications, please get in touch.

www.rowanvalebooks.com
info@rowanvalebooks.com

Printed in Great Britain
by Amazon

84999956R10187